THE AMBASSADOR'S SON

Recent Titles by Kenneth Royce

THE
AMBASSADOR'S
SON

Kenneth Royce

This first world edition published in Great Britain 1994 by
SEVERN HOUSE PUBLISHERS LTD of
9–15 High Street, Sutton, Surrey SM1 1DF.
First published in the USA 1994 by
SEVERN HOUSE PUBLISHERS INC., of
425 Park Avenue, New York, NY 10022.

British Library Cataloguing in Publication Data
Royce, Kenneth
  Ambassador's Son
  I. Title
  823.914 [F]

  ISBN 0-7278-4713-9

Typeset by Hewer Text Composition Services, Edinburgh.
Printed and bound in Great Britain by
Hartnolls Ltd, Bodmin, Cornwall.

With acknowledgements to
Sir Michael Wilford

Prologue

The hysteria increased with the deluge. Uncontrolled laughter pealed out into the night to be almost lost against the pounding of rain on car roofs and near empty streets. Anyone with sense had long since dived for cover from the cloudburst. But the group of seven somehow held together, perhaps drawn to each other by uncertainty generated by the primeval forces unleashed at them, and by the unrealities they themselves had created. In the state they were in, to be soaked to the skin and legless was a bonus.

Don Hayes slipped and fell against a car. His legs went and he crashed down, striking his head against a wing mirror which snapped off. Someone bawled out, "The Don's dead," and several sets of footsteps rushed towards him. They got him up, held him against the damaged car. "Come on, you yankee sod, stay on your feet." The plea might have come from any one of them; the rain was so heavy that it was impossible to see who was doing what and voices were so disseminated as to be sexless and random. The group had become one milling mass, a squirming heap without direction or coherence embodied by inane laughter and physical inability. They were stoned out of their minds.

They somehow managed to make a rough circle, holding on grimly to one another to perform "A Ring of Roses" in the middle of the street. And then they fell in like an implosion, at which point one of the two girls in the party slowly collapsed. They all fell on top of her still laughing and giggling.

When they finally disentangled and unsteadily scrambled to their feet, the girl remained down. Someone bawled, "She's spaced out."

And then another voice, yelling to penetrate the roar of the storm, "Get the hell out of here or we'll all be in trouble."

The American, already barely able to stand, hearing the disembodied voices and seeing virtually nothing but torrential rain and suggestions of shadows running away, suddenly felt his head explode and he was falling into an eternal abyss.

It seemed that nobody realised the girl was unable to move, far less that she would never move again. And two days after that, very sober by now, that the girl, Paula Smith, ostensibly an undergraduate at Oxford as they all were, had in fact been an undercover policewoman from Special Branch. And that she had been shot dead from close range.

Chapter One

"It's good of you to see me so late. I really do apologise for the hour." Stuart Wilson stood under the canopy of the porch and made no attempt to enter.

"I figured it was important or you would not be here. Come in." Marvin Hayes, United States Ambassador to the Court of St James, closed the heavy front door behind them and ushered his visitor into the spacious drawing-room. "Everybody has gone to bed, including Zoë. She guessed it wouldn't be a social call at this time of night. Drink?"

"I think I need one. I have a chauffeur with me so I'm not restricted." Stuart Wilson sat down wearily.

"That sounds like you need a large one. Scotch?"

Wilson gazed round the splendid room but noticed little. In any event he had visited here before. He felt wretched and wished someone else was doing this job. He took the heavy cut glass almost full with whisky and reflected that this was no time to be calibrated. But he needed the drink.

Marvin Hayes sat down opposite him, aware of the unease of the Home Office Minister and inexplicably depressed by it. Suddenly he did not want this meeting at all. He had met Stuart Wilson at various functions but would not claim to know him well. A few years younger than himself, Wilson was a ministerial type: dark hair neatly brushed and receding, well-cut suit and rather good-looking features. Deep-set brown eyes seemed always to be thoughtful, though Hayes knew him to have a wicked sense of humour which was not evident now.

"How much more liquor do you need before you spit it out? It is very late, Stuart." Hayes remembered the first name in time.

Wilson looked up. He liked Hayes, the rugged honesty of the man, one who had spent much of his earlier career on the outside rather than deskbound. He was tall with good bearing. A popular figure on the diplomatic circuit, a government man to the core with a pedigree which covered many departments.

"Please bear with me, sir. This will not be easy to say." Wilson took a swig then put the drink down and clasped his hands. He found it difficult to look the Ambassador in the eye. "You will have heard of the wild party in which your son was involved at Oxford a few nights ago?"

"Of course. There were other parties. It was an exciting time for them – finals. I gather some of them went over the top and I had words with Don as soon as I heard. Nothing has been made of it so what's the problem?" Hayes was unaccountably churning and he wished Wilson would get to the point.

"The other parties were not involved in a killing."

"Killing? What killing? I heard that one of the girls died of alcohol poisoning or drug abuse. I've heard nothing about a killing. Stop pussyfooting."

"You've heard nothing from the college?"

"About what? Where is this taking us?"

"The girl did not OD, nor did she die of too much drink. She was shot dead."

Hayes was still for a few seconds, expression blanked out. "Are you talking of one of the girls who was in Don's party?"

"Yes. There were two girls. The one who was shot was in fact an undercover policewoman from Special Branch."

Hayes was confused and considerably concerned, feeling that something he would rather not hear was about to be said. "I've heard none of this. I'm terribly sorry to hear about the girl. Presumably she was shot some time later?"

"No. While they were revelling. It happened while they were all together."

Hayes knew something was still being held back but suffered a strange reluctance to continue. "A Special Branch undercover agent? Why was she there and why wasn't I informed at the time of the tragedy?"

"There's been a cover-up. It was hasty but seems to have worked better than could be expected given the time factor. You will have seen little in the press."

"I've seen damn all in the press, well, just a paragraph that an undergraduate had died whilst out celebrating. Don rang to say they had been over the top with the celebrations and that he and his friends had been censured by the college. He did not mention the death. Are you sure he knew about it at the time?"

"Oh, yes. He knew about the girl. He fired the shot."

Hayes put his drink down slowly. He felt sick with shock. His hands shook and he folded his arms in an attempt to hide them. He could not think for a moment, but he was used to dealing with crisis and his wits gradually returned. "What crap are you giving me here? Don doesn't have a gun and if he did he would hardly take it to Oxford."

"As yet the police don't know whose gun it is, only that he fired it."

Hayes was still trying to recover. Too much did not add up, yet an HM Government minister had personally come to give him the news and he had to take it seriously. "Has he been arrested?" It was best not to think about the political repercussions both here and in America.

"No. We are hoping to avoid that happening."

"Then you are not sure. This is beginning to stink. Why the hell would my son want to kill a Special Branch agent?"

Wilson reached for his drink and finished it. "The police are sure. Would you prefer that he is arrested?"

"That's a damn fool question. You talk of cover-up; how can that happen and so quickly? The college must know

5

what has happened. The press. The police know. You know. What about the girl's parents? Of course I don't want him arrested but I would need far more convincing that he did it than you've managed to give. The only thing that is holding this together, giving it any credence at all, is your own presence. This is a nightmare you've thrown at me, for chrissake."

"I understand. I really do. Do you imagine I cherished the idea of coming here with news like this? It is a nightmare for me too and I cannot, at the moment, see how it will end. The chief danger is not those sources you have mentioned but Her Majesty's Opposition."

"You haven't begun to answer my question."

"May I have another drink first?"

"Can you help yourself? I'm not sure my legs will carry me after that bombshell. It does not rest at a shooting, does it? We've got politics wrapped in here." Hayes turned his head as Wilson crossed the room with his empty glass. "Will you top mine up too? Jesus, what a goddamm mess."

When both men had their glasses recharged, Wilson, a little more sure of himself now that he had told the worst, said, "A whole chain of circumstances is involved here, and a good deal of luck. When the local police came on the scene the dead girl's warrant card was enough for them to immediately contact SB. This in turn set off a chain of events during which SB took over the whole incident and warned the locals to keep it quiet. Other lives could be at stake, other agents; they had to be warned.

"I'm guessing a little now but I imagine the press were quickly stifled on the 'other lives at risk' basis and the story was put out about celebrating too much. The shooting as such was squashed at birth."

Hayes shook his head. "Your people must be easily satisfied. What of those celebrating with my son? Presumably they all know it was a bullet?"

"I would think so, but don't underestimate us. I've been briefed for this but there are some gaps I'll have to close later. If SB warned the college and gave them the story to be put around, the members of the party, now reduced to one woman and five men, would have been warned that their careers hung in the balance. They would have been told to keep quiet, and it does not need much conjecture that that was what they would want to do anyway. And SB would quickly have got to them. Your son gave no indication to you and it would be best if you did not raise it with him. The whole business is hanging by a thread but if nerves are steady it will work."

"What will work?" Hayes, now partly over the initial shock, was looking for flaws and wondering why this should be happening at all.

"Getting your son off the hook. It was probably all a terrible accident."

"And why would you want to do that?"

Wilson looked surprised. "I'm only the messenger boy. But I should have thought it much better all round if this particular business did not come to light."

"And in what form would you expect my gratitude?"

"That was never in our thoughts. We don't want this kind of scandal any more than you. We've taken quite a lot of flack recently. And so has your good friend the President."

"Wouldn't it be better if someone from Special Branch dropped by to explain all this to me? It is after all a police matter."

"If someone from SB came it would admit a police presence in the affair. Is that what you want?"

"I want the truth. And as yet not even you seem to know it. I want to know exactly what has happened here."

"I haven't all the case details. I'm here because the Home Secretary asked me to contact you personally. I've had no direct contact with the police, but the Home Secretary most certainly has. It is not exactly the type of subject to joke about. We're trying to help you more than help your son. It is in our interests as well as yours. We don't want something like this to get out any more than you do. We don't want a change of Ambassador."

Hayes left his drink on a side table and started to pace the room. "I shall still want more evidence than you have provided. Indeed, you've provided none. This is a monstrous accusation you've made."

Wilson inclined his head in agreement. "I'm here as an early warning. We want to avoid you making any direct contact with the police. At least you can explain me away in a dozen different ways. Trust us."

Hayes turned away from the draped windows and stared down at Wilson, wondering just how much he really knew. "Trust you? I can't do that until I've seen some hard evidence and have spoken to my son."

Wilson drained his drink, wondering why he still felt so sober. "I'll do what I can, I'll try to get the case notes. Although we don't want you to make direct contact with the police you should bear in mind that the police forces come under the jurisdiction of the Home Office. We can't stop you from seeing your son but I doubt you'll get anything from him. Anyway, I've finished what I came to do. I am deeply sorry to bring such rotten news. It must be clear to you by now that we are doing everything possible to help you both."

"At what price, Stuart?"

"That's a cynical remark, sir. Would it make you happier if we arrested your son? For murder?"

It was the first time the word had actually been mentioned and it created an uneasy silence. Hayes was struggling with his conscience. He was immensely fond of his son, an only child since his elder son had died in an air crash three years ago. He was still confused, not just by the impact of the news but of the various repercussions it could create; they seemed to be endless, not least of them the effect this would have on his wife Zoë. He could not see how he could tell her but he knew that he must. He shook his head. "No," he said. "I wouldn't want you to do that."

Wilson said, "I'm sorry I had to say that. Look, if it will help I'll try to arrange a meeting with a senior police officer, as long as you understand that it is the sort of thing that the press are so adept at winkling out, no matter how careful we are. But it will be up to the police to decide. They might object strongly to being used in this way and I would not want to force them. May I contact you at the Embassy tomorrow?"

"Sure." But Marvin Hayes was still trying to come to terms with the news that his son had shot an undercover policewoman. There was something not right about it. He said, "How old was this policewoman?"

Wilson showed surprise. "How old? I don't know. Does it matter?"

"As male undergrads range roughly between nineteen and twenty-one and women from around eighteen to twenty, she would be a bit young, wouldn't she, for an undercover cop?"

"I hadn't thought about it. Undergrads are not all that young. Some go abroad for a year or so before starting. My own daughter was in India for over a year before she went to Cambridge. It depends."

"But she would still have been young."

"Are the police suddenly old men and women?"

"And what of her parents? Wouldn't they be just a little curious about the nature of her death?"

"I understand they have been told. They would be among the first to recognise the dangers of undercover work. They would understand the need for secrecy, the need to mislead. I understand the girl had been doing undercover work for the last eighteen months."

"Aren't you curious about the work she was doing at Oxford? What was she investigating, for God's sake?"

"At this stage I don't think that matters. It might complicate things to follow that line at this time. Undergraduates are not all saints."

"That's not good enough. If my son is being accused I want to know why he might have done it."

9

"It can't all be answered at once. One step at a time. Let's make sure your son is off the hook first. Then we can sort out the rest. I must go."

They shook hands and when Stuart Wilson had gone Hayes stood wondering why the Home Office were trying to help him so much. Somehow he had difficulty in attributing it to the special relationship between the two countries. He would motor down to Oxford first thing tomorrow.

Chapter Two

It was difficult to avoid the Diplomatic Protection Group, many of whom assigned to him he had got to know. Marvin Hayes wanted to go to Oxford alone and this meant without a chauffeur either. He was already drawing attention to himself by detaching himself from normal routine, but it could not be helped. He telephoned his son in the morning, and had then to make various excuses to his staff or otherwise raise an alarm. Privacy was hard won in diplomatic circles. As yet he had decided against telling his wife Zoë, choosing to wait until he had more to go on.

Motoring out of London against the early morning traffic was easy enough, even enjoyable, and he reached Oxford in good time, but he had overlooked the possibility that the Oxford one-way traffic system might be hostile to strangers and no more friendly to the locals.

The colleges were well scattered and he found himself constantly passing the prison, an unwelcome reminder of his mission. In the end he pulled up and asked a policeman, who could not fail to notice his American accent and gave him concise instructions. Hayes found his son waiting at the foot of his college steps, barely giving him sufficient time to get in the car before driving off.

"How the hell does anyone find their way around in this place?"

"Instinct and habit. Dad, what's happened for you to be down here?"

Don Hayes was taller than his father and almost gangly.

He was a pleasant-looking young man with an engaging manner. He had been surprised and worried when his father had telephoned for an urgent meeting.

"Give me a route out of this place and direct me to somewhere where we can talk."

"We can talk in the car."

"Don't be too clever, son. This is far too serious a matter. You just tell me which way to go."

From then on no word passed between them as Hayes drove grimly and Don recognised when it was best to keep quiet. They finished up in a layby on a minor road with a tractor covering a field on one side and a tall hedge on the other. They did in fact talk in the car because there was nowhere more private.

Marvin Hayes came straight to the point. "Right, now tell me in detail what happened the night you celebrated the end of the finals."

Don stirred uneasily, his long legs trying to find space that was not there. "Gee, Dad, we've been over this. Nothing has changed."

"Everything's changed, son, so cut the bullshit. You've been accused of murder."

"What! Are you kidding me?"

"No, I'm not kidding you. You must have been seen by the police."

"Sure I've seen the police. We all have. And we've kept out of each other's way ever since. How can anyone be accused of murder when Paula died of natural causes? She did, didn't she?"

"Is that what you were told?" Hayes was puzzled by his son's attitude; there was nothing of the guilty man about him.

"I guess that's what we assumed. I believe there will be an autopsy but nobody has said anything about the result of one."

"So who had the gun?"

"Gun?" Don awkwardly eased his body round in order to face his father. "What gun?"

Hayes rubbed his face. He felt drained. "Just give me chapter and verse of what happened that evening."

"It was the end of the finals. Along with other colleges we went celebrating."

"What do you remember about it?"

Don suddenly looked vague. He spluttered round a reply for some time until he said, "Look, the early stages were okay. We just had fun. I don't know who started it but at some point we detached ourselves from the rest and from then on we got a bit wild."

"How wild? I want it all, Don."

"To be honest I can't remember. Everything blacked out. I could hear voices, laughter, but nothing coherent. They tell me I fell down a couple of times."

"Did the others help you up?"

"I think so. Yes, they did, because they ribbed me after."

"So they were sober enough to help you but you were legless?"

It sounded bad put like that. "I think they were as bad. It was just the way it went. We all fell over when Paula went down." Don tried to brazen it out. "Okay, so we were all climbing the pole without a parachute. We were way over the top. I don't suppose we were the only ones."

"You were the only ones who carried a gun. Whose was it?"

"I wish you'd stop it about a gun. I haven't a clue what you're talking about."

"Then you'd better think harder. The police apparently have evidence that you fired it. I have it on best authority that the girl died from a bullet wound. And you didn't even hear it? Just how spaced out were you, Don? For God's sake, level with me."

"Okay, I was bombed out of my mind. We all were. But I know nothing about a gun nor did I hear a shot." Don held his head in desperation. "Goddamn it, the noise of the storm nearly burst our eardrums, and we were singing

13

and laughing and shouting through that. None of us knew what we were doing."

"You weren't spaced out enough to miss killing a young policewoman with a single shot. If it was done under the influence of drink or drugs it was a remarkable shot, unless it was not intended for her. Had you taken any drugs?"

"Policewoman? What are you talking about?"

Hayes eyed his son in disbelief. "Are you saying you did not know the girl was an undercover cop?"

"Paula? Are you sure we're talking about the same girl? A cop? What the hell would she be doing there?" Don was by now in a state of despair. He had expected a hard time over the nature of the celebration but nothing like this.

Hayes realised he would have to see Stuart Wilson again. Better still, the Home Secretary. Was it possible for someone to be so allegedly guilty, yet not only know nothing about a gun but have no idea his victim was an undercover policewoman? He supposed it possible if Don had been full of drugs at the time. "You haven't answered my question about the habit."

"I never had a habit. I haven't taken any drugs since arriving in this country. I have not broken my promise to you and Mum. I wouldn't let you down."

"Is it possible that someone spiked your drinks?"

"Of course it's possible. Once we were under way anyone could have done it."

"Do you reckon someone did?"

"I don't know. We didn't have a blood test. I think we were all spaced out, not just me."

Hayes, grim faced, more confused than ever, drew out a notebook and pen. "Give me the names of all those in your party."

"For chrissake, Dad, you're not in the DEA now. You're supposed to be a bloody diplomat."

"You've caught on quick to English idiom. I don't intend to interview them, I just want their names."

"Okay." Don leaned back as far as he could but there was no comfort in the car. The names came easily to him:

14

"Neill Barker, Tammy Rees – Welsh girl – Phill Marshall, Walter – known as Wally – McQueen, Jamie Burke, Paula Smith – the girl who died – and myself. Dad, believe me, I didn't shoot anyone. I haven't got a gun and this is crazy. If I had, why haven't the police arrested me?"

"To protect me. So I am led to believe. And thereby avoid a scandal both here and back home. It wouldn't go down well back home, that's for sure. They've had a spate of scandals and they are apt to shake things up a bit. They've had a few here but nothing like this. Give me a route back to the college."

"You don't believe me, do you? You don't believe your own goddamn son."

"I believe you were not aware of what happened. Beyond that I know no more than you. I haven't yet told your mother by the way, so be careful what you say when she gives you a call."

Don was close to tears. "I wouldn't foul anything up for you. You should know me better than that. I wouldn't hurt either of you."

Hayes concentrated on his driving. "I know you wouldn't. Not consciously anyway. And that's the crunch, isn't it? You were so hyped that you don't remember a thing. So we start from there. Hang in, I'll be the last one to crucify you." He reached across to squeeze his son's shoulder. "Keep a low profile. With any luck we might have this thing sorted out before you leave Oxford."

There was a long silence, the misery between father and son building up. And then Hayes broke the strained silence by asking, "Am I on the right road? I'll drop you off at the college and then I must go straight back to London."

Hayes was totally bewildered on the drive back. He did not think his son was lying but was certain that a lot had happened he did not know about. One way or the other, Don had blanked out. Or had been blanked out.

By the time he returned to the Embassy in Grosvenor Square there was little of the working day left and he had a lot of catching up to do. He made calls to the private numbers of both the Home Secretary and his minister Stuart Wilson but both were in the chamber of the House of Commons on what would appear to be a long session. He felt frustrated. And angry. He could not brush aside Wilson's assertions but he needed to know far more than he did before making his next move.

It was a frustrating day all round and he was unable to make contact until the next day when he agreed to meet Wilson at the House of Commons.

The bad weather had completely disappeared and had switched to a mini heatwave. It was a little too early for ripe strawberries but they went on to the terrace just the same and it was here that Stuart Wilson introduced Marvin Hayes to the Assistant Commissioner of Police, John Cordell. Wilson had somehow arranged some seats at the extreme end of the terrace. As it was early and the House not yet sitting, the terrace was fairly empty, but there were still too many people about for Hayes' comfort.

Hayes belatedly realised that Wilson had been right about not being seen with a policeman, although Cordell was in plain clothes, looking more like a banker than, arguably, the second most powerful policeman in the country. Cordell could have stepped straight out of the City, but he still had a policeman's eyes; they missed nothing. Johnny Cordell had played midfield for the Metropolitan Police soccer team and had kept himself fit. In his mid forties he appeared younger for such a high rank but he had an exemplary record and was certainly not unknown to Hayes by reputation.

For those who might overhear, Wilson said, "The Ambassador is concerned about aspects of the Diplomatic Protection Unit, Johnny, I am sure you can allay his fears."

They sat down in a semicircle, backs to the far parapet, as if to accommodate TV cameras, but in reality to keep

16

an eye on anyone who approached too near, so that the topic could be quickly changed. Hayes could now see the advantage of meeting so publicly; it was far less sinister than a clandestine meeting.

The sun had yet to reach its zenith and changed the colour of the Thames to a more acceptable hue. The river traffic was quiet and St Thomas's Hospital on the opposite bank appeared to have had a spring clean. It was pleasant and warm, marred by the subject being raised by the three men.

"Did you see your son yesterday?" asked Wilson.

"I suspect you know very well that I did. He says he has no recollection of any shooting that night. He recalls the girl falling down, it seems that they all fell on top of her, but heard no shot and until I mentioned how she had died believed she had done so by natural causes. There is no doubt he was genuinely shocked by what I told him. None of it makes sense and I would like to know how the police reached their conclusions."

Cordell had an A4 buff file with him which he had placed on the table but had not opened; it lay there like a mystery object and was too thin to have much in it. He tapped the file and said, "There's not a lot in there, as you can see, but what there is is damning. This has come up from Oxford, sir. I've had words with the chief there, but you will appreciate I have not been personally involved in the case. I'm pig in the middle and merely trying to help."

"Thank you, Commissioner. I do appreciate it. So what is in the file?"

Cordell smiled. "I'm not yet Commissioner, but everyone above my rank calls me Johnny and those below refer to me behind my back by that name."

As that left only the Commissioner himself sufficiently high up the tree to use the familiarity, Hayes could not help but smile; Cordell had a sharp sense of humour. He noticed Wilson smiling quietly.

"What's in there, sir, is the testimony of a witness who

claims he saw your son having a row with Paula Smith earlier in the evening."

"That's it?"

"It doesn't seem much, does it? The witness was in a bad state even the day after the parties. If he was in anything like the self-admitted condition of your son the previous evening it is possible that his evidence is fantasy. Meanwhile it must be heeded."

Cordell laid his hand on the file and looked Hayes straight in the eye. "I believe you were once a policeman yourself, sir?"

"Some would say not. I was with the Drug Enforcement Agency for some years. But I was operating a good deal outside the United States. Is there a reason for mentioning that?"

"Only that you will realise the devastating importance of the fact that your son's prints are on the gun."

Hayes was stunned by this news and for a few seconds was groping. Then he cleared his mind and said, "This is the first intimation I've had that you found the gun."

"Oh, yes we found it. Under a hedge and reasonably dry so the prints had remained. I'm sorry to tell you this."

"How did you check the prints? Don has no recorded prints in this country."

"We took prints from all the students involved. But I could have raised your son's from the FBI in Washington, as I am sure you are aware. I thought you would prefer us not to."

Hayes felt shattered. "It was a small matter at the time. A young student's stupid excursion into drugs, but it lasted no time at all and there has been no problem since."

"Just long enough for it to go on record. There's a lot of it about, sir."

Hayes raised his hands in a hopeless gesture. "Just where do we go from here?"

"Nowhere, sir." Cordell glanced at Wilson and it was obvious that the two men had already discussed it. "We leave it on file."

"That's very magnanimous of you. May I ask why?"

Cordell showed his first sign of discomfort and again glanced at Wilson who had remained remarkably reticent throughout. "I thought Mr Wilson had already explained that to you, sir."

Hayes searched Wilson's bland expression before saying, "To some extent. I can understand the need not to rock the international boat, to enjoy the present stability and co-operation between our two countries. We are cousins, are we not? Keep it in the family, so to speak. It's not good enough, gentlemen. There's a price to pay about which you are being deliberately obtuse."

"You think we're the Mafia? That we'll call in the debt?" Wilson was openly smiling.

Hayes searched the expressions of each of his hosts in turn. They were ostensibly open, honest faces. Wilson was a politician, so that let in a myriad of doubts, but John Cordell was in a position where he had to be believed. He would not cover up a murder unless there was an incredibly good reason, and even then he would not do it alone. He was being backed. Cordell was as straight a policeman as one could find, and yet Hayes was left in deep doubt.

Hayes turned to look at the Thames, a therapeutic exercise which provided no conclusions. "Gentlemen, I'm sorry," he said at last. "I can't accept what you say. Emotionally, I'm immensely grateful to you. I don't want to see my son on a murder rap. Particularly if it was an accident arising from a drunken escapade. I once saw a young soldier shot by a friend of his. They were playing the fool, not having checked that the gun was still loaded. I was a witness at the trial and saw a young man go down for a long prison sentence for one careless act of crass folly. It ruined his life and his best friend was dead. I wouldn't want that sort of thing to happen again.

"But this is a policewoman who has been shot dead. An act that sends any police force in the world into an orbital crusade of revenge. Yet you sit there calmly telling me

19

that you know who did it but because of international repercussions you are willing to let the perpetrator go free. How do you cover up something like that? How do you explain to the girl's parents that you cannot find the culprit? And the press? And the local police who were first involved? I find it difficult to swallow."

Wilson lowered his voice as the terrace began to fill. "You don't have cover-ups in the United States? When the reason arises? You've had more than your share, from assassinations down. And they are still being talked about and new books written about them. But still nobody knows for sure. Why should *this* be so difficult to accept?"

Hayes screwed his eyes against a reflection of light. He shrugged. "Johnny here will agree with what I say. As he intimated, I was once in law enforcement; no cop will let anyone off the hook for the killing of a fellow cop. Maybe things are different here but I can't swallow it. I have a strong gut feeling that letting Don go is far from the end of the story."

"You accept the alternative?" Wilson was showing just a little pique.

"I understand the alternative, yes. And that's even more difficult to swallow."

"You are a man of considerable integrity, sir." Cordell was quite sincere. "We are trying to help you but in so doing are being corrupt." He leaned forward. "But perhaps not as much as you think. We may have your son's prints on the gun but there are other aspects of the case which are shaky."

"Will you tell me what?"

"I can't go that far. I've already stepped well beyond the bounds of propriety in telling what I have. I'd have to resign if any of this came out, and there might well be legal action against me."

"So you are taking all that risk for me?"

"Not for you personally, but I think there would be quite a few people relieved if they knew of these issues and the course we are suggesting. From the Prime Minister down, and certainly the Foreign Secretary, to your own President. This one is best swept under the carpet."

There was a long silence while Hayes mulled it over. Whether what was being done was for the stated reasons or not he knew he would still be indebted to these two men, and perhaps others. He still did not like it, but they had at least offered the hope that the case was not so straightforward as it appeared. It was a loophole for his conscience. There was something else, too, which had impressed him with the way they had played their hand. "Thanks for not bringing Zoë into it." It would have been an extra pressure on him had they done so. "And I still want to know the final answer. I don't want everything left in limbo so that we never know what to believe."

Cordell inclined his head, content with the way matters had gone but uneasy at the way the place was filling up. "We will, of course, continue our enquiries. It is true that we have enough to arrest your son for murder but there is plenty we're unhappy about. Continuing enquiries will keep everyone content and might produce something more acceptable to all of us here. Are we in agreement?"

Hayes nodded and said, "I'm not mad about it but I guess so. It still leaves me feeling uneasy. You've put up a case for letting it ride but I hope you come up with more than you seem to have. Is there any chance of my seeing that file?"

Cordell smiled. "I'll pretend I never heard that. We've gone as far as we dare."

The three men shook hands, a bond of conspiracy rather than a gesture of friendship, and they left the terrace talking about the Diplomatic Protection Group."

Later that day Stuart Wilson telephoned Michael Sealy at Century House, the headquarters of the SIS, and requested an urgent appointment.

Chapter Three

Marvin Hayes had again lost much of his day and his secretary had suffered in trying to reschedule appointments he should have honoured. Anna Brus, thirty-eight years old and a career woman, went for the Ambassador as soon as he returned to his office. A pretty woman with almost elfin features and close-cropped, beautifully cut hair, and the brightest of brown eyes, she remained single for reasons clear only to herself. Anyone who knew her never raised the matter for fear of pulling the pin; she could be very touchy on the subject. Petite and fiery, she was highly efficient and the only person who could upbraid him in the way she did and get away with it. The problem was, as Hayes knew to his cost, she was almost always right.

"Okay, okay. I surrender. I should have warned you."

"You've upset a lot of important people." She had a last shot at him.

"Okay. So let's get on with it. Make no more appointments until I tell you. I must go to Washington."

Anna stood before him in front of the huge desk and couldn't believe her ears. "How can you do that? I've had to squeeze people in. When are you thinking of going?"

"Tomorrow if I can get to see Bill Fuller. Give him a call around three." Fuller was deputy head of the FBI.

Anna was about to explode again when she saw something was wrong. Her boss was not himself. He was distracted and wan, and clearly had something on his mind. "What's the matter?"

He was searching through papers on his desk. He looked up and there she was, small and challenging and clearly worried about him. "Don't ask. I mean it, Anna. Don't ever raise it again. You just get hold of Bill Fuller."

"So suddenly I'm a pariah. I'm here to help you."

"And so you do, but cut the bull because it won't work. It's personal, Anna. Nothing to do with anything here." But suddenly he realised that that might not be true. He could feel the problem all around him, clinging like a shroud. His mind was clouded and would remain so until something was settled. He almost wished he had left Don to take his chances, but it was virtually impossible to do that while there seemed to be doubts about him, and even then, right or wrong, it would be the most difficult task of his life to condemn his son to a life in prison for a murder he was far from satisfied he had committed. Such an act would also ruin his own diplomatic career and completely devastate his wife Zoë. The former he could cope with, but the latter would be a cruel, cruel stroke to a sensitive woman who still mourned the loss of her eldest son. The whole matter needed a lot more thought and some sound advice from a friend – he was too near to the problem to make a satisfactory judgement. But the discerning Anna was right: there was something wrong and it had not gone away with the end of the meeting with Wilson and Cordell. There was a nasty aftertaste to that meeting.

In an effort to catch up with desk work he was home late that evening. The light was beginning to fail as he gave a friendly greeting to the armed policeman at his front door and went inside to find that Zoë had ignored his telephoned instructions to eat without him and that he would simply have a snack when he arrived. She had arranged a cold salmon salad so they could eat together.

Zoë was an elegant woman, given to shyness although well capable of holding her corner. She socialised because her husband's job demanded it, although many an evening she would much rather have curled up with a book than dress up and attend the many functions that came with the job. Over twenty-eight years of marriage she had suffered

Marvin's many absences, particularly when he was with the DEA. Half the time she did not know where he was until she received a telephone call, sometimes in the middle of the night.

Since Marvin had been appointed Ambassador her life had changed completely, but she quickly adapted and made little complaint. She saw more of him now, but not always alone. This particular night she had dressed nicely for him – she never let him down – and they had a quiet supper in the large kitchen. If she was largely uncomplaining, she was still no fool. She noticed almost at once that he was not his usual self.

"What's on your mind, honey? And don't tell me it's work. You're worried about something."

In a quiet way Zoë was more discerning than Anna; her inner vision was deeper, and suddenly she was worried.

Hayes almost told her then; almost gave her the full story. Then he could see that she was waiting for bad news and he made the effort to trivialise his all too obvious despondency. "I've had to cancel some appointments; I'm flying to Washington tomorrow. It's a nuisance but something's cropped up."

"And you're not taking me? I don't want to be alone in the house." The huge house, a gift from a wealthy American to the nation, stood inside Regent's Park at the north-west corner.

He did not mention the staff who lived in; she would be far from alone. "I'm not even leaving the airport over there. A quick meeting on a delicate matter, and I'll catch the first available plane back. I'll get someone to fax you when I know which flight I'll be on."

"What's happened to the telephone?"

Hayes smiled. "And let Signal Intercept pick up the call at Cheltenham?"

"It must be delicate, then."

But he would not be drawn further, and in spite of his efforts it became increasingly difficult to be halfway normal and he felt the rest of the night deteriorate into

24

sometimes badly handled evasion. He did his best, but he could see that Zoë was far from happy. What would she be like if she knew the truth?

American diplomats are expected to fly American but he flew Concorde to save time. He did not attempt to reset his watch and spent almost the entire journey in going over what was happening to him, for as matters now stood he was the only one affected by the bizarre sequence of events. Zoë did not know anything and Don was temporarily off the hook. He dozed towards the end of the journey and was woken just before touchdown to feel dreadful. He braced himself for the coming meeting.

After landing he was hustled away from the mainstream passengers and guided to a separate room. As he entered, a man detached himself from the table he had been sitting on and came forward with hand outstretched and a wide grin of welcome.

"Marvin, good to see you."

The two men embraced. They had often worked effectively together and it was clear that recollection was not far from either of them. It was a friendship that had endured some tough times.

"Customs lent me this room, as you probably guessed. Much nearer than the special VIP lounge." Bill Fuller looked an academic, which was not too far from the truth. Like many in the FBI he had trained to be a lawyer, even practised for a while, but had now been with the FBI sufficient years for him to be Deputy Director. He was tall, almost thin, wore frameless spectacles and was generally quiet of manner.

They faced each other across a plain wooden table on plain wooden chairs like two prisoners given special privileges. A top post ambassador and the Deputy Director of the FBI talked in a room full of echoes; apart from the table and chairs there was waiting but plain walls.

"What's on your mind, Marv?"

Hayes told him and Fuller made no interruptions and

expressed no surprise until Hayes had finished, and even then he sat still for quite a while. Eventually he slowly shook his head, gave a strange sort of grin, almost of embarrassment, before offering one word which perhaps summed it up: "Weird."

"I've flown over three thousand miles for that?"

"I can offer you a cup of coffee as well."

"Is that it? Come on, Bill, you worked on assessment with the Company for a number of years, so assess."

"You obviously think there's an angle. That they want you in this position. You would owe them something."

"Well, don't you? What I don't understand is how could I possibly help them? If I was in your position, or high up in the CIA I can see that they might want a few favours as a quid pro quo, but what can an Ambassador possibly provide?"

"There's nothing left to lobby for over the return of some of the IRA men who were resisting extradition here. The Noraid funds are not a problem just now. They know you and the President are old buddies." Fuller grinned. "How else would you get such a prime post? You're more cut out for the field."

Hayes managed a smile. "No, the IRA is a dead issue since the cease-fire."

"Then, maybe there is simply nothing. Years with the DEA have taught you to trust nobody; that's not smart for a diplomat. Maybe there's a good deal of sense in what they say. It would make a terrible mess when it hit the fan. Capitol Hill wouldn't be too pleased."

"Is that what you really think?"

"I haven't had the time to think about it as you have and you've come up with nothing or you wouldn't be here. Don't expect too much of me."

"Isn't there anything going on you can link me with. Something the Brits want and we're not too keen?"

"Oh, there's plenty of that. But I can't see one that needs the US Ambassador to the Court of St James as pig in the middle. Ambassadors have been neutered, they haven't the power they used to have. You know that or I wouldn't have said it."

"What about trade? Anything there I might help them with?"

Fuller leaned sideways on his chair, long legs crossed and one arm along the back head turned towards Hayes. "There's plenty there, although where you'd come in is difficult to say. As I understand it there's an underlying trade war with Europe. Trade tensions are always high. The G7 meetings seem to be improving but you could not influence anything there, as you well know."

Hayes silently agreed and then said, "There's something, just the same."

Coffee was brought in by one of the airport staff and discussion was suspended for a while. When Fuller had half emptied his cup, he said, "I've had dealings with Johnny Cordell. He's a straight cop and a very good one. There are only two ways of reaching his rank at his age: graft or efficiency. He's there because he's good. He'll have given it to you straight."

"As straight as he knows it to be," Hayes conceded. "Maybe he hasn't the full story either."

With some exasperation Fuller said, "Why can't you accept it for what it is? Stuart Wilson is right. Nobody wants an Anglo/American flare-up. Getting back to the special relationship with the Brits has taken some time, and nobody would want to destroy that." Fuller swivelled round in his chair to face Hayes more squarely across the table. "Listen to me. I'm talking like a goddamn politician. That's listening to you. You should have given up all that diplomatic stuff, it's not you."

"I did it for Zoë. I was never home. Now at least she thinks she can be proud of me and knows where I am. She thinks I'm the most important American in Britain. I wouldn't want any of this to go sour on her. She's not all that fit as it is."

"I know why you did it. But you could have come into the FBI with me, a desk job."

27

"I couldn't work under you. I'm much better than you."

Fuller laughed softly. "That's more like you, an awkward son of a bitch. This has really got to you. I guess I'd feel the same if it was one of my sons."

Hayes pushed his chair back, hands clasped between his knees. He gazed at the floor. Suddenly he looked up. "I expected too much. That was unfair of me. At root, I guess there's a limit to how much, no matter how bright they might be, an ambassador can influence anything these days. Old Joe Kennedy thought the Brits would lose the war when he was Ambassador in London. He was a much more powerful man than me and they ignored him, so what chance have I got to affect anything? I'm sorry I wasted your time."

Fuller rose. "It was worth coming just to see you. But it might not have been a waste of time from your point of view. If you're unhappy about this and think you're being used, there is someone in London who might just possibly help you, do a bit of digging."

Hayes looked doubtful.

"He used to be a detective superintendent at Scotland Yard. Resigned for a reason that's escaped me, dabbled around with antique clocks for a while but couldn't totally keep clear of the game. The truth was he was too good to let go. Both MI5 and 6 used him and probably still do. He's been useful to us a couple of times. Try him. Maybe he can help."

"Hire a private eye, you mean."

"That's up to you. You're the one who's been doing all the beefing. If you came to me for help then that's the best I can do. He's a bristly character and quirky. Used to wear gloves, even in summer, but the last time I saw him his hands were bare so maybe he's stopped doing it. Studied at the Open University over there. Father served in what was then the King's African Rifles during the Second World War. His name is George Bulman."

"You seem to remember a lot about him."

28

"I've good reason to. If you're interested, I'll fax the address over to your personal machine. It will save you enquiring locally and keep it away from the Embassy." Fuller glanced at his watch. "I must get back."

Hayes pushed his chair back under the table. "Isn't there one of our boys I could use? There must be the odd Company man twiddling his fingers over there who wouldn't mind the work."

Fuller was about to open the door but returned to the table. "You're not thinking straight, Marv. In the first place if you want a Company man you should be talking to Hank Rosario at Langley, not me."

"I barely know him. And what I saw I didn't like."

"You're not the only one who doesn't like him. But you couldn't use one of our lot, anyway. Think about it. Supposing it went wrong and they found our people were being used on what to them is a purely domestic issue. That could only make things a lot worse."

"I just thought there might be an agent at a loose end."

"There are plenty if you know where to look. But don't use Americans. If you want to carry this through see Bulman first. He might not want to touch it but he has a reputation for being an anti-Establishment man. He can't stand bullshit."

"I don't know what he could actually do but I suppose you're right. Better than doing nothing. Can he be trusted? I mean, this is a delicate business."

Fuller stared hard at his friend. "That's a query against my own judgement. You think I'm getting careless?"

"I'm sorry. This business is getting to me. Anyway, thanks, Bill. It's good to see you. I'd better sort out a flight back."

"Leave that to me and I'll get someone from the office to inform Zoë. Don't forget to give her my love."

"Sure. And, Bill, this isn't one to be filed, okay?"

Fuller offered a cynical grin. "You didn't have to mention that. There's no way I would want something

29

like this on file. That way it can never be found by anyone. We do not want this to be official at any level. You're on your own, Marv. Good luck."

During the flight back Hayes realised he had been so bemused by the situation that he had imagined his friend Bill Fuller, with the vast resources of the FBI around him, would wave the magic wand instead of opting out. Maybe Fuller saw the international complications clearer than Hayes himself who was too close to the problem – if there was a problem at all. When national interests are at stake close friendships can be very tenuous if views differ greatly on an issue. Bill Fuller was concerned only with the effect Hayes' problems might have on the State. Hayes was worried about his son first and then the State.

Hayes felt he had been let down by an old friend. Bill Fuller had listened, made some of the right noises, then offered up a clapped-out limey cop whom he doubted strongly he would contact. You find out your real friends when in serious trouble. Perhaps he was being unkind; Fuller had to protect himself just as everyone did.

By the time they touched down at London Heathrow, Hayes was convinced he had made a wasted journey. And he felt isolated and lonely. That Zoë was at the airport to greet him in spite of the late hour was a bonus he enjoyed. She drove him back and he dozed off to avoid answering awkward questions.

The fax was already there when he went into his study soon after they arrived home. He slipped Bulman's address into a drawer and went to bed, Zoë lying awake at his side wondering what he was keeping from her.

The next day was so busy at the Embassy Hayes had no opportunity to contact Bulman, something he would prefer to do from home in any event. The work kept his mind off things and it was not until eight that evening, while Zoë was putting the finishing touches to a meal she insisted on preparing herself, that he went to his study to ring the number Fuller had included on the fax.

A gravelly voice answered, gruff and verging on the point of rudeness uttering just one word: "Bulman."

"My name is Marvin Hayes. A mutual friend suggested that you might be able to help me on a private matter. Would it be possible for us to meet?"

"Sure. Bill Fuller rang me to say you might be in touch."

Hayes was stunned by this. How could Fuller be so careless? "He shouldn't have done that."

"Why not? I might not have agreed to see you if he hadn't phoned. I don't do private jobs any more. But on his say-so I might make an exception for you."

There was no way he could pull rank here. Hayes asked, "Did he say anything about the problem?"

"Bill wouldn't do that. He's not careless. When would you like to meet?"

It was not easy to arrange a clandestine meeting when in the public eye, complete with a bodyguard who may well have instructions to stay with his charge at all times until safely home. It was not a situation which was likely to arise in normal circumstances. Murder was hardly normal.

The obvious place to meet was the Ambassador's house in Regent's Park, and George Bulman duly arrived the next evening, tidied, complete with briefcase, trying to look like a successful lawyer. The policeman outside the front door had been warned to expect him.

Hayes opened the front door himself, which further worried Zoë when there was someone paid to do it for him. Hayes took Bulman into his study and offered him a cognac but Bulman preferred Scotch with or without water but never with ice. They sat down in big leather chairs like club chairs, indeed the room had a club atmosphere about it, sombre and rather dark but comfortable.

Bulman was bigger than Hayes expected. The hair was still dark but thinning, and the eyes, set deep in craggy features, gave the impression of being whisky soaked, baggy and difficult to find until the laughter in them registered, as if Bulman found the funny side of everything he saw. Or perhaps his eyes reflected a deep cynicism of everything he saw.

"I didn't expect malt," Bulman said after sipping his drink. He noticed that Hayes had opted for the cognac. And then, "Before you start, sir, I would like to know just what I should call you. I'm a bit out of touch with titles and designations. Would Your Excellency do? Mr Ambassador?"

Hayes fingered the stem of his brandy balloon and took his time gazing at his guest, trying to stare him down without success. "Are you taking the piss, Bulman?"

Bulman's lips twitched and Hayes suddenly smiled, feeling at ease in this man's company. "Does Mr Hayes sound too formal, Mr Bulman?"

"Mr Bulman does. I'll settle for George or just Bulman, it doesn't matter which." He glanced down at his glass. "This really is a fine drop of Scotch."

Hayes sat back, comfortable with his visitor but uneasy with the situation. "I'm trying to decide just how much to tell you."

Bulman said bluntly, "You tell me everything there is to tell or I'm leaving." His tone had changed. "I haven't yet decided to help but the only way I can decide is to have all the facts as you know them. There's no halfway on this, Mr Hayes. You trust me with everything or I'm away."

Hayes moved uncomfortably. Even telling an old friend like Bill Fuller had been difficult enough, but he knew nothing about this man except what Fuller had told him. He would be opening himself up to a stranger and he found that difficult.

Bulman said more reasonably, "You must have thought this through before ringing me. Why is it now so difficult to tell?"

It was a little while before Hayes could speak at all and it was then that the unreality of what he was about to do struck him. What the hell was happening? "Okay." He drained his glass. "This is how it is."

Like Fuller, Bulman made no interruptions and sat transfixed as he heard the story through. It was not until Hayes had shakily finished that he raised his glass to his lips. He put the glass down carefully. "That's everything?"

"Right up to meeting Bill Fuller. Can you do something?"

"I would like to try. Something stinks in the State of Denmark."

"You feel that too, just from what I've told you?" Relating the problem was like reliving it, almost as if he had somehow witnessed the murder itself. "You don't think I'm being unkind or fanciful?"

Bulman shook his head. "Oh, no. The events themselves would appear to be more fanciful by far than your reaction to them." Bulman sat reflectively before saying, "I know Johnny Cordell. We worked together for a while. Straight copper. But I understood he had retired or was about to."

"That makes a difference? Perhaps he was no longer a policeman when we met?"

"I don't think he'd do that to you. If he was introduced to you as Assistant Commissioner then he still is."

"But why would he leave?"

"The usual reason. He's had an offer from industry he couldn't refuse." Bulman dismissed the question. "Happens all the time to the best coppers. Although it didn't happen to me."

"So you'll help?"

"It will be difficult. You want me to find out what the hell is really going on. Is your son guilty or innocent, and is what they are offering you too good to be true? And if so, what's the little game? Maybe not so little. And you'll want me to do this without involving you. That will be the difficult part, because on whose authority will I be operating? I mean, they won't believe I'm on a self-imposed refresher course and they'll know who put me up to it."

"My son? He could officially hire you."

"Without you knowing? Anyway, you haven't told him about the various approaches you've received. Have you?"

Hayes shook his head, worried by this complication. He had not thought things through as Bulman was doing.

"The girl who was killed. The policewoman. I'll have a word with her parents. They can't be too happy with what's happened. Maybe I can persuade them to hire me on a non-paying basis." Bulman straightened. "We can discuss terms later but I'm not cheap. I'm sure you've got the money. But expenses I will need from day one and they won't be low. I can guarantee no results. I have a gut feeling that we're up against much more than a murder. May I have that list of students who were with your son that night?"

Hayes felt drained. He had got his problems off his chest and transferred them to someone else, but he recognised that that was an illusion. He hoped he had done the right thing, and when he considered that he realised there was no other course if he wanted to expunge uncertainty. Just the same, he felt sick at heart and suddenly very exposed. He had now to trust Bulman right or wrong. He was a man used to control but now felt he had lost it, and that made him feel very vulnerable. They might speak the same language but Bulman still remained a foreigner and Hayes would have been happier dealing with one of his own countrymen. And that was not permissable. His doubts grew even as he shook hands in a bond of agreement.

Chapter Four

About two hours before George Bulman called on Marvin Hayes, Michael Sealy left the weekly meeting of the Joint Intelligence Committee and searched for a cab to take him to his Chelsea home. The meeting, as usual, had covered worldwide reports, discussed by the heads of each main intelligence organisation, in addition to senior representatives of the main departments. With diplomats, soldiers, and others seconded to the Cabinet office, they formed the very hub of the country's intelligence network.

Emphasis had changed a good deal, but even with shrinking military forces, and seemingly fewer enemies, there was still much ground to cover. The plight of arguably the most important foreign diplomat in the country, arising from the antics of his son, never arose. The Committee could only know of it if Sealy told them and Sealy was keeping a very tight lid on the affair.

There was nothing unusual in keeping certain issues under wraps until their purpose was clearer. There was no benefit from talking endlessly on what might be when one had only to wait to see. Sealy had always been reluctant to put all his cards on the table, even at the Joint Intelligence Committee meetings, which were really designed to cover general ground and what should be done about problems in various parts of the world, as well as domestic ones. The actual details of how things were done were kept to the departments concerned, or would otherwise need far more than a weekly meeting to cover.

Sealy arrived home to a lonely flat with nothing but his thoughts to keep him company. He put his briefcase in a floor safe, warmed up a can of soup, took a French loaf from the freezer and defrosted it in the micro. It was a frugal meal but, unless he went out to eat, was typical of his evening fare. He relied on lunches for sustenance.

His wife had died just over a year ago, still grieving the loss of their only son. The emptiness was something he had got used to. A strong-featured man, for some too much on the serious side, just fifty he was still very much on the matrimonial market and there were a few women who would consider him a catch. But the simple truth was that Sealy's seriousness extended into commitments and nobody could ever replace Meg.

They had married very young, had a son during the second year of marriage and Meg suffered two miscarriages later. In all they had almost thirty years together. Up to five years ago Sealy had worked mainly abroad, and when he started to slow down he was pulled in, and his son Ray maintained the tradition. A few years ago Ray had died at an age when he had barely begun to live and less than two years later Meg committed suicide.

After Ray died the marriage had drifted. Sealy's love for Meg was still strong, but it was never to be the same, and when he finally finished up alone Sealy's bitterness burned into his guts.

His closest friends recognised the problem and saw the buoyancy go out of him. He had always been a serious man and he hid his pain and the legacy of guilt behind his seriousness. He buried himself in the work at which he had always excelled. He carried on believing that no woman could ever replace Meg.

He had agreed to a meeting with Stuart Wilson the following day and realised he must give it some thought. He sat back with a drink and let his agile mind wander.

Bulman returned to his North Kensington apartment which occupied one floor of an Edwardian house in one of the old squares. The area had gone slightly up-market over the last few years and the famous Portobello market was only a block away – a happy hunting ground of his for antiques and old clocks.

His mind was not on clocks when he entered his steel-covered front door, ostensibly there as a deterrent against burglars but which had been more than useful on those occasions when Bulman's life had been at risk. Not all his cases were straightforward.

By the time he'd made himself a coffee and taken it into a living-room that looked like a junk shop until one looked deeper to find the rarer pieces, he was not at all sure that he had done the right thing in taking on the Ambassador's job. It wasn't that he was unsure of his line of enquiry, but the certainty existed that in no time at all the police, including Special Branch, would know about it, possibly raising many ghosts – dangerous ones.

He sat down in a regency armchair and gazed at a magnificent, mounted Boulle clock which chimed almost as if he had willed it. His first instinct was to contact those people he already knew, like Johnny Cordell, but if he did that it might kill enquiries at birth. And that was the problem. He had a strange feeling of *déjà vu*. But this time the US Ambassador was involved and that was an added complication which would far from protect him. "You're a fool, George," he said out loud. But taking on the occasional job like this helped him cope with the emptiness, the loneliness of the apartment, and the absence of a woman in his life. Sometimes it could be very lonely indeed.

The next morning he had a little trouble locating the dead girl's parents. He was already restricted by being unable to use press and police contacts without raising questions so the only course left was to contact one of the Oxford don's who knew Bulman well and had even put him forward for an honorary doctorate without success. He obtained the name and the town where her parents lived and a local telephone directory provided the rest.

This was all he needed; he had no intention of calling on the girl's parents to add to the burden they already carried.

In any event he doubted very much that they would know precisely what their daughter was engaged in at the time she was shot.

There was only one obvious area where he could start and he went down to Oxford the next day in his twenty-three-year-old Daimler Sovereign which he garaged in a lock-up two blocks away. As he motored down on a fine morning he realised he was doing this more for Bill Fuller of the FBI than Marvin Hayes. He had worked with Fuller a couple of times on crimes which had stretched between the two countries. They worked in quite different ways but had built up a mutual respect and above all trust. But during those jobs they had all the back-up and help they needed. Now he was strangled, and as he neared Oxford, accepted that he would have to take some risks of exposure or get nowhere.

It took almost a full day to locate Neill Barker, who did not return to his digs until late evening.

"Neill Barker? I wonder if I might have a word with you, sir."

"Oh, God, not again. How many more times?"

Bulman smiled. He had not said he was a policeman nor made any attempt to produce identification; he simply acted as he had done for so many years. "Is there somewhere we can talk? Can I buy you tea or something?"

Barker was rather an effete-looking young man with a highly polished accent. Tall but slight of build, Bulman later discovered that the blond Barker was an Oxford blue at middle distance running.

"Is this about Paula? I've really had enough and I can't tell you chaps any more than I have."

They stood on the pavement as a horde of under-graduates milled round them and an invasion of bicycles apparently tried to hack them down.

"I'm not the police," said Bulman at his kindest. "And there is nothing to stop you walking away. But I have gone out of my way to come and I've waited most of the day for you. I'm representing Paula's parents. The police are a cold-blooded lot and the Smiths have really been told nothing. I just want to paint a picture of her last night to them, not just offer an official statistic."

Memory of the event made Barker uncomfortable. "Take my word for it that they won't want to know. We're all trying to forget it. And people like you won't let us. I'm sorry you've wasted your time."

"Isn't there a pub where we can go?" Bulman looked round in desperation. "Just a drink and we'll call it a day. It'll be on my expenses."

Barker led the way to a bar which was too crowded but Bulman managed to get treble Scotches. The two men thrust through the mêlée and finally stood on the pavement outside the pub which was in one of the older streets, in spite of its reproduction beams.

"Cheers! So what happened?"

"I can't change the story no matter how many times I tell it. We had a massive booze-up after the finals. Our group went wandering off into the night bombed out of our minds and enjoying every conscious moment when the sky burst open on us as a massive retribution for mindless behaviour."

"Conscious moments?"

"Well, most of them weren't. None of us realised we had drunk so much until the next day. We were all in a terrible state. Terrible."

"Including Paula Smith?"

"Well, yes. We were in no condition to single anyone out. We were all in it together. Absolutely smashed."

"Except the person who fired the shot."

Barker had no wish to relive it. "We did not bloody well know she had been shot. It was pissing down. We couldn't see blood or anything like that. We could barely see at all. I suppose we simply thought she had had too much to drink. She wasn't the only one to fall down that night. We didn't know she had been shot until Don told us the other day. He was very secretive about his source but Don is reliable. The police said nothing about a shooting

39

although they asked some very strange questions. We've been heavily warned by the college not to discuss this with anyone; none of us wants to cock up our results; to be sent down at this stage would be absolute disaster. But as you're representing Paula's parents it seems only right that they . . . look, I've said far too much. If this comes out I shall deny every word."

"You won't need to. Have you told me anything you haven't told the police?"

"Not a word."

"Then stop worrying. Were you taking drugs that night?"

"We talked about it afterwards. We had no drugs but someone might have set out to fix us."

"Did you know Paula well?"

"Fairly well. She had toured India or somewhere before coming here. She was a nice girl. I liked her."

"Are the others still at their digs or have any of them gone down?"

"We've been told to stay put for the time being. You'll have a job talking to Wally McQueen, he was taken very ill the next day and is still sick. It's a miracle we weren't all taken away."

Bulman caught Barker glancing at his empty glass, and spotting the weakness insisted on getting another round. He half expected Barker to have gone by the time he returned with the drinks but he was still there leaning against the wall of the pub, hair hanging down, gaze reflective and evidently in need of the whisky which Bulman passed to him.

"Don't you find it strange that nobody mentioned it was murder?" asked Bulman pleasantly.

"Extremely." But Barker's expression had changed, his thoughts almost readable. "Murder! I have never thought in those terms. If Paula was shot it would have been accidental."

"It wasn't accidental that someone was carrying a gun."

"It need not have been one of us. It could have been anyone passing by. I suppose that as she was some form of undercover policewoman the police might want to keep it quiet for whatever reason. They were certainly fast to gag us through the college authorities and to keep the details out of the press. Very impressive."

"Presumably it was Don who told you Paula was undercover?"

"Oh, yes. Well, he'd have got it from his old man, wouldn't he? God knows what she was investigating." Barker drank half his second treble and was well on the way to being drunk but retained a furtive defence against saying too much. "I sometimes think the whole thing is baloney. She wasn't shot at all and certainly not undercover."

"So where has she gone, Neill?"

Barker gazed out into the busy street as if he might find her there. "You have a point." He stared at Bulman's craggy face and said, "I don't know where it started to go wrong. All we wanted to do was to celebrate the end of a three-year slog. It had been bloody hard work. I sometimes wonder if it would have happened if there hadn't been the deluge. We weren't the only ones caught out in it."

"The storm probably offered up a sudden opportunity to a very patient person. You say you were all smashed out of your minds; do you mean to say that you have never considered that one of you might have been putting on an act?"

Barker shifted his feet uncomfortably. "I'm sure that we have considered it but perhaps it's something we would rather not face."

"Who would be your choice of the one who stayed sober?"

"Oh, no. Don't try that on. I know it wasn't me. We were largely together by chance. It was just the way it went. One minute there's one almighty party, the next

41

it's breaking up into groups going off in a number of directions."

"One last thing. How do you get on with Don Hayes?"

"Don? He is good at sports and I think he's quite popular. Nice chap. Yes, I like him."

"Thank you for your honesty. I won't let the others know that we've met. Don't worry about word getting back to anyone. Now, any help you can give me in locating the other addresses to save my legs would be really welcome."

"Bulman, you say your name is?" Barker's words were slightly slurred but he had already had half a dozen Scotches. And when Bulman nodded in assent Barker added, "You're a gent, Bulman. A pleasure to know you. I can't help you with the others. When they are not in college they could be anywhere. Why don't you speak to Don? All you have to do is to follow a trail of undergrads until you find one with an American accent."

Bulman shook hands and walked off hoping he had not made matters too complicated for Barker to cope with. When he glanced back Barker was trying to get into the pub against the tide.

They did not want to be seen together, particularly at Century House, but meeting places for clandestine meetings were not always readily accessible. So they met in a small café off the Charing Cross Road, which Sealy referred to as the "little taximen's". The size appertained to the café and not to the taximen who no longer used it anyway due to a change in the traffic system which made nearby parking impossible.

They had come early to avoid the lunchtime crowds and squeezed in behind a table for two and ordered a mixed grill, something neither had had for some time.

"I used to come here years ago," said Sealy. "They use a good oil and change it regularly. Their chips are better than those served at the Ritz."

"And it's safe here?" Wilson was surprised at Sealy's

good mood, as if the café produced nothing but pleasant memories.

"It wouldn't be if the taximen were still around. One of them might recognise you. Me, I'm part of the distemper."

The food was as good as Sealy had suggested and they enjoyed eating, interested as the place gradually filled up. Sealy had selected the table well, it being one of two which had any degree of privacy. They waited for coffee and Wilson eventually said, "I'm not happy about this Oxford business, Mike. It leaves a nasty aftertaste."

"You think I like it any better? That's the name of the game. Opportunities cannot be missed."

"That's all right if the game is worth playing. I'm not sure that the benefits here warrant the risks. I'm uneasy about it."

"The benefits can be considerable. It's a matter of choosing the right time and the right issue. But that apart, we're doing Marvin Hayes an immense favour."

"I wonder if he sees it like that?"

"It's true. His son's prints are all over the gun. And with his drug record he could be in really deep trouble."

Wilson shook his head. "The drug record was a brief excursion many students are stupid enough to try, and lasted no time at all."

"But it's on his record. Juries don't like drugs. We could have pulled young Don in right at the beginning. The local police take exception to our interference but can do little about it. They are very much on best behaviour; the consequences have been spelled out to them. So that leaves you and me and Barry White of MI5. Does anybody else know?"

"That Don Hayes' prints are on the gun?"

"The whole bit. The Ambassador knows only so much. His son was so stewed he really knows nothing at all unless he's much cleverer than I think. The gun was not found immediately, which gave us time to grab it and do the forensic here in London – something else the locals don't

43

like. But they have had to face up to the fact that Paula Smith was with SB and there is little they can do about that. They have had to accept that it is all out of their hands."

Listening to these reassurances made Wilson even more unhappy. "And you're the only one at SIS who knows about it?"

Sealy grimaced. "Of course. As indeed I hope you are among the politicians. You know better than I that it is imperative that the PM, or any senior minister, is able to say honestly under challenge that they knew nothing about any of it."

"Which leaves me carrying the can," replied Wilson bitterly. "The SIS get away with murder. If this blows up everyone calls for a public enquiry, which never happens, into the behaviour of our intelligence services, while people like me are thrown to the wolves. I think I should tell the PM."

"Don't you dare. He would not thank you for involving him. Leave things as they are. Whichever way you look at it, right now we are doing the Americans a big favour, and saving them from a scandal. I have to hope that Don Hayes is sufficiently strong a character not to do a runner to the US. They would be livid if it came out that way."

"Can't you take his passport?"

"For God's sake, you're Home Office. You must know bloody well we can't. He's not holding a British pass-port."

"Of course, I'm sorry, I simply wasn't thinking. I'm sure his father wouldn't want him to run, it would be the worst possible thing to do. Tell me, what was Paula Smith doing there?"

Sealy looked around for a waitress to serve another coffee. "There have been whispers of an assassination or kidnap attempt. There is more than one politically important Arab undergrad at our universities who could be under threat. At the moment we have more than one undercover agent at Oxford, which was another reason we did not want the murder of Paula Smith to be made public. There is also a drug ring involved and we think they are integral. We are pretty sure Don Hayes and his merry band were drugged up, probably without them knowing it. Paula Smith might have been near to something. That is another facet we must control."

Wilson said warningly, "You're overstepping boundaries. This is an MI5 job."

"I already explained it to you. Don't try to opt out of this, Stuart. It's a fifty-fifty job, always has been. The effects and the benefits of this business lie mainly overseas, although from a protection point of view the domestic boys would come out smelling of roses. They put the SB girl in with others to keep an eye on known subversives and that was their pigeon. Because of the overseas links and the finance coming from various sources they accepted our involvement. There has been little, if any, friction between us. It's an interservice operation and always has been. There's a lot of twaddle talked about interservice rivalry; when the chips are down we know how to pull together very effectively." He paused to smile. "Besides, we are far less accountable than they are and they know it.

"Admittedly we were lucky to come in so quickly after the shooting but someone had to act to keep the lid on it. We've explained the situation without the detail to Barry White and he supports me. In due course he's got plenty to gain. The biggest problem was, and perhaps still is, Special Branch. It was one of their girls who was killed and they don't much care for the idea of being brushed aside. They are livid at the loss and want to handle the enquiry themselves. Have they approached you?"

"You know they have. I've held them off. I agree that there might be advantages in doing what we've done but they want an arrest. I placated them by saying they could have an arrest any time they liked, that evidence was strong, but so was the reason for sitting on it for the time being. By waiting we will gain far more than an arrest. I'm not sure they believed me but they're professionals and have to take it as it is. But I need some firm ideas from you, Mike. Something I can pass on. Johnny Cordell was not at all happy with his part. He's not convinced he's been told the whole truth. And nor am I."

Sealy shrugged. "Who knows the whole truth? It's something we have to determine. At the moment nobody knows exactly what happened that night."

Wilson pushed his chair back. "Somebody does," he said drily. "Whoever squeezed the trigger."

Sealy sorted out some notes to pay the bill. "When the time comes we'll put real pressure on young Hayes. But the time is not yet right." He held out a hand. "Thanks for coming, Stuart. We'll soon have the buggers where we want them."

They separated outside the café and Wilson left wondering what Sealy meant.

Sealy, on the other hand, knew exactly what he meant and was well aware of confusing Wilson. Back at Century House he made a strong effort of will to push the whole matter to the back of his mind and to catch up on other issues. At half past three Barry White telephoned him from MI5 at Curzon Street and dropped a little bombshell.

"SB have just informed me that some of the undergrads are being approached by an outsider."

"Do they know who and why?"

"Bulman is the who. The why is anybody's guess although the word is he's acting for the parents of Paula Smith who have been fobbed off by SB."

"Bulman! George Bulman?"

"The very same. I haven't heard about him for so long I thought he must be dead."

"We should be so lucky. Interesting."

"With SB dissatisfied with everything about the case what do you think we should do?"

"He should be discouraged. I'll deal with it."

"He's not an easy man to intimidate. I had a feeling something like this might happen."

"I can't see how the girl's parents would get hold of someone like Bulman, and certainly not so quickly. Marvin Hayes flew to Washington the other day. Didn't leave the airport and we lost track of him because he was whistled off. He had obviously made arrangements to meet someone and if it was anyone from the Company or the FBI, Bulman has friends in both camps – not many but influential. Perhaps he was recommended to Hayes. They wouldn't want to use any of their own for obvious reasons."

"If you're right then the Ambassador is far from satisfied with what he's been told."

"Well, he wasn't just going to take our word for it, was he? Dammit, his son's future is at stake. And his own. And a resulting mayhem back home if any of this came out. He was bound to do something if only to badger Stu Wilson from time to time. Bulman is a bit special, though."

"So what will you do?"

"You don't want to know what I'll do. Don't get yourself involved."

"I am involved, for God's sake. We've been acting concurrently."

"Not with Bulman we haven't. Play it safe your end. Forget Bulman and calm the SB down; they've been acting like recruits. I'll take the can for anything that happens. Just leave Bulman to me. But thanks for the tip-off, Barry. I owe you."

It would be easy to be self critical and say he should have expected it. But Sealy was a realist. He had slightly underestimated the American Ambassador, but only slightly. He could not forget that Marvin Hayes had served a long time with the Drug Enforcement Agency. It was not something he was likely to forget. But so often there was a joker in the pack and they didn't come any wilder than Bulman. The combination of Hayes and Bulman was almost impossible to anticipate. But it made no difference. He would have to deal with it and he did not see it being resolved by a head to head. It would need much stronger methods than that.

Chapter Five

Bulman ran Don Hayes down to earth the day following his talk with Neill Barker. It was tedious work trying to find students who did not want to be found and certainly not to be questioned. From a gregarious, riotous bunch they had suddenly become reclusive. Seeing each other reminded them of that they wished to forget and created suspicion in their minds about their colleagues that they did not really want to entertain. They were afraid of the situation, realising the trouble they were still in and which simply would not go away.

In this respect the presence of Bulman did not help but he had to find them one by one. When Bulman caught up with Don Hayes he took the quickest way to get attention and to stop the young American from storming off. "Your father sent me," he said. "He's employed me to help you, but as that gives you an advantage over the others, I'd rather they did not know I'm on his payroll. Ostensibly I'm working for the dead girl's parents. I've an old banger parked somewhere, where can we talk?"

They drove out of town to a stretch of the river and sat on the bank to watch the ducks and swans and distant people throwing bread to them. It was pretty and peaceful, English countryside at its best. "Will you miss all this?" asked Bulman.

"Yes. Yes, I will. My father thinks I killed the police-woman." Don Hayes watched the ducks, his young face drawn, eyes brooding.

"If he thought that, I wouldn't be here. I'm trying to get at the truth."

"None of our bunch knows the truth."

"One of you does. And he or she made damned sure that the rest of you didn't."

Don turned his head, eyes squinting against the lowering sun. "You really think that? Is it possible to kill someone without knowing a thing about it?"

"Of course. Drink and drugs can blot anything out. What are you going to tell me that you didn't tell your dad? And I'll respect your confidence."

"Nothing. I told him all I know."

"Bullshit. If you were so stewed at the time how can you be so sure? Where were you when this happened and what happened next?"

Don put his head in his hands. "I can't take much more of this. I've been through it all with the police."

"Cut out the self pity and just tell me. I'm wandering in the dark here, and I'm trying to help you."

"How do I know Dad sent you? You could be anyone."

"Okay. Let's find the nearest phone, ring him up and ask him."

"No, forget it." Don waved an arm. "He wouldn't thank me for doing that." He gazed at Bulman again. "You're a crafty sod. You knew I wouldn't."

"And you've been in England too long, using language like that. Get on with it, Don. I haven't much longer to live."

"I think we all fell on top of Paula; that's more of a vague impression than an actual memory. We were shouting and giggling and generally acting insane. I think it was still teeming down. I don't remember getting up although I must have done. I think I heard someone call for an ambulance but I didn't know why and it seemed to come from another world and I probably fantasised. My head was revolving on my shoulders. My sight had gone to join my senses which had left me much earlier. I'd never been in such a state. And then I think someone whacked me. Either that or my brain exploded. It was really dark then."

"You didn't tell your father any of this?"

"Are you kidding? I've done him too much harm. I told him enough."

"So why are you now telling me as your father's representative? I'm bound to tell him."

"But it won't be in my presence and you'll know how to handle it. And I can always deny it."

Bulman smiled, his crusty face changing completely. "And then?"

"It was still raining when I came round but apart from the blow, I was suffering from whatever had spaced me out in the first place. I just about managed to get on to all fours. Enough sense crept into me to wonder what had happened to the others. I was still unable to get to my feet. There was a street lamp and I must have crawled over to it for I remember standing up and clinging to it, and I think I was singing. I could see nobody. They had gone. Including Paula. Either that or I'd moved away from where we had been."

"Or had been moved?"

"I guess that could have happened but my thoughts, those few I conjured, did not go that far. I must have passed out again because my next conscious thought was that I had a terrible headache. I had been sick, the rain had stopped but it was still very wet. I tried to look at my watch but couldn't read it even in the light of the lamp. I climbed up again and must have moved off. I fell quite often and have bruises on my knees to prove it."

"Have you one on your head? Where you were whacked?"

Don felt the back of his head. "I can't feel a bump, but it's tender."

"Did you tell the police?"

"I think so. I can't remember what I told them. I was still in terrible shape. But whatever I did say as sure as hell didn't impress them."

"Do you know what the others said?"

"We were interviewed separately, and none of us was in

51

a condition or the right mood to exchange notes. We were all scared out of our wits. We still are."

"All of you?"

Don appeared uncertain. "I suppose so. I assumed they all felt as I did."

"That was before you were accused of the killing?"

Don said sharply, "I've never been accused of the killing."

"Your father told you the police were satisfied it was you who fired the shot."

"They haven't told me direct. That's strange, isn't it? Why didn't they arrest me?"

"Apparently they are trying to help your father and to stop a special relationship go up in smoke. Surely he told you that, so stop digging for something that isn't there. I've already seen Neill Barker but I shall need your help to run down the others."

"I'll do everything I can. Wally McQueen is sick. Nobody's seen him since that night."

"Is he in digs? Home? Hospital?"

"I heard he went to hospital. He must have been really bad. He never could hold his drink."

Bulman chuckled. "He certainly didn't stand out that night. Do you own a gun?"

"I've never had a hand gun. I had a .22 rifle which I used to pink with back home. But I haven't got it over here."

"Pink?"

"Sure. Pinking. Aiming at empty cans and that stuff. Never hurt anything with it. Do you think I did it?"

Bulman went into noncommittal repose. He followed the antics of a duck leading her young up the river bank before saying, "I've met a few murderers in my time." He turned to look Don in the eye. "Some have even been as unlikely as you. It's too early to form a view."

"Thanks a bunch. That really makes me feel good."

"If you want me to help you you'd better start helping me. Consider yourself guilty. The police do. Now you use any trick you can think of, but I want to know exactly what happened long before the girl was killed. Just when did it first start to go wrong? What were you drinking and whose idea was it to break away and how did you manage to finish up with those particular people? Are they all your usual friends? I think this was planned and the weather arrived as a godsend."

Bulman tore a sheet from a notebook and passed it across. "I'm going back to London tonight but I'll be down again tomorrow. That is my address and telephone number. If anything crops up give me a ring. Meanwhile line the others up for me. If they object they'll be under immediate suspicion." He rose as if it was an effort and stood gazing towards the river. And then he placed a hand on Don's shoulder and said, "Where did we leave that old banger of mine?"

Bulman saw the movement in the shadows as he turned into the square. He kept walking without turning his head, passed the entrance leading to his own apartment, rounded the nearest corner and continued away from the square. He crossed the street and turned right to see the warm beacon of a call box. He was lucky to find it unoccupied and not vandalised. He reflected that Neighbourhood Watch was more effective than he realised. He sorted out his change and dialled a local number.

"Spider? Will you do me a favour?"

"What sort of favour? The last time I did you one I almost got killed."

"This isn't breaking and entering, just a quick surveillance job. I'm ringing from the call box just round the corner from you. I want you to wait outside my place and to follow a guy when he comes out and to let me know where he goes. That's all there is to it."

"I'm watching a film with Maggie, for God's sake. She's already wondering who's called."

"Tell her it's me. Maggie will understand. She can fill you in on the film when you get back."

"Damn you, George. Is this life or death?"

"I don't know. But this guy is good apart from his first guff. But maybe he wanted me to see him. I've no one else to ask, no one as handy as you."

"How long have I got?"

"Ten minutes or so. If it falls flat I'll come out and tell you."

"Don't expect too much. I'm out of practice."

"Thanks, Spider. Always could rely on you."

Bulman took his time leaving the kiosk, checking his money as if he might make another call. He then walked slowly back to his apartment, fully aware that he was taking someone with him.

The light in the entrance hall was invariably out, the lightbulbs constantly vandalised. He was used to that. Instead of going straight up the stairs he dived under the stairwell and waited.

A man entered, briefly framed by the faint light from the street and then came right in to allow the door to close. It was pitch black until the visitor pulled out a narrow beamed flashlight and went to the stairs. He made no sound.

Bulman judged the man's progress by the disappearing light and he stepped from under the stairs and noiselessly mounted them. At the first landing he could not miss the glow of the flashlight above him and continued to climb. Just a few steps from the upper landing he saw the man standing in front of his apartment door, running his fingers round the steel frame. There seemed to be no hurry in the movements and Bulman watched with interest.

Then, as the light beam moved, Bulman stiffened, at first unable to believe the recognition. The man eventually rang the bell and waited and from behind him Bulman said quietly, "There's nobody in."

Most people would have jumped, some might have panicked from the shock, but the the only move the visitor made was to remain with his back to Bulman while his right hand crept inside his jacket.

"There's no need for that, Aleksei. I'm not armed."

Bulman stepped forward and switched on a landing light. "It's downstairs where the vandalism occurs. They do the damage and then dash straight out into the street. Want a cup of coffee?"

Aleksei showed no sign of unease at being caught though his right hand still remained inside his coat. He switched off his flashlight. He was a tall thin man with bleak eyes and a noncommittal expression. "You have a good memory. But I don't think we have actually met." The voice was harsh and grating.

"No. We haven't." Bulman produced his keys and opened the apartment door. As he led the way in he said, "But I've seen plenty of your mug-shots and even a video taken in Paris. I'm surprised you are still in business. There is not so much work for assassins these days."

Aleksei made no comment as Bulman offered him a seat in the living room. Bulman slipped off his jacket and went into the kitchen to make the coffee. He found Aleksei at his elbow.

"Can't trust anyone, can you? I suppose it goes with the job. If you intend to follow me like a puppy then sit by the kitchen counter and I'll bring the coffee over. Who sent you and why?"

"Don't ask stupid questions." Aleksei had a heavy accent. His gaze never left Bulman as if he felt under threat.

"Relax, for God's sake." Bulman took the coffee into the living-room and asked Aleksei to bring the cups and sugar if he needed it. They sat quite close to each other but facing, Aleksei on the edge of his chair trying to assess a changing situation.

Bulman was smiling. "If you'd come to kill me you'd have done it by now, not left your prints on the coffee cups to give yourself extra work cleaning up. Are you working for us now? There can't be a lot of work around for unemployed assassins these days. I mean the Social Services wouldn't know how to find you a job. Or is it just difficult to adjust and you are living here illegally or have they set you up?"

Aleksei Chernov enjoyed his coffee and put it down. His movements were all steady and calculated. "You don't expect me to answer any of those questions so why do you ask them? Don't try to be clever at my expense, Mr Bulman."

"George will do or just Bulman. You still haven't told me why you're here."

"To make your acquaintance. I hear about you. In the old days I hear quite a lot about you. Make sure you keep away from this man, I would be told. And, to an old professional, that is intriguing. We don't warn these days. We advise. And we give good advice."

"With good back-up, no doubt. And what precisely are you advising me to do?"

Aleksei shrugged, showing an increasing indifference to what Bulman had to say. "You have been seen to be mixing with young boys. You must stop."

"Young men, not young boys. And why should you be interested? An out-of-work hit-man scrounging off the British taxpayer when you should be in prison, or splattered in front of a train. Don't try to intimidate me on my own patch, Aleksei, or I'll get someone to look closer at your domicile here."

Aleksei offered a faint smile. "We are not much different, you and I. Neither can back down. I have advised you. That is all I came to do."

"And if I tell you to stuff your advice?"

"I thought you had already done that. Then I take further instructions."

"And obey them to the second trigger pressure. Can't we do a deal? You tell me who wants me barred from Oxford and I'll tell you whether I can meet your request."

"It is not a request, Bulman. When people like me take up this sort of employment, and I would like to retire from it if they'd let me, then we have to be exceedingly efficient as there are so many waiting to take over."

"Now that's the first real threat you've made. Didn't you make enough money to retire?"

"Our money is worthless. This is like starting out all over again. There are so many youngsters about these days ready to step in, that I don't expect to finish the course. Things aren't what they used to be, even in our business. Standards have slipped. Meanwhile I do my best and stick rigidly to my instructions. I am not allowed the luxury of likes and dislikes."

Bulman smiled slowly. "That was almost a hand of friendship, Aleksei. But I do understand your restrictions. I'm afraid the answer still has to be to tell you to piss off and not to try to interfere with what I do."

Aleksei nodded sadly. "It's good to meet a fellow pro. So many would have been shaking in their shoes. What a pity it is my job to eliminate people like you. Soon there won't be any of you left and then what will I do?"

"Write your memoirs. *Autobiography of an Assassin.* That should encourage the youngsters to blow your guts out and set themselves up for a similar fate." Bulman looked at his watch. "I'm knackered having done all the things you don't want me to do."

Aleksei gazed slowly round the room. "Ah, you do have a telephone. I wondered why you felt need to use a call box."

"I've been in and out of so many security scams that I never know when my phone is bugged. You know how it is. I always make certain calls from outside. It's time you went and made your report. I'll see you out."

Aleksei rose. "I can let myself out."

"I know you can," Bulman said drily, "but I want to make sure you go."

Willie "Spider" Scott was waiting in exactly the same position Aleksei had used when he left the building opposite. Scott's association with Bulman went back years to when Bulman was a detective sergeant and Scott was one of the best "creepers" in the business. There are few, if any,

57

cat burglars who would even consider breaking into the Chinese Legation. Scott had done it, but that was a long time ago.

During that time it was said by others that Scott could pick up a tail in his sleep. Bulman could testify to the almost impossible task of following Scott even with a full team. They had been enemies then, disliked each other intensely, but the mean streak that in those days had been part of Bulman's make-up had gradually disappeared and the dislike Scott had for Bulman eroded with the years. Certain events had also drawn them closer together and they had found a common need during which they were forced to rely on each other. From this came an increasing mellowing and a mutual trust and respect. Scott left crime the day he married Maggie and had resisted the pull of offers from the security services who had used his expertise from time to time. It had not been easy for him to resist.

And now as he watched Aleksei walking down the street he wondered why he had been so stupid as to agree to follow. He was rusty. But as he slipped from the shadows he realised that old instincts never die. He was out of practice but that was all; he still knew exactly what to do.

After a couple of ploys used by Aleksei he knew he was up against a pro and his reflexes sharpened with the warning. He followed for a couple of blocks expecting the man to go to one of the many parked cars, but he kept walking and Scott dropped back a little.

They weren't alone on the streets but there were not a lot of people about either. After a while Scott hoped that the man would find a car and drive off so that he could not continue. If Bulman thought he would then steal a car to follow he would be out of luck; those days were over.

There came a point when Scott considered they had been walking for too long, yet they had not basically changed direction and were still roughly heading north. And then, almost catching Scott unawares, Aleksei mounted some steps without hesitation and Scott stopped.

With his quarry out of sight Scott held back; it could be another ploy to draw him out. He waited much longer than he wanted and cursed Bulman for dragging him into something like this. Finally he made use of the long line of parked cars to approach the house. There was nobody at the top of the steps nor under the porch. The man must have entered the house.

When Scott finally mounted the steps he was aware of warnings he had not suffered in years. There was no name board but there were four unmarked bell pushes. The front door was locked. He crossed the street and stood opposite. There had been lights showing on two of the three floors and now there were lights on the third, which was the top floor, that had not been on before. The basement was in darkness.

Scott suddenly realised he had got hooked on what he was doing and was looking for information that Bulman had not requested. He smiled to himself and said quietly, "The crafty bastard." Bulman had gauged him well.

Scott took one last look across the street – not even a twitching curtain – and went back as cautiously as he had arrived until he was certain that he was well out of sight of the house. He then broke into a jog.

He called on Bulman as he lived so near to his own place. The two men shook hands and Bulman had already poured two large whiskies, a fact not lost on Scott who said, "You're a cocky sod at times, George. It's worth more than a whisky." He sat down thinking it was time Bulman changed his furniture.

"I'll put it on expenses and square up later. Cheers! Nice to see you, Spider."

"So you're on expenses? Got yourself a job? They sat back in easy silence, enjoying each other's company. Eventually Scott said, "He lives at 56 Jupiter Street. You know it. A few blocks from here. Right on your doorstep, George."

"Did he see you?"

"Probably. I'm not in top form and he's either totally

innocent or a bloody good pro as you suggested. No name plates. He might live on the top floor."

"He's an ex-KGB assassin," said Bulman as if passing the time of day. "Maybe not so ex. Name is, or was, Aleksei Chernov."

Scott stared in disgust. He had open, good-looking features and a rich crop of hair. It was difficult for anyone to see him as an ex-villain. He had enjoyed doing it but had never entered the world of criminal violence. What oldtime coppers would call an honest villain. But suddenly he was angry. "You sent me after a killer? What the hell do you think you were doing?"

"Calm down, Spider. He wasn't going to top you. Those types don't top anybody unless they've been paid for it."

"Even if they find they are being followed?"

"He'd probably expect it. Forget it. Do you think it's an easy place to break into?"

Scott stiffened. He knew what was going to happen next and he both hated the idea and was roused by it. "I can't fall for that one, George. Maggie would kill me."

"I asked your opinion. Don't read too much into it. Is it an easy one?"

"I didn't case it. I don't know. A bloody assassin is bound to have a few defences up his sleeve. I did find it odd that each flat had an outside bell without a name tag. How would a visitor know which one to press if they hadn't been there or been told? It doesn't allow for stray callers. The street door is kept locked, unlike this dump."

Bulman offered one of his secretive smiles. "I knew a 'safe' house like that."

"A safe house for an assassin? Who would supply that? And take that knowing smirk off your face."

"It would be interesting to find out what name he travels under. As sure as hell it won't be Aleksei Chernov." Bulman gazed thoughtfully at Scott. "Do you know how many organisations are used to set up a new identity? Up to thirty outfits are needed to make a safe change, a new life for someone."

"Thirty? Government organisations? Thirty cock-ups?"

"In some areas they can be very good. Insurance, medical records, employment, mortgages, bank accounts, false educational qualifications, social security, pension rights, passports. It goes on and on. New names and birth and marriage certificates are the easy parts. I wonder to what extent a helping hand has been offered to Aleksei?"

"Perhaps he's just living on his wits. Taking his chances as an illegal."

"Or perhaps he's become a security supergrass with all the benefits that breed enjoys."

"Enjoys? They probably live in constant fear."

"Not Aleksei. He's seen death too often to flinch from facing it himself. He expects to be killed, even perhaps from his own lot. Trained assassins go dead inside after a while. They go on killing and wait for the day."

"Who do you think he's working for?"

"That's exactly what I'd like to find out, Spider. If we could find out if he has a new identity it would at least be a pointer. Easy for you, a job like that."

"Forget it," said Scott. "I'm beyond it."

"You'll never be beyond it. You're the best."

Scott sat there shaking his head. "Get stuffed."

"I'm trying to get right to the root of this thing. This is a certain way of doing it. Help me, Spider."

"It would break Maggie's heart if anything went wrong. I'm sorry, George."

Bulman could see that Scott was in torment. Scott wanted to do it: he always had and always would want this kind of challenge; it was like offering a drink to an alcoholic. Scott had enormous skills which had not been exercised for some time until the appetizer of following Aleksei.

"And if I'm caught? I couldn't face stir again, George. You know damn well I couldn't cope with that again."

"In that unlikely event I'd come clean with authority and get it sorted. Now we've got to make sure Aleksei isn't there."

Chapter Six

Michael Sealy went into the office earlier than usual. He carefully placed on his desk a silver-framed photograph of himself with his wife Meg and son Ray; a family studio shot, familiar to all who called in his office. Some knew the circumstances that had led to this habit but few knew why he took it home with him every night only to bring it back the next day, when it was perfectly possible to get a copy print made.

Connie Taylor, Sealy's P.A., knew why he did this. Or she thought she knew why. She believed that by leaving it in one place it would no longer be seen so often. It would become part of the furniture and Sealy had pledged himself never to forget.

Connie, a tall elegant woman in her late thirties, had carried the flag for Sealy these last few years. She was patrician in both looks and manner and some found her unnecessarily aloof. This opinion was formed mostly by those who worked with her, not understanding that it was the only way she could get through each day while so close to the unattainable man she wanted so much. Those friends she had outside the sphere of her work saw a different person, still elegant, sometimes reserved, but a warm caring person who could laugh wholeheartedly or act with dignity. The daily proximity of Sealy had taught her control.

Now that both Meg and Ray had gone Connie Taylor was finding it more difficult to hide her feelings, particularly as she saw the changes in him. He had always been tough, a mode he could slip from, but now he was becoming hard and she did not know what to do about it. And he rarely discussed anything any more, although he had never been under any obligation to do so. He was gradually changing into someone she did not know and it both worried and hurt her. These last few days had concerned her even more; it was reaching a point where she hardly knew him at all. It was obvious that something was on his mind, but what?

As he sat at his desk she stood before him, a sheaf of files in her arms, and said, "Are you all right?"

When there was no response she stood looking down at him. He was obviously deep in thought. He was dressed as neatly as ever as if to make up for the years he had spent in the field, but his features were frozen.

"Are you all right, Mike?" She had called him that for some time now following a spate of late work.

He looked up at last. "I'm sorry, I was miles away." He smiled but it was forced and he clearly wanted to get back to his thoughts.

"There are some files here that should be tackled. They have fallen rather behind." And then she suddenly remembered which day it was and she felt terrible. Today was an anniversary of Meg's death. She prevented herself from being too insensitive just in time and stole a glance at the silver-framed photograph mounted at an angle on one corner of the desk.

Perhaps Sealy saw her. He made an effort to rouse himself and reached up for the files. "I don't know how you put up with me," he remarked with a more genuine smile.

And that, reflected Connie, was the trouble: he really did not know how she put up with him and she doubted now that he ever would.

Later that day, she received a call from her friend who worked at the US Embassy, Anna Brus. Both women were attached to their bosses in different ways. Anna was proud of Marvin Hayes, considered him a fine ambassador who well deserved his position, and she would do anything to

63

protect him and, if necessary, keep him in line. She was worried about her boss too.

The two women had first met on the Embassy circuit, and had been good friends ever since. So physically different, they had much more in common than was obvious. They had both been married, Anna to an US Air Force officer who left her for a German woman while serving there, while Connie had suffered rape from a drunken husband who was still technically married to her pending separation settlement. But apart from that there was a spark between them which tossed aside the past and enabled them to enjoy each other's company without probing each other's job. They knew the rules. There was also another bond, which as yet was unknown to them and was building up without their knowledge, and neither could have known the devastation it would cause.

"He's a shit. A spoiled American brat. Takes advantage of his father's position and rams it down our throats every opportunity." Jamie Burke was vehement and had clearly entered Oxford by his brain power and not the way he spoke. Wild eyed and fiery, a born troublemaker, he must have been brilliant not to have been side-shifted to one of the lesser-known universities. His voice had travelled well from Glasow; nothing in it had changed.

"So why did you celebrate with him?" Bulman had trouble understanding Burke at times. He had met the type before: everything was wrong with society – the same society that had enabled him to reach Oxford. At base he was an anarchist, for no change of any government would satisfy him.

"He'd cotton on to people. That night it happened to be us. He can't hold his liquor. He doesn't belong here."

It was raining mildly so Bulman's return to Oxford found him in a tea shop after making use of Don Hayes' information on how to contact Burke. Only the time of day dictated the venue, for Burke was a young man who looked eternally in need of a drink.

Burke's appearance matched his character: unruly dark hair over thick brows, fiery brown eyes, strong features and a shortish, stocky body. As he claimed to be all for the underdog it had been difficult for him to refuse to see Bulman, who was still using the ploy of representing the dead girl's family.

"And you can?" prompted Bulman.

"Can what?"

"Hold your liquor? You obviously did that night. Along with the rest of them."

"Aye, it happens that was an exceptional night. None of us did that night. And there's no need to be sarky."

"Were your drinks spiked? It's a question for all."

"Of course they bloody were. I'd never get in that state if they weren't. Someone chose his moment."

"Or her. There were two women with you."

"Tammy wouldn't do a thing like that, she's too much sense. And the other girl was shot, so they say. It's more likely to be the Yank."

"Why?"

"He's been at it before, across the pond. Aye and probably here too."

"How do you know that?"

The question arrived like a whiplash and Burke realised he was being carried away by his own rhetoric. He took a mouthful of cake, which gave him time to think. "You hear these things around. You know how it is." Crumbs came with the words.

"Rumours, you mean? I thought you were the factual type, all black and white. Good guys and bad guys and change the world guys. I'll mention what you say to his master. We don't want junkies in our universities, do we?"

"There's no need for that. I was trying to be help-ful."

"You were trying to stir it up for someone you dislike intensely for a reason you have not made clear and which I would have to put down as blind prejudice. You don't like Americans. Okay, that's a viewpoint. I bet you don't like the English either. How the hell did you get to Oxford? Why not Glasgow or Edinburgh, or wouldn't they tolerate you up there?"

Burke almost tipped the table over, realised where he was, and quickly recovered. He glared hatred at Bulman who smiled back sweetly. Burke snarled, "You make a crack like that again and you'll be walking like a bent old man."

Bulman, still smiling, said, "That's more like you, Jamie. I prefer it when you don't pussyfoot around. You haven't answered my question."

"I live in England. South London. And I'm not answering any more of your stupid bloody questions."

"Like so many of you brainy types, you've got no common sense. Is that what you did on the night of the finals? Lose your cool? Shoot a policewoman because you don't like the police?"

Burke looked murderous but made no move.

Bulman added, "You're not very good at self control, are you?"

"Just what do you think I'm doing now? You'll never see so much control when all I want to do is to smash your stupid sassernach face in."

"That's not control, Jamie. That's because we're on public view and you don't want to balls things up. A crumb of common sense at last. Well, did you shoot her? Did you find out she was in the police? And did you discover why she was there?"

Bulman really did think the table was coming at him then. Burke had gone white with rage and was barely holding on to his senses. Bulman suddenly saw how it might have been, that Burke was capable of killing in a red hot fury. Perhaps he had much to hide.

And then Burke managed to avoid exploding and said in a shaking voice, "I don't have a gun, you stupid bugger. And I didn't know she was police. I didn't even know she was dead. If we could think at all we probably all thought

66

she had passed out. Don't try to pin anything like that on me."

"And you told this to the police?"

"No. I told them I wasn't there and the rest were lying. What do you think I told them?"

Bulman wondered why Burke was still with him in a half-filled café, answering awkward questions in a vile mood when all he had to do was to walk out of the door. It was then he realised that Burke was trying to glean something from him. There was something Burke wanted to know and was afraid to ask him.

"How do you get on with Neill Barker?" asked Bulman quietly.

"He's an upper-class pratt."

"Is he another one who cottons on? I mean, he's hardly your type, is he? Just as Don Hayes isn't. That leaves three other people, apart from the dead girl, to make up the party. How many of those were your type?"

"We were all mixed up. It was the way it went. Some of my usual friends got lost in the scrum."

"Or you became detached from them or were dragged away by someone. Can you remember who?"

"If I'd been sober at the time it wouldn't have happened at all, so how can I remember who? I don't think there was a who. I told you, we just finished up that way."

"Did Wally McQueen have a gun? A fellow Scot, now he'd have been your type."

"Why would I know if Wally had a gun? Why would I know if anyone had a gun? You're asking pretty dumb questions. Anyway, Wally's in dock."

"So people keep telling me. Have you any idea which hospital he's in?"

"No. Why don't you check at his lodging or with the college?"

"I've already checked his digs. You mean you haven't tried to find out so that you can visit him? None of you seems to have done."

"He wasn't a very popular guy. Anyway I heard he was

67

not critically ill. We don't want to know each other since this thing happened and the college has advised us to keep apart, seeing us as trouble together. We'd have done it anyway. It was a one-night stand for the lot of us."

"So McQueen wasn't popular but was there. Evidently another one you didn't like but who cottoned on. That only leaves Tammy Rees and Phill Marshall. You're a hard man to please, Jamie. Have the police had you in for more questioning?" Bulman was trying to draw out what was on Burke's mind.

"No. None of us has been contacted again so far as I know."

"You seem to be surprised by that."

"It's typical police, isn't it? Bloody useless."

"Unless, of course, they know who killed Paula Smith."

Burke was now uneasy. "There's been nothing in the papers. Nobody's been arrested as far as I know. Maybe she did die of natural causes and all the rest is bullshit."

"Maybe you're right." Bulman caught the eye of the waitress and signalled for the bill. "Thanks for your help."

"Did you learn anything?" Burke had calmed down.

"Yes. I learned that nobody knows a thing, everyone was conveniently spaced out and nobody owns a gun. You are all, more or less, saying the same thing. You all claim to keep apart so there is obviously no collusion."

"Aye, well, maybe the collusion is elsewhere."

Neither Tammy Rees nor Phill Marshall were at their lodgings and their respective landladies had no idea when they might return so Bulman returned to his hotel on the outskirts of Oxford and sat in his room tracking down local hospitals and ringing them to try to locate Walter McQueen. As he did not know which hospital McQueen was in and nobody else seemed to know, nor which ward he was likely to be in, it was a long tedious task and got him nowhere.

If the checks had been thorough Walter McQueen was in

none of the hospitals within a fifteen-mile radius. Bulman then took a step he had been avoiding for several reasons. He rang the master of the college, could not get him immediately so had to leave a message and then hang around the hotel hoping for a return call. When it did not come within two wasteful, long hours he called again. He could still not raise the master but did get an assistant who told him that as far as he knew McQueen had been taken to an out-of-town hospital which had a wing that specialised in drug addiction. The name was not known off hand but it was thought to be in London.

Bulman put the phone down. Drugs in a university were no longer rare, even at times common, but no one would want it publicly discussed and certainly not with a stranger. Bulman could understand the negative stance but he really needed to know where McQueen was.

He returned to London that evening unhappy about his day's work. Apart from goading Burke he had got nowhere. He would have stayed on in Oxford until he located Tammy Rees and Phill Marshall but had arranged to make a direct report to Marvin Hayes that evening. When he returned to his flat he called Spider Scott to find both he and Maggie out and left no message on the answering machine in case it upset Maggie; she had endured a lot during the early days of Scott's escapades. His frustration continued.

He did not call on Marvin Hayes until after nine. To his surprise Zoë Hayes answered the door. He liked her on sight and she seemed to know who he was and asked him in. He had never met the Ambassador's wife but had seen her photograph in the newspapers. He was instantly aware of her nervousness.

"Marvin's expecting you," she said, glancing over her shoulder as if she expected her husband to confirm. "I'll take you to his study." But Hayes entered the hall just at that moment and was clearly surprised to see his wife there, but was quick to hide his irritation.

"I was at the back of the house," Hayes explained

quickly. "I'd have answered the door, honey, there was no need for you to disturb yourself."

Zoë Hayes shot Bulman an almost despairing look as if she had been hoping to have a few words with him herself. Bulman bowed graciously, aware of her good looks and sorry to see her clearly disturbed. "I hope we'll meet again, ma'am."

"I hope so too, Mr Bulman." She disappeared at the rear of the large hall while Hayes led the way to his study.

When they were seated with the usual drinks Bulman observed, "Your wife knew my name. Have you told her any of this business?"

"That worries me, too. She glimpsed you leaving the other night but I have not discussed you with her. She's guessed something is going on that is not Embassy business and she knows that I'm worried even when I don't show it. She must have listened in to our last call."

"And she wanted you to know that she had."

"I guess so. It's not like her at all. I don't want her to know what's going on. It could kill her if she finds out about Don."

"Maybe she's stronger than you think. She's just shown a glimpse of determination."

"You think I should tell her that the police have proof against our only son for murder? I can't take that risk. What have you found out?"

"Nothing concrete. Someone doesn't like my nosing down at Oxford to the extent of sending an ex-KGB hit-man to warn me to lay off."

"You're kidding me. Are you serious?"

"He was. I've had him tracked down by an ex-cat burglar I know. We'll have a look inside his apartment. But it does show there is something to find in Oxford."

"Ex-KGB? Ex-cat burglar? What are we entering into here?"

"If you want this kept under wraps the underworld is the only place for me to turn. I can't make it official because I believe not only will I get no help but there'll be road blocks all round to stop me. Someone already knows what I'm doing, but that might be isolated information. I don't think an assassin would be sent if it was general knowledge, the press will co-operate only so far – if they smell a story so strong then they'll go for it."

"So you think Don is innocent?"

"I didn't say or suggest that. But I do think he's the centre of some strange goings-on. And I do think the lack of action on the part of the police is very strange indeed. Certainly they'll co-operate with the security forces, even if they don't like it, if the issue is big enough or the name in Whitehall, Curzon Street or Century House is powerful enough. They would have a job not to co-operate. Having said that, I think they would continue to make enquiries if only to offer an illusion of activity."

"But they say they can prove Don did the shooting. What other activity could they make?"

"Well, you see, even with Don's prints on the gun, I don't think they believe he did it. There are plenty of ways his prints could have got there in the state he was in. So they would not want me messing around, or at least whoever is pulling the strings wouldn't. The use of Aleksei Chernov might point us in the right direction."

Hayes stretched his legs out, glass in hand, gaze firmly on Bulman. "This is beginning to look sinister."

"It always was sinister. There's a mixture here. I can't find out what Paula Smith was doing down there in the first place. There may be two or even three issues that are somehow connected, perhaps by design, or perhaps by opportunism, or a combination of both."

"Look, George, perhaps it's time I called our own people in. If there's some kind of conspiracy here, they can make bigger noises than you. They have the muscle. Please don't be offended, I think you're doing a terrific job. You're given me hope, for one thing."

"I'm not sure I intended to do that. All I'm pointing out is that there is something bloody queer going on, and that the reason given for not arresting Don is not necessarily the right one. Are we trying to twist your arm about anything?"

"No. Not yet anyway. Diplomatic relations are quite normal. You think they might do? There's a limit to how much I could help them."

Bulman shrugged. "Well, call your own people in by all means. You can settle up my account here and now if you prefer. I need the expenses settled anyway. But perhaps you'd better keep me on a retainer for a few days."

Hayes clasped his hands and smiled crookedly at Bulman. "You don't think they'll help, do you?"

"Why should they? They didn't before."

"Well, there's now an element that was not there in the first place."

"You are grasping at straws, sir. The element has been there all along. We still don't know what it is, we're still groping but with just a little more conviction that there is something to find. But do please try them again."

Hayes stared at what remained of his drink, then at Bulman and then finished his drink quite slowly. "You know, the truth is," he said after putting down his glass, "I'm not really a diplomat. I don't come from the mould of diplomats. I'm not a high-powered businessman being rewarded for subscribing to party funds. I was, as you were, a policeman. A specialised one, it is true, but still a cop at heart.

"I'm here because the President's wife and my wife are old schoolfriends and it was noticed, only just in time, that Zoë was cracking up through some of my antics helping Uncle Sam. I didn't want this job, it's not me, but Zoë wanted me to take it against all the odds and jockeying and competition. Maybe I'd served my country better than I realised but I was still surprised when I was offered the post. I accepted for her because I owed her." Hayes leaned forward. "And look where it's got us, George. Just about the biggest crisis of my life, which looks like doing to my wife what none of my field play managed to do. It's tearing my guts out. And hers too because she

72

knows something is going on and is worried sick because I won't tell her."

"You're being very frank with me, sir."

Hayes raised his arms in despair. "Maybe I've got to like you. I need to talk to someone. But you're right: they won't help back home for fear of showing themselves to you Brits. They'd need to know far more than we do before they risk rocking the boat on this delicate issue. Will you carry on?"

"Of course." Bulman pulled out a list of expenses. "Don't think me grasping but I don't live on your kind of salary. By the way, do you normally answer the front door yourselves at night? After your bodyguard has signed off for the day?"

"Our live-in butler would normally do it. But I don't want the staff involved in this." Hayes went to a wall safe and withdrew some cash. "This should cover you." He handed over some notes. "By the way, I've been increasingly thinking of bringing this whole thing up with the Prime Minister."

Bulman smiled cynically. "That's your prerogative. And he will, of course, listen very sympathetically. And when he's looked into it he'll come back and say, 'Ambassador, we are doing everything to protect you and your family. Please don't worry about it.'"

"Then who's pulling those sort of strings, George?"

Bulman shrugged. "There are some, as in the USA, who are unaccountable. In the end we might all have been barking up the wrong tree and find that the original reason is true."

"Do you believe that?"

"No," Bulman said without hesitation. "I'll plod on."

Wally McQueen lay on the bed, gazed up and made rude signs at the two television scanners high in opposite corners of the room. After a while he rolled off the bed and took stock as he had done so many times before.

It was a fairly large room with a small table and chair

73

and an upright armchair. Behind a fixed screen were a washbasin and WC. There were two rows of bookshelves filled with a mixture of fact and fiction, and embedded high above them, a microphone sensitive enough to pick up his breathing. It was a cell, whatever its amenities, and the door was steel with a food flap. Meals were regular, much better than normal prison meals, and were served on plastic plates with plastic utensils.

Recessed lights were permanently on but there was also the addition of two square armoured glass recesses well out of reach on one wall. He knew the glass was toughened when he had first tried to break them with anything he could find to throw.

McQueen was well built, bearded, small eyed, and occasionally aggressive. He spoke with a London accent although he had been born in the Midlands. He had no known political affiliations and no criminal record, although he was known to the police.

He had been imprisoned since the day after the finals and was well aware that this was no ordinary prison. It was this that concerned him most. There was virtually no communication. He had not been interviewed and the only sign of life was when the meals appeared. As the food flap opened only one way he was unable to shout through it although he had tried. So he had vented his frustration on the door, kicking it repeatedly until his feet were sore. He finished up shouting obscenities at the microphone once he had located it, but no reaction came back to him.

Once he realised that a psychological war was being waged with him, he calmed down to cope with it. It was either that or slowly go mad. He tried to read, occasionally demanded an explanation from the unresponsive microphone, and tried to stifle his frustration. They couldn't keep him here for ever. Which led him to wonder just who held him. Meanwhile, he realised with growing fear that nobody would find him here because none of those he knew would have the slightest idea of what had happened to him.

74

He increasingly reflected on the night of the party and wondered what had happened to the American. And then he would veer away from the subject as if the microphone could pick up his thoughts too.

Chapter Seven

When he got back to his own flat Bulman rang Spider Scott and was thankful that he answered and not Maggie. "Sorry about the hour. When are you going to do Chernov's place?"

"You've got me out of bed to ask that?"

"You weren't in bed. You're a night hawk. What about it, Spider?"

"I didn't say I'd do it. And I wouldn't even consider it without someone outside with a bleeper. Go back to bed, George, and when you are organised let me know. And don't ring at this time again."

"Hang on. I've got to go back to Oxford tomorrow. Finding people there is worse than finding a camel flea in the desert. Take a daylight look and see what you think." He hung up before Scott could answer.

"Nice room," observed Bulman. "Are they all this good?"

Tammy Rees smiled. "I share it with another girl. It's not bad. Nice landlady and not too far from the college. If you want some tea you'll have to take me out and buy it."

"Can we do the talking first? If we're not interrupted this will do fine."

"Have you talked to any of the others?" Tammy Rees spoke with a muted Welsh accent, a very attractive girl, bright eyed and fair skinned, though her hair was dark with deep waves. She seemed to look out on life as if round every corner was a pleasant surprise. But Bulman already knew that she saw this was not true. She had either

76

recovered remarkably quickly from the event or had yet to suffer an over-delayed shock.

"Most of them. I haven't seen Phill Marshall, and Walter McQueen seems to have disappeared into thin air."

"He's in hospital," said Tammy brightly. "God knows why."

"So everyone tells me," said Bulman drily. "But no hospital around here seems to have him." He left it at that to see if Tammy had anything to add but she knew no more than the others and seemed to be surprised by what he said.

"And you want me to give my recollection of what happened that night?" She had suddenly become serious as if she did not want to recollect at all.

"I'm just trying to get a general picture of what actually happened."

"Well, my own recollection is absolute zilch but as you can see I survived to tell the tale. I never want another night like that again. Poor, poor Paula."

"You were friends?"

"Good friends. She was a couple of years older then me but wanted to get India out of her system before studying seriously. I got the shock of my life when I was told she was a policewoman. Special Branch, too. Couldn't believe it."

"Does it make any difference to the way you feel about her?"

Tammy curled her legs under her on the slightly shabby settee. "Not really. It made me realise that she'd been spying on us but she was a lovely girl and must have had good reason."

"Good girl. Why do you think she was spying?"

Tammy shrugged. "I've thought about it. There have been a lot of drug rumours. And the colleges are very sensitive to the dangers some of the foreign students face, particularly those from the Middle East. But I really don't know. What I do know is that some stupid pratt put something in our drinks that night."

77

It was the most positive assertion yet. Bulman said, "Do you know who did it?"

Tammy shook her head. "Whoever did it, did it to us all. I'd like to catch the idiot."

"But he wouldn't have done it to himself, would he? He'd have acted the part. What about Don Hayes, could he have done it?"

Tammy noticeably bridled. "You're on dangerous ground, Mr Bulman. I love him. Don wouldn't hurt anyone, and think what this must be doing to his mother and father. He wouldn't have done this to them."

"Nor to you?"

Tammy offered an impish smile. "You are not a very subtle detective, are you? Ask it straight out: does he feel about me as I do about him? Well, I don't yet know the answer. Do you?"

"It's possible that he does. He was careful to leave you out of any comments relating to that night. That could be interpreted as protective, couldn't it? What about the others?"

"Jamie Burke and Wally McQueen are a pair. I don't like either of them; they're too radical for me. They are both clever but very basic. Burke is definitely mixed up in the extremist end of organisations like Animal Rights; he'd go to any lengths, even to releasing animals to a fate worse than the one they face, if it came to it. I've heard him talk when he didn't know I was there. I advised Don to keep clear of him."

"So why didn't he?"

"I've thought about that, too. It affects me as well, you know. I would like to think it just happened by accident that the seven of us just hived off into the night. But I don't think it was that way at all. It was somehow engineered. If drinks are spiked – and it may not have been drugs but a deadly mixture of alcohol – and people lose their minds it is possible that they forget likes and dislikes and follow whoever might lead them. If one is sober and convincing and cunning enough it would be fairly easy to get others to go with him on a wild chase. We were all celebrating, for God's sake. We weren't fussed who we were with; it wouldn't have mattered that much after a while."

"Did you hear a shot?"

Tammy shook her head. "I sometimes think that's a load of rubbish, that she's not really dead. But I have to ask myself what happened to her if that's true."

"Yet a shot was fired. Nobody seems to have heard it."

"Maybe it didn't happen while we were all there. Maybe it was done some time after she fell down. Someone made us panic, called out for someone to ring for an ambulance and for the rest of us to scatter quickly if we wanted to avoid trouble. We could barely stand, unable to think straight or even at all. Survival comes top of the list in that situation – I could do a paper on it. It was shameful the way we left her. But whoever called out said they would stay with her."

"You couldn't identify the voice?"

"It sounds dreadful to say so but I couldn't have identified anyone's just then. Not even my own mother's. It was just a voice penetrating the wind and the rain and doped minds. We would probably have done anything just then. We were still laughing and giggling even though Paula was down. Don had fallen earlier; we helped him up."

"You remembered that all right."

"Only hazily, but mainly because it was Don. I can't speak for the others. Supposing one of these silencer things had been used? Should we have heard the shot then?"

"I shouldn't think so. Not with the racket you say was going on."

Tammy uncurled her legs and Bulman noticed what nice legs they were. "I haven't been much help, have I?"

"I think you have if only to give Don Hayes a glowing tribute. That will help him."

Tammy straightened. "He's not in trouble, is he?"

"No more than the rest of you." Bulman reflected that the girl was sharp. "I'll see Phill Marshall and try to run down Wally McQueen and that will finish my enquiries. Thanks, Tammy, don't let the torch go out."

Phill Marshall had not returned to his digs and nobody seemed to know when he would be back so Bulman once more returned to London.

When he arrived at his flat he checked the answering machine to find no calls, rang Spider Scott and was again frustrated to find the answering machine on. Both Scott, who owned a travel business, and Maggie worked but Bulman could at times be impatient when he wanted something done. To Bulman's surprise Scott called round at six p.m.

"I don't want you to keep phoning while Maggie's there. She's already smelled a rat and she'll always be suspicious when you suddenly turn up. Can you ring this guy to find out if he's in?"

Bulman laughed. "You've been going straight too long. How can I ring him? You don't think he's using the name of Chernov, do you? Let's wait until it's dark and then go see what happens."

"I'll need a camera and a bleeper. I need to know if he's creeping up on me."

"I might have some bleepers somewhere. Haven't you got any of your own?"

"Never used them. But then I did my homework properly first. It seems you want this done yesterday. I'll call back at nine."

Scott went and Bulman wondered if he was doing the right thing in endangering his friend.

Scott returned at nine with some story he had given Maggie to cover his absence. Before leaving with Bulman, Scott took out a small bottle of nail varnish and painted his fingertips. He hated wearing gloves. The two men set off together at half past nine.

They stood where Scott had previously watched the house from across the street. It was not fully dark, but some of the lights were on. The basement was in darkness and so was the top floor; the middle two floors were clearly occupied and faint music drifted from one of them.

Scott gave a warning to Bulman to stay where he was and then crossed the road, mounted the steps and rang the bell of the top apartment. He was not as calm as he used to be; his confidence had remained on hold for far too long. But it was almost impossible for him to back down from a job and his fingers were tingling.

He rang the bell again, waited for much longer than normal then turned to wave at the shadowy doorway across the street. He could not see Bulman but hoped that Bulman could see him as he approached the front of the porch and waved again. His bleeper pinged once and he grinned as he turned back to the door.

He had half a dozen dummy security keys on him which he had removed from a ring of picklocks he kept hidden at home. The third sprung the tumblers and he opened the door cautiously. It had been years now since he had done this and it excited him as it always had except that now there was an underlying fear he used not to experience.

He closed the door quietly, weighed up the well-lit hall, then went up the stairs keeping to the edge to minimise squeaking. He briefly rested at each landing. There was no light on at the top landing so he produced a small flashlight and found the door to the right of the stairs.

He beamed the flashlight over the door to find no obvious attempt at security and that worried him. An ex-KGB assassin would take precautions, it would be second nature, but there wasn't even a hair stuck across the tiny gap between door and lintel. Perhaps it was the wrong apartment but he somehow thought not.

It took him a little time to open the door and he pushed it carefully. It was completely dark inside. He closed the door behind him, crept into the hall and stood with his back to the wall. Something was not right. It should never be this easy.

He resisted the temptation to put on the hall light and examined the two doors leading off from the hall. He found

81

a dead fly in the gap between floor and door. He grinned in the darkness; this was more like it, anyone breaking in would open both doors. He hooked out the fly with a nail file and placed it carefully to one side.

There was a fair-sized living-room nicely furnished in a contemporary way, and off that a small kitchen. The other door off the hall led to a bathroom and toilet. The apartment was comfortable but without character. Scott settled down to examine a small desk in one corner, at the side of which was a stacked stereo system. If this was Chernov's home he was certainly not on the dole. All the desk drawers were unlocked except one. He found what he wanted in the central drawer.

An unsealed envelope contained a crumpled birth certificate, a marriage certificate, a death certificate, an insurance policy, an old mortgage book, cancelled some years ago, a British passport with about six months to go before expiry, and naturalisation papers. There was also a cheque book and a bank statement. Scott laid them out and photographed them one at a time with a small flash camera Bulman had supplied. When he returned the envelope he found another, smaller one with a bundle of BP option certificates indicating that the owner had a car and had being buying petrol in this country for some time.

Scott was feeling quite satisfied but was intrigued by the one locked desk drawer and felt compelled to open it. It took some time and he cursed his staleness. He had almost given up when the lock clicked and he slid the drawer forward. The drawer was crammed with pornographic photographs and some videos he guessed were of the same ilk. He took two shots with the camera and then discovered one had the name, address and telephone number of a dating agency on the back which he snapped before putting everything back. He had intended to leave it at that but because of his surprise discovery he searched the rest of the room and found some soft porn magazines in a rack behind the stereo. He was returning everything to its place when the bleeper pinged twice.

Scott moved quickly to the window, pulling one of the curtains back just a fraction but he could see nothing in the street and moved towards the living-room door. He stuck the fly back under the door, noticed the telephone recessed on a small hall table, crossed to take the number and found the disk blank. He hurried to the front door and put his ear to the wood, heard nothing, then let himself out. He was trying to relock the door when he heard the footsteps on the stair.

Scott kept working away at the lock; it was essential to turn it. He had already accepted that there was no way out without passing whoever was on the stairs. His fingers started to tremble and then he began to sweat as he experienced his first real attack of nerves. The lock finally sprang, the noise far too loud on the dark, quiet landing. He went to the furthest point away from the door that the landing permitted. This was the top floor and unless there was an attic the only way out was the stairs. He pushed himself back against the opposite wall. It was the best he could do but he felt totally exposed.

Then the landing light came on and he had nowhere to run. Scott just stood there trying to push himself into the wall. A man was fiddling at the front door of the apartment with his back half turned towards him. Scott heard the faint click of the tumblers turning and stood absolutely still. He could only see a half-turned back view but from Bulman's description the man could well be Chernov. The door opened and closed again after the man had gone in. Scott did not move.

The light went out and Scott was glad of the darkness but remained where he was for a little longer, intrigued by the fact that the landing light could also be controlled from inside the apartment. He moved quickly and silently down the stairs. He let himself out the front door, locked it, and then strolled up the street on the same side so he could not be seen by anyone looking through the curtains of the top apartment. He knew that Bulman would understand and follow in his own good time.

They met up round the corner a few minutes later.

"I thought he had got you," said Bulman with some relief.

"He almost did. You didn't give much warning and I had trouble closing everything down." He paused, finding difficulty in adding, "I had a bad dose of the shakes. I've never had that before. I'm beyond it, George."

"Don't talk daft. You're just rusty. You made it, didn't you?" But Bulman could see that Scott was still shaken.

They were walking slowly together and Bulman glanced at the subdued Scott. Both were tall men over six feet. "You haven't lost your touch, Spider. You've done a great job."

"I was beginning to wonder. I think I've got what we needed. By the way, he's into porn, probably for his own pleasure."

They reached the street where Bulman lived and Scott handed over the camera and said, "Have you facilities for developing these yourself? I wouldn't trust them with anyone else."

"No, but I know someone who will lend me his darkroom. Do you remember Bluie Palmer? I'd better find a cab."

"Bluie? I thought he was tucked away inside."

"So he was. But he's been out for a bit. He didn't win the name Bluie for nothing. When I show him your shots of Chernov's porn, he'll probably be able to identify who's taking part, the date, where it took place, the main actors and who took the films. Probably himself. It shouldn't take long."

"You mean you're going now? How many friends do you manage to keep? You're a ruthless sod, George."

"I know. But Bluie's hardly a friend. He just owes me a few favours. I could have put him away for ever. I'll give you a ring tomorrow."

"It's all in the camera. I'm off. I'm late."

The two men parted to go in opposite directions.

*   *   *

It was four thirty in the morning and Bulman was at home with copies of the snapshots spread over a small table. He had taken his jacket and tie off and he looked tired and haggard, the stubble on his chin reflecting in the light from the desk lamp he had pulled over.

Charles Dubas had been born in Estonia in December 1945. The birth certificate was a good job, aged and seemingly genuine. The naturalisation papers showed that Dubas had been accepted as a British citizen in 1960. It would have been interesting to have seen his parents' birth certificates but they were not on the roll of film. The used cheque book, old mortgage book, valid passport, and the rest, had been nicely placed for anyone to find. Do most people keep all these documents together? Or do they tuck away those they are hardly likely to use from day to day, like a will which was absent but might have been interesting to see.

There was no telephone number and it was unlike Scott to slip up on such a vital point. He searched the directory in vain. In spite of the hour he rang directory enquiries and learned that the number was ex-directory.

Bulman was disturbed by his findings. And more disturbed by what he had not found out. He had a shave and shower and made strong coffee. It was too late to go to bed, he would only get up feeling worse. He sat down with his coffee beside him and considered why Chernov's papers had been packaged together and too easy to find, for an assassin with a great deal to hide. And Chernov was not the type to make things easy for anyone.

Bulman found much of what he had was contradictory. Although Chernov was involved, if only as enforcer, Bulman had a strong gut feeling that the issue had nothing to do with espionage at any level. True, cast-offs from that profession were being used, but that was because they were very experienced men, as hard as nails, and looking for work like many others. Most people like Chernov were redundant yet still had a lot to offer. As he was not the kind to go touting for business in his particular line without the best of contacts, someone who knew the game at least as well as he was involved and pulled his strings.

Ambassadors had not the power of a few decades ago. It has been suggested that they were no longer of real value, an expensive ornament on an enormous expense account paid for by the public. Showpieces, no more. The world had shrunk too much, and techniques were quite different from the old days. Their roles had changed. So of what possible use was Marvin Hayes outside that envisaged by his own employers?

Bulman left the photos spread out on the table and sat before them, scrutinising them until he dozed in the chair and almost fell off it.

He awoke with a start to grab the table. He checked the time: ten minutes past six a.m. He rose wearily, searched in a small music rack which he now used for magazines and found a tattered exercise book which he took to the telephone. He checked a number, punched it out and waited for some time while it rang out.

A woman eventually answered, angry and tired. "Whoever it is I'm not in so get stuffed."

"It's George," Bulman got in quickly. "And you've got it the wrong way round, Julie. I hope I'm not interrupting anything. Have you someone in bed with you?"

"George? Which George? Do you realise what time it is?"

"I didn't think it would matter, you being a night worker and all."

"*That* George. I should have known. For God's sake, I could have been busy."

"I know," Bulman admitted. "But I'd have been quite willing to hold on until you were finished. You awake yet?"

"You bastard. You haven't changed, have you? What do you want, George?"

"If you're still on the game, I want you to do a job for me. Well paid."

"Then it can't be your money. You'd want a refund on a freebee. I'm listening."

"Are you still freelance or are you working through an agency?"

"Money's tight. I use an agency or get forced out of the game."

"It's not the DLA Agency, is it?"

"That cow. You've got to be joking. She's a rip-off."

"I want you to join them for a short period and aim for a particular client. Never mind the rip-off, you'll be well covered for money. Just for a spell."

"You don't even tempt me, George. And this isn't the time to discuss it. I'm going back to sleep."

"I'll buy you a lunch at Romano's. See you there at twelve thirty." He hang up before Julie Clarke got round to thinking he was becoming really reckless with money.

They had not met for well over a year and Bulman could see some of the changes. Although she was still attractive, he was saddened to see the premature ageing of Julie Clarke. She had kept her figure though, and he supposed it was an essential part of the game. He recalled that she should be in her late twenties but appeared to be about ten years older, and it would not get better for her if she continued to live as she did.

They had talked about it a long time ago when a restraining order had been placed upon a husband who believed in total possession, violence and, when he finally decided to cut loose, non-payment of maintenance.

Bulman understood all the economic arguments from a woman he liked, for her to do what she was doing. She had somehow missed out on modelling, had done a little film-extra work, but was difficult to discipline into routine hours and would never admit that that was precisely what she had descended to. Perhaps she had been through enough not to want to be owned by anyone again and had set herself for all to enjoy but none to possess.

He had always found her to be warm and generous with an impish personality and a kind of recklessness that would probably always be part of her. He believed, too, that there were times when she enjoyed her profession. When it came down to it, trying to analyse her got him nowhere and in the end he took her as she was. Trying to be the big brother to her had not worked, nor anything else.

"You're still at it," Julie said with a twinkle in her eye. "You always think you can start afresh. I'm okay, really. And I'm sorry I was so rude to you over the phone. It was a shocking time to ring but I guess neither of us is going to change, George. You've put some weight on, by the way."

"I'm always putting weight on." He watched the waiter serve the meals. "And this lot won't help. So you're coping?"

"I'm more than coping. And I've got some put by. I'll give it at most another five years and then I'll be set for life."

That's what they all say. But Bulman did not say it. He had forgotten just how much he liked this girl and was beginning to have serious doubts about the job he had in hand. "You bring back a lot of memories, Julie. Some of them very good."

"Very good indeed." She gazed coquettishly across the table. "And we had some laughs." She could be vivacious and was at that moment. It was then that he realised she was putting on a show for him. She always looked her happiest when covering pain and he wondered if things weren't as good as she said.

"What is it you want me to do, George?"

"I'm having second thoughts. This place is as good as I remember. Eat up."

"At six o'clock this morning you were quite happy to think of using me. I haven't changed that much. I can still pull them in."

Bulman dabbed his lips with his napkin. "Of course you can. I've always fancied you myself. But this could be dangerous."

"More dangerous than a few hours ago? Something's made it worse since then?"

"No." Bulman shook his head. "But I was tired out at that time, not thinking straight. Let's enjoy the meal, each other's company after so long, and forget the rest."

"Well, damn you, George Bulman. A sudden conscience? Have you suddenly stopped using people? What's happened to you?"

"It's riskier than I first thought." He smiled. "But I'm glad I phoned you, Julie. It's really good to see you again."

"You don't want me to get in bed with the guy?"

"That's the easy part. This man used to earn his living knocking people off. He's a professional killer. I don't know what possessed me to ask."

"Has he a reputation for topping brasses?"

"Oh no, nothing like that. It would have been political, paid jobs."

"And apart from sleeping with him what else was I expected to do?"

"I wanted to know who he is working for."

"And how would I find that out, George? Ask him? Slip him a 'micky' and go through his pockets?"

"No. I just wanted him out of the way for a specified time so that we can take our time going over the place. What we want may not be there but it can't be a snap job. We need most of the night. If he found out what had happened he could get nasty. Very nasty. I believe he's a lot to hide."

"Then you'd have to be damned careful, wouldn't you? And make sure I get the wink if you cock it up."

"No, I'm sorry. I wasn't thinking straight. I'm sure you can keep him occupied for the night but I should have thought it through before ringing you. This man is living a lie and he won't get slack in protecting it. He'll go through life looking over his shoulder but that's the type of life he's always led. It's second nature to him. If you try to keep him with you that little bit longer than he expects he'll start to think. I'm a bloody fool to have raised this at all. You're entitled to be paid for your time so you won't lose out."

"I wouldn't take it without doing the job, George. I've always worked for it."

"There are times when I'm very stupid indeed. I could bite my tongue off."

"I'll bite it out for you if you don't stop it. It's very simple." Julie gazed at him and was as near to pleading as he'd ever seen her. "I need the money, George. And I think you know it, you bastard."

Chapter Eight

Connie Taylor was about to open Mike Sealy's office door and found it ajar. If she entered unexpectedly she always tapped first; if summoned she did not bother. She should have tapped now, as she had just returned from a colleague's office and was passing Sealy's door when she remembered there was something he had given her which needed clarifying. Normally she would have buzzed him on the intercom.

She did not know why she reacted as she did. Later, worried about it, she believed it was because she was becoming increasingly concerned for him. The door was ajar, she gently pushed it, and there was her boss standing in front of his desk with his back to her, fiddling with the silver-framed family group photograph which lately had so seemed to obsess him. Connie at once felt a sense of guilt and she knew she should move away or announce herself. Instead, she watched, fascinated by what he was doing.

Sealy unclipped the back of the frame, laid it down carefully, then removed what appeared to be a letter from behind the photograph. It was folded and he straightened it carefully then read it. As far as Connie could see the letter was handwritten. There were two sheets and when separated she could see the light from the window behind them. They were so thin they must have been rice paper.

Connie found she could not move. From that distance there was no way she could read anything but it was Sealy's reaction that so disturbed her. His hands were shaking and by the time he had finished reading the second page she was certain he was quietly crying. She felt her own tears well up, just watching his clear distress.

The hand holding the letter drooped and he stood staring out of the window for a short time before reading the letter again, this time in a more controlled state. The watching Connie had the strong impression that he had no need to read the letter at all, that he had probably read it so many times he knew it by heart. The reading of it would seem to be some self-inflicted punishment of something he would never allow himself to forget. Connie was rooted by what she saw and forgot the dangers.

Sealy straightened as if even that small move was difficult, placed the two sheets together and folded them with great care, before returning them to the back of the photo. His fingers fumbled as he replaced the board over the letter.

Connie suddenly realised she must move. She pulled the door towards her until it was just ajar and hurried back to her own office to hear her intercom buzzing long before she reached the door. She raced the last few yards and tried not to sound breathless as she spoke to Sealy; he had obviously recovered quickly from his sad ordeal.

They both went to lunch at the same time, but rarely ate together. When Sealy had left for his, Connie felt a pull she was not prepared for. The temptation to go to Sealy's office while he was out was too strong to resist although she fought the urge as much as she could. She could not understand why she even thought like this.

She had a key to his office because she did so much admin for him. She rarely used it but now she wished she had not got it. She gave him a few minutes to clear the building then went along to his office, full of guilt and trepidation and wondering what was happening to her. As she turned the key to his office she convinced herself she was looking after his best interests.

She left the door partly open so that she could hear the movement of other people and be able to make a quick escape if needed. She felt like a traitor and the feeling was so strong that she nearly gave up. Then she remembered his shaking hands and his tears and she went in and picked up the silver frame and turned it over. She saw at once that it was easy to open and judging by the wear around the clips had been opened many times before.

She glanced towards the door and took up a position much the same as his when she had watched him. Her hands also trembled while she fiddled with the catches around the frame but for a quite different reason; she had never in her life done anything remotely like this before. She removed the letter, laid down the frame and realised just how fragile the two sheets were.

Well fingered and almost holed in one place, the letter was very difficult to read, with writing that varied in style and was sometimes almost unreadable. At first she thought it was a child's writing, but as she read on guessed that it had been written with great difficulty under tremendous stress, almost as if someone had been trying to prevent it being written or it had been done patchily at odd moments, very furtively.

When she was halfway through she wished she had never started but having done so could not stop. She felt her legs go and grabbed hold of the desk for support, having to wait for a few moments before carrying on. When she had finished she tried to fold the letter as it had been but was shaking too much and began to panic. As she tried to get a grip on herself she was sorry she had not tried harder to resist temptation.

Stumbling on human tragedy in so lurid a way was not for the faint hearted and as she slowly recovered enough to make a better job of folding the delicate sheets of paper she could not avoid the fleeting thought of what her critics might think of her if they could see her now: the haughty bitch was falling apart.

She got the letter back in place and put the backing on, fumbling again as she tried to move the clips. She was putting the frame in its usual position when she felt the presence of someone behind her.

*   *   *

93

Zoë Hayes was finding it increasingly difficult to get her husband alone. He constantly worked late, attended what invitations came their way, even though he hated most of the formal parties that went with the job. By the time she got him alone in the bedroom he was too tired to talk about almost anything and was soon asleep, although she was certain that he was often just lying there pretending.

The fact that he was avoiding her, although he swore he was not and was simply a victim of this crisis and that which called on his reserves, did not help her own problems. She knew he was keeping something from her; it worried her sick and was affecting her health.

Zoë increasingly began to wonder if she had been right to use her various influences in landing her husband the job. Many had wanted it, while Marvin had been completely indifferent to it. She knew why he took it in the end and she loved him the more for it. And although now they were seeing more of each other, in real terms they were seeing far less. It was bizarre.

They had spent little time together while he was with the DEA, but the times they'd had together were marvellous. She knew that when Don had made his brief excursion into drugs, while Marvin had spent most of his life fighting those who created and pushed them, it had scarred her husband terribly. She had the same feeling now as she had then; impending disaster, but doubted if she could ride it again. If Don was in that sort of trouble it would finish them, for she was barely holding on to her sanity now and Marvin's avoiding tactics made things worse.

She got him alone at breakfast. She usually rose later but this time she made sure she was with him. He was going through a pile of newspapers when she entered the breakfast room. Breakfast was the one meal he insisted was free of staff. He liked to sort things out before going to the Embassy.

He glanced up over a news-sheet as Zoë entered the room. He saw her deepening lines, the haggard eyes and the despair behind them. He well knew what he was doing to her and saw no way out. His trust was in Bulman, and while that had grown into something solid, he knew more than most just what a slow game detection could be.

"Good morning, honey. Good to see you up so early. Would you like some coffee?"

"Cut the bullshit, Marv. I'm perfectly capable of pouring my own. I want to know what's going and why we need a private detective. You tell me now or I book myself into the nearest nut house. I can't stand your evasion any more."

Hayes folded the paper, his mind working furiously. He had seen what Don's brief jaunt into drugs had done to her, so what would happen if he told her that the British police, at high level, claimed they had proof that Don had committed the murder of a female Special Branch officer. Just what should he tell her? If he lied it could come back at him and make things considerably worse. He had known this day would come and that sooner or later he would have to face it.

"You're terrifying me, if it's that difficult for you to tell me. For God's sake, Marvin, just don't sit there like a dummy. Talk to me before I talk to the walls. It's about Don, isn't it?"

If he said nothing she would crack as she was doing already, and if he told her the truth he had no idea what she might do. His burden was as great as hers, it was just different. If he told her anything it would have to be the truth for there was no way he could see to bend what he knew.

He gazed at her, knowing what she was suffering and that he was about to plunge the knife in. "It's not drugs," he said. "It might turn out to be nothing at all. They had a wild party after the finals and someone got hurt. Someone's trying to lay the blame on Don. That's why I've got this ex-cop looking into it."

"And that's it?"

"Sure. It'll all sort out. Don't worry about it."

"That's what you've been keeping from me while I've

been half out of my mind with worry? Why couldn't you say so when it happened?"

"I didn't want to worry you."

"You didn't notice how sick with worry I've been?"

Hayes avoided her accusing gaze. "Well, that's it. Enquiries are going well from our point of view."

Zoë sat facing him, lips trembling and tears welling. When he put out a hand to her she suddenly cleaned the table of what was in front of her with one despairing sweep of her arm. As crockery scattered on the floor she yelled, "You lying bastard. Why are you doing this to me? What's happened to you?" Tears were flowing down her cheeks and Hayes felt as if he had committed her to a nursing home.

Hayes rose shakily, came round the table to comfort her, but she backed away and cried out, "Don't touch me. I want to know who got hurt? *Tell me, damn you.*"

"A girl. An undergraduate. Look, try to understand, honey. I've been trying to protect you from exactly this situation. Leave things to me. I'm dealing with it."

"What happened to her?"

Oh Christ, she was going to drive them both over the cliff. "What does it matter? It's done. Goddamn it, Zoë, calm down."

"Is she in hospital?" Zoë was backed against a wall, a crying, pathetic figure in need of a convincing lie to comfort her because she was afraid to face a truth she did not really want to hear. And yet she must. "Answer me, Marvin." It was a whisper.

"No, she's not in hospital."

She knew he was still evading her and could barely get the next words out. "The morgue, then?"

It had taken the agony of her persistence to reach this point. Hayes did not know what to say or to do to help her. His effort to help so far had turned to disaster. He had considered her nervous frailty while underestimating her determination and intelligence. In his heart he supposed it would always have come to this point and yet he would probably have done nothing different given it all over again in the hope that time would provide the right answers. There was no point in further evasion.

"She's dead," he said, and it sounded far worse now than when he had first been told. He sat down heavily on the nearest chair. "I'm sorry. I had hoped to have some useful answers by now which would have avoided this. I did it for you."

Zoë quietly slipped down the wall to a squatting position where she could hide her head in her folded arms. She was quietly sobbing and Hayes knew it would be a mistake to try to comfort her. From a gap in the arms came a muffled and tearful, "How did she die?"

He had already acknowledged it was over. "She was shot. I am quite satisfied it had nothing to do with Don and I'm trying to prove it."

"So the police think it was him or you wouldn't be doing that?"

"I don't think they're quite happy with what they have. No charge has been made. That's terrific news, isn't it?"

Zoë placed her chin on her arms and looked up at him with wet and reddened eyes. "I want to go home. God, I hate this place. You stay on here while Don and I go back."

And then he said perhaps the hardest thing of all: "I doubt that they'll let Don return until this business is really cleared up. The police are helping us by pressing no charges but I think they'll need a few more answers yet before he'll be free to go." At least he had so far avoided telling her that the dead girl was an undercover cop. If she found that out he did not know what would happen. He just had to hope and pray she did not push it any further.

He thought she was about to make another outburst but with a clear stroke of insight Zoë asked, "So who's doing this to us? Do you trust your precious Bulman to find that out?"

*　　*　　*

97

Sealy did not go to his usual haunt for lunch but settled for a scratch meal at the mews set-up just fifteen minutes from his office. There was a short line of garages and he unlocked the double security locks and entered through a door let into one of the large double doors. He closed it behind him and locked it from inside.

He switched on a light to reveal two cars in the garage, a Jaguar XJ12 drophead and a Porsche just to show community spirit. The garage was clean, shelves neatly lined and floor, so far as could be seen, clear of oil.

Sealy went to the rear where there was an off-white plaster wall with shelves stretching the width of the interior and rang a buzzer which looked like a protruding nail. He gave a certain signal and quite quickly a section of the wall and shelves swung back and he passed through into something quite different. A young man wearing an empty pistol holster greeted Sealy with some reverence.

The irregular-shaped hall was stone floored with an L-shaped corridor running off. The air was cool and the faint hum of an air-conditioning plant could be heard coming from the rear of the small complex. The walls were clinical white and nothing hung on them.

"How is he?" asked Sealy as he followed the younger man to a comfortable rest room at the end of the corridor.

"Brooding. Would you like to see some clips?"

"I'd like a sandwich first, Tommy, if you can scrounge one up."

"No problem, sir. Coffee?" Tommy Wise was in his early thirties, fair hair and skin with a moustache which made him look older and did not suit him. His automatic was lying stripped on the table where he had been cleaning it. He did not miss Sealy's quick look of disapproval – on duty was not the time to clean a pistol; he should be wearing it and it should be serviceable.

Sealy sat down in a comfortable chair and ate a pre-packed egg and cress sandwich with a mug of black coffee, perched on the edge of the pine table. While he ate, Tommy Wise assembled his gun, checked it and slipped it into his waistband holster.

Wise was not comfortable in the presence of Sealy, who was a very senior officer with quite a reputation, particularly recently when his compassion seemed to have disappeared. Even during the last few days it seemed to Wise that Sealy had changed for the worse: he had become more remote and his moods were all on short fuse. The word unpredictable sprung to Wise's mind but he kept his thoughts very carefully guarded.

When Sealy had finished his sandwich and coffee they went into the observation room where the whole of one wall comprised television monitors flickering with varying pictures of McQueen. Wise ran a few clips through to show Sealy McQueen's behaviour patterns and Sealy watched impassively. After a while Sealy said, "I'd better see him. Make sure you keep me covered."

There were two similar well-separated cells. For staff there was one bedroom with two comfortable bunk beds, and a very modern bathroom with shower. There was another, smaller room which could also be used as a bedroom. A store room contained a chest freezer and refrigerator packed with convenience foods. In the same room was a sink and a micro oven.

Watching the external cell monitors Wise led the way to the cell where McQueen was captive. At the door Wise spoke into a microphone and told McQueen to stand at the far end of the cell and not to move; he had a visitor. He drew his gun because he did not trust McQueen whose actions could be seen on the monitor. Once certain McQueen was at the end of the cell Wise opened the door while Sealy kept an eye on the monitor.

The two men went in, the armed Wise first. The door closed behind them and Sealy could see that McQueen was looking for a half chance.

Sealy said, "Even if you overpowered us both, and you'd be shot if you tried, you'd find no way out and

99

an alarm would sound elsewhere after which you would be killed and disposed of. I thought it time we had a little talk."

"There's nothing to talk about. You have no right to hold me and there's going to be real trouble if you don't let me go. People will miss me."

Sealy sat on the edge of the bed, much to Wise's dismay. "People have already missed you but with no concern. You are not too popular at Oxford, McQueen. Everybody thinks you are in hospital recovering from the night of the finals. Nobody I know of has set out to find out which hospital, and if they did they would find it difficult to do because word is that you have been sent to a special hospital in London which has a drug unit. Nobody wants to be openly associated with drugs. So, for the moment you are on your own."

McQueen was trying to make up his mind whether to rush Sealy. "You'll not get away with it."

"Why not? So far we have."

"What do you mean?"

"You know perfectly well what I mean. You know why you're here. Your best chance of getting out of here is to co-operate with us."

"My God, Britain's a sham, a bloody police state."

"Of course we are." Sealy smiled without humour. "Doesn't that frighten you just a little?"

McQueen was glaring, back to the wall, ready to pounce like a trapped animal.

"Before you commit suicide by making a reckless move, bear in mind that we know a lot about you. The teenage wife you deserted would like to know where you are. Your family couldn't care less, even with your presumed academic success, for I feel certain you will have passed with honours. You have very few friends at Oxford and by now most will know that something is going on. You're already on your own. No one will come to help you even if they know where you are. You'll be one more mysteriously missing person, but the manner

100

of your disappearance is already well fazed. In due course I'll tell you what we want of you."

McQueen weighed his chances. Wise had moved to one side so that he had a clear target and with the gun raised he was obviously expecting one. "I want to see a lawyer and I'm entitled to a phone call."

Wise grinned widely but it was Sealy who answered. "You'll get neither. We are not the police and you have not been charged. In effect you've been kidnapped. You're lucky. With your slimy and violent past we should have executed you. Instead we've given you books to read and a radio to listen to and I promise you we'll let you know the exam results as soon as they come through. You are getting attention you in no way deserve."

McQueen watched Sealy rise, ready to fling himself at him if Wise dropped his aim. But there was something about the way Sealy gazed at him that chilled McQueen right through. Suddenly it was not the man with the gun who worried him but the man without, almost as if Sealy was willing him to try something in order to solve a difficult problem. McQueen remained still.

Sealy offered the faintest of smiles and said, "Good day."

Bulman went into the office, glossy portraits of attractive women hanging round the walls. A man was speaking silently on television and Bulman noticed the video beneath it and guessed that this was a client stating his credentials for the record, but with the sound turned off. The woman behind the desk was all lipstick and smiles and very blue eyes lost in heavy mascara. He could see, as he was meant to do, her long crossed legs in the kneehole of the desk.

He flashed an old police warrant card which should have been handed in when he resigned from the Force but which he claimed he had lost, swearing that it had inadvertently been destroyed by fire with a pile of old rubbish he had burned. It had passed Reception and now it had been accepted by the woman who ran a dating agency with a dubious reputation.

She was clearly edgy and fiddled with the ends of her blonde hair as she gazed up at him. She did not offer him a chair so he remained standing, which he had always considered to be a position of advantage.

"What can I do for you, Superintendent?"

"I take it you're Lottie Devine."

"Yes." She was already wary.

"Is that your real name?"

"I think you know that it's not. But it's the one I use and it will do. I'm busy. Will you get to the point?"

"I want to know if you have a certain man on your files. He's foreign with a Russian accent." Bulman gave a fair description of Chernov. "Do you mind checking it out?"

"I don't have to. I know the man. He's been registered with us for about a year. Uses us regularly and pays promptly. Does that help you?"

"It does." Bulman pulled out a snap of Julie Clarke and handed it over. "Do you know her?"

Lottie shook her head slowly. "She not one of ours."

"She not one of anybody's but I want you to take her on as from today until you can arrange a date with her and what's-his-name. What name have you got him under?"

Lottie tapped out on the keyboard of her desk computer. "Charles Dubas. Is that the same one?"

"That's him." He was mildy surprised that Chernov was using his adopted name with an outfit like this, but too many names could be confusing to the user. Has he got any requests in?"

"I don't like what you are asking me to do."

"I'm asking you to do what you are doing all the time, bringing two people together. And to save a lot of time don't come out with any morality crap because we know too much about some of the types you have on file and the peculiar habits of some of your women. Don't make it difficult for yourself or I'll get you closed down. And I'll leak the story to the *Sun*."

Lottie considered her options behind a glare designed to kill and said, "He's a frequent user. I've arranged a girl for him tonight."

"Does he ever have the same girl?"

"Never. He made that clear at the start. Each date is a different girl."

"So he doesn't know who he's getting tonight?" And when Lottie shook her head he added, "Then change the girl. Let's get it over quickly."

"For God's sake, the girl has already been lined up. I can't cancel now."

"Yes you can. You ring her up and tell her it's been reported that her date has been seen at an Aids clinic. I'll go part way towards compensating her but I'm not covering the lot."

"So what's in it for me? This is all extra work."

"Salvation, Lottie. We'll let you stay in business." Bulman became icy in a way that scared Lottie. "You'd better not cock this up. It won't be just closure that will happen to you. Do the girls call at his home?"

"He doesn't allow that. He meets them at a small hotel, usually one we have an arrangement with. I don't think any of the girls has ever seen his home; he's a very private person."

"I want your assurance that you will fix this up. I'll then get my girl to contact you straight away and you tell her what time and where. You understand?"

"Of course. Anything to help the police."

Bulman took out his wallet and removed some notes which he placed on the desk. "That's for the girl who is losing her date. I'm sure you'll hand it over to her." He was certain that the money would not go beyond Lottie but it suited him for this to happen.

Lottie gathered up the notes and placed them in the middle drawer. "Is there anything else I can do for you? A date, for instance?"

Bulman gave Lottie one last hard look. "I'm not that desperate. But I warn you, Lottie, nothing had better go wrong with this arrangement. I want nobody to know but you and me. And under no circumstances are you to let Dubas know the girls have been changed. You understand what I'm saying?"

"You're making me nervous. I don't need that kind of talk."

"Oh yes you do." Bulman moved to the door, looked back at the over-made-up Lottie and said in a tone she could not mistake, "This is no game, Lottie, no casual favour to keep your business afloat. This is life or death, girl, and don't you forget it for one second. God help you if it goes wrong."

Chapter Nine

Scott hated being rushed. He liked to work at his own pace and now suddenly, and obviously hurriedly, Bulman had arranged for Chernov's absence for that very night.

"What's wrong with you?" Bulman complained to Scott as he passed over a whisky. "Tonight, tomorrow night, next week, it was opportunist. We want it over and done and we don't want Julie to have time to change her mind."

"Okay. I just don't like arrangements out of my hands." He gazed round Bulman's flat. "This place needs decorating."

"You've already said that. Take the drink."

"I never drink on a caper and neither should you. We want our wits about us."

"Well, I can't put it back in the bottle." Bulman drank some of Scott's whisky. "Do you want any tools?"

Scott hooked his long legs over the end of the settee in disgust. "What the hell's wrong with you? How did you ever become a copper? I used to carry all the tools I ever needed on a bike." He glanced at his watch. "What time do we go?"

"Julie's meeting him at eight p.m. They have a meal and then get down to a night's work. The room is booked by the agency so it's all plain sailing."

"I hope we don't need anything like all night. She might wear him out and he could come back early."

Bulman finished Scott's drink and eyed his own. "According to the agency he's a very regular customer; probably gets a headache if he can't get a woman, like Jack

105

Kennedy used to. Heavily stressed jobs can have that effect on some people and there's nothing more heavily stressed than knocking people off."

Scott unhooked his legs and stood up. "If you're trying to put me off, you've just done it."

Bulman smiled. "You do take it seriously, Spider."

Scott shot a warning look. "And you'd better do the same. Leave that other drink alone." It was time to go.

It was nine thirty by the time they reached Chernov's house and fifteen minutes later before they entered the apartment. The dead fly had disappeared from the living-room door, but the more usual hair routine was found at the base of the second internal door. As Scott fixed the hair to the lintel with a small piece of chewing gum he wondered just how many times a day did Chernov set his little traps.

Scott preceded Bulman into the living-room, pulled the heavy curtains making sure there were no cracks and switched on the lights. He went back into the small hall and examined the ceiling.

"Where do we start?" asked Bulman. "You want us to split up?"

Scott gave him a scornful look. "The first thing we do is to find a way out. I don't want to be caught like last time."

There were two possible escape routes: the hatch to the loft, which was in the hall, but with the hatch release catch out of reach; and the fire escape which ran close to the bathroom which, unusually, had a narrow door opening on to a small gridded landing. Neither was ideal.

Scott turned on Bulman who had been following him around like an overgrown puppy. "What the hell are you doing? You're the bloody detective, get on with the search."

Bulman accepted the rebuke. "We were trained to find them but you were trained to hide them. So where to first?"

They split up and took separate rooms, searching diligently, taking time to replace everything as found. They were searching for anything that might give an indication for whom Chernov was working. If it was there it would be well hidden, but the two men knew all the usual hiding places, and as they worked considered what might be the unusual ones.

Because Scott had searched the desk during his first break-in he left it until later and when he did get round to it was sorry he had. He called out softly to Bulman in the next room, "The porno stuff has gone."

Bulman came into the room as worried as Scott. He leaned against the door jamb, pulling at his rubber gloves. "Do you think he knows you've been here?"

"I can't think where I could have gone wrong. I know I'm rusty but I'm not careless. He may have seen me on the landing and simply reported back."

"No." Bulman shook his head. "I know about this man. He'd have gone for you. If he had no gun on him he'd have had a knife, something lethal. Men like Chernov survive on their instincts. If he found out, then it was later. Maybe he moves the stuff around, thought it time to get rid of it. Have you found anything?"

"Three telephone numbers on the bottom of the bread bin and one scratched on the bottom of a carton of milk. I've made a note of them."

"What happens when the milk goes off?"

"You've never been the hunted, have you? You transfer it to the next carton and the next. He's taking precautions day by day and changing them all the time. He's living in the heart of a volcano that could erupt any time. If someone doesn't get him, eventually his blood pressure will."

"People like Chernov don't have blood pressure. And they go on killing because that's what they do best. The precautions he takes are routine, like catching a train or changing his toothpaste. We'd better get on with it."

They did but were no longer comfortable about the time they had. Scott made a breakthrough when he found some weapons fixed to the underside of the bed. He did not remove them but accounted for a rifle with telescopic sights

107

ady fixed, and two automatic pistols. He found them by untacking one end of the hessian fixed to the underside of the bed and by shining his flashlight into the cavity. A board had been fixed across the bed and operated on a pivot. By tilting, the weapons were revealed, fixed to the board by plastic clips.

Scott called Bulman to see. "There'll be more," said Scott. "Ammunition, other equipment which he'll have spread around, but this is enough for us. The man is still very much in business. Let's go."

As Bulman climbed awkwardly to his feet he remarked, "I noticed one of those clips was empty," and when Scott was not drawn added, "We still haven't got what we came for."

"We might have in the telephone numbers. He's shown himself to be too careful to have a name hanging around and even if he has it will be a coded one. Why the hell am I telling you this? You know damn fine."

But Bulman was showing his own brand of unease. "The more we've looked around the place the more anonymous it's appeared. Spider, I reckon this is a safe house. But whose?"

"Let's go. We'll take the fire escape."

"That's bloody difficult for my weight. Why?"

"Maybe we're beginning to scare each other but I've not been comfortable since those porno shots disappeared. He's on to us. I have a nasty feeling that the front might be watched."

It had been a very long time since Bulman had heard Scott talk like that. Scott was too experienced to panic but his instincts had been honed on danger and expertise. Bulman made no further objection. Scott was suddenly very edgy and that worried him more than he would care to admit.

Scott refixed the hair on the door and removed the gum, went round the apartment to make sure they had left everything as it was, switched the lights out and pulled back the curtains. They felt their way round the furniture to the bathroom door, closed it behind them and unlocked the fire escape door. The platform was barely large enough to hold them both and Bulman had to move to the edge while Scott fiddled to relock the door.

They moved down the creaking metal steps of the fire escape with Scott leading.

They descended into a litter-strewn alley and picked their way to the street behind the main entrance to the building. It was two a.m. and the streets were dead with little pools of orange light from the street lamps.

At the corner Scott led the way even further from the block and Bulman did not argue, happy to leave himself in the hands of an ex-cat burglar who had survived most crises by reflex action, and that worried Bulman too, because he knew Scott was uneasy.

When Scott was reasonably satisfied he stopped and turned to Bulman. "Can you find your own way back from here?" He picked up the occasional sound of traffic from a main street a couple of blocks away.

"Sure." Bulman shrugged his heavy shoulders. "It's nippy now. The walk will do me good."

Scott grinned: Bulman hated walking. "We can compare notes tomorrow." But Bulman was already walking away quite quickly for him, and Scott sensed it was not just because he wanted to get home. Scott watched him disappear into the gloom, could hear no footsteps beyond Bulman's and started to walk home.

Bulman had one thought in mind: to get to his telephone. He cursed Scott for putting so much doubt in his mind but at the same time knew he was being unreasonable and that Scott was right. He was in such a hurry to get in that he dropped his keys and the faint tinkle was like cow bells in the night. When he finally entered his apartment he switched on the lights and went straight to the phone. He tapped out Julie Clarke's number and as it continued to ring out he became illogically irritated.

He hung up and kept his hand on the phone. He kept telling himself that he had paid Julie to spend the night with

Chernov so how could he possibly expect her to answer the phone in her own home? That was the logic. But he had picked up some of Scott's misgivings. He knew the name of the hotel at which they were staying but dare not ring there. Julie was right, he did use people, but he believed that he did not do so recklessly; everything was thought through first. He had pointed out the risks and had paid her extremely well. So why was he suddenly worried. For the second night running Bulman had little sleep.

After a restless night, dozing on and off in a chair, Bulman awoke at six a.m., shaved, showered and changed clothing, then went to the small row of lock-ups to drag out his old Daimler. The traffic had yet to build up and he had little problem in parking. He walked the short distance to the DLA Dating Agency.

The small, profitable business was two floors up and there was no lift. He climbed the stairs feeling he was the only one in the building. He was so anxious, that he reached the landing before wondering why the street door had been unlocked. He faced the glass panelled door with the now fading agency name on it and turned the handle. He already knew the office did not open until ten a.m. so was not surprised to find the door locked.

He bent down to examine the keyhole and noticed the scratch marks around it. It was an old door and an old lock; there was nothing to steal here but information. Even so, it took him a long time before he was able to spring a lock Scott would probably have breathed on to open. He went into the brightly decorated reception room with the glossies of beautiful women lining the walls. He stopped just inside the door, and quietly closed it behind him.

The young receptionist was slumped over her desk, the hole in the back of her head almost big enough to fit his fist. Her copper-coloured hair was matted with congealed blood and her back was spattered with gore.

Bulman had seen a number of murder victims, but not for some time and seldom as young. He felt sick. To be impassive to this kind of sight needed constant contact with violence. What made it far worse was the feeling that he was responsible.

The door to the inner office was ajar, and with terrible foreboding Bulman crossed the floor towards it. As he reached it he saw the reflection of the VDU and as he entered the room could see the blank screen flickering, the video still switched on beneath it with the sound off. The tape must have finished hours ago.

Lottie Devine was at the side of her desk, half propped up against it, the maroon-tinged hole in the centre of her forehead like an Indian beauty mark. There was a dark mess on the side of the desk behind the head. Her skirt was rucked and she was showing her legs to the last. From her unnatural position Bulman guessed that she had tried to make a run for it once she realised what was about to happen.

Video cassettes were scattered everywhere. He had to pick his way through them and then he stopped because he knew he would not find what he wanted. It had already been found and taken away.

He bent over Lottie, whose eyes reproached him as he touched her. Judging by the smell, the amount of rigor, and the congealing of blood, Bulman reasoned that both women had been killed the evening before, and that made him cringe.

He returned to the reception room, pulled the young head back by a streak of unstained hair and saw the same type of bullet hole as on Lottie. He lowered the head carefully as if she would feel it if he just let it drop.

He had Julie Clarke's hotel number with him so he took out a handkerchief and picked up the phone. He used a knuckle to tap out the number. When he got through to Reception he said slowly, "This is the police. Just answer what I ask you and we'll leave it at that. Don't try lying because we know what your sleazy doss house is used for. A male client of the DLA Agency was booked a double room for last night." He gave a fair description of Chernov, knowing it was pointless giving a name. "He'd have had a fair-haired attractive woman with him. You know who I'm talking about?"

"Look, I'm day shift. You want the night clerk and he's gone home. But I can tell you that nobody from the DLA is here now. Hold on while I check the book." The waiting Bulman heard a rustle of paper, then, "They had two reservations for last night. One lot left before I came on. The other cancelled last night. They never came."

Bulman's mind went blank. He quickly got a grip on himself and asked, "Do you know what time it was cancelled?"

"You'll have to wait for Norman to come back on duty. I'm sure he'll be able to tell you."

"One last thing; have you a description of the couple who left this morning?"

There was an awkward silence. "We go blank on descriptions so don't pay much attention. The least we know the better. But as I say they had left before I came on."

Bulman put the phone down. It had all gone terribly wrong. He picked up the phone again, dialled 999 and reported the double murder. He moved quickly to the door.

The traffic had built up considerably on the way back, but at least he was going against the stream. He parked the car on double yellow lines outside his own apartment block and went in. At first he did not know what to do. He made huge quantities of coffee to stave off the tiredness arising from two almost sleepless nights, feeling very alone with knowledge it was difficult to share without compromising others.

His overriding concern was what might have happened to Julie. He rang her home repeatedly but at last did what he knew he should have done in the first place; he drove to her address in north London. He had trouble getting past Julie's landlady but a small bribe settled the matter and he was given the key to her rooms.

The Julie Clarke Bulman remembered had always been

tidy and he was relieved to see that she had not changed in this respect. Then he got angry with himself for mulling over trivia when he did not know if she was alive or dead. He was running away from the issue because he had placed her in danger in the first place and it was no use arguing that he had no idea that something like this would happen.

Something like what? It was an admission and he sat down wearily on one of her fussy chairs. Julie was dead. Chernov wouldn't have killed the other two and left her alive. There was no point in going through her things; there would be no clues here. He was torturing himself and perhaps that was why he had come. He checked with the landlady that Julie had not returned last night and then went to the hotel where she should have stayed with Chernov.

He got no further than he had on the telephone. The manager, believing Bulman to be a senior police officer, thought he was walking a tightrope, and showed Bulman the room where Julie should have stayed and the room of the couple who had left earlier that morning.

Both rooms had been made up by now and there was nothing to learn. Norman, the night clerk, would not be back until late evening. Bulman examined the reservation book, and the cancellation in the name of Mr and Mrs Hope was clearly marked as being actioned at five p.m. the previous evening.

Bulman realised before he started that he was making token gestures. He drove home, garaged the car and walked round to Chernov's address, feeling he had little to lose. He rang the unmarked bell but no one answered and he rang again, a good long peal. He stepped back into the street and gazed up at the blank windows. There was no sign of life.

He climbed the steps again and rang the remaining bells repeatedly. The house was apparently dead, confirming his belief that this was a safe house. He returned home again and studied the numbers Scott had obtained from the bread bin and the milk carton. He was tempted to ring

113

them, but thought it might be wiser to use other means first to find out to whom they belonged. He rang Scott at his travel agency: "What about a snack lunch? That place in St Martin's Lane? Twelve thirty?"

It had been a long time since they last met in this particular pub. Bottle windows and real ale, it was one of the few places Bulman would drink beer instead of whisky. They took a pint each to a window seat; within fifteen minutes of them sitting down the place was crowded to overflowing. The noise level was high and they had to bend close to hear each other without being overheard.

Bulman told Scott what had happened at the DLA Agency and Scott spilled his drink. Scott had never carried arms although army training had taught him how to use them. And he had never used violence on a caper. He was badly shaken by what Bulman told him.

"So what happened to Julie Clarke?" asked Scott, upset and uneasy.

"I was hoping to raise that first." Bulman took a long pull of his drink and wiped his lips with the back of his hand. He found it difficult to face him because Scott, ex-burglar or not, had his own code of conduct. It was often difficult to equate these two friends in cops-and-robbers terms. "Spider, she has to be dead. Chernov wouldn't slip up on that. I'm bloody sorry, mate, but I honestly didn't think it would go anything like this far. Okay, I know what Chernov is, but he won't kill gratuitously, there's too much risk."

Scott eyed Bulman critically. "Evidently there was more risk in letting them live. They could finger him in a way he would obviously prefer not to be known. Killing is a bit extreme to cover a sexual appetite, isn't it?"

"Thank God we agree on that. Why did it happen and how did he find out Julie was sent to keep him busy?"

"Maybe Lottie warned him. Told him you had called and what you wanted and saw extra money in it. You didn't scare her enough."

"Then why didn't he knock us off instead?"

But Scott was looking beyond Bulman to a small head-line on somebody's newspaper. Without a word he left the pub and went to the newspaper stand next door, bought the *Standard* and returned to the unsettled Bulman. Scott skipped through the pages and finding what he wanted folded the paper back and handed it to Bulman. "Might that be her?" asked Scott.

Bulman read the small, graphic piece about a woman found strangled and mutilated on Tooting Bec Common in the early hours of the morning. She had not been sexually assaulted, which puzzled the police as to motive. "That's her," said Bulman.

"How the hell can you be sure?"

"He didn't touch her sexually, leaving no risk of a DNA match. They won't find a weapon and they won't find witnesses. The mutilation was to warn us. He wouldn't get satisfaction from that sort of perversion: he'd have killed her first. That's her. I'm telling you."

"So after killing her why didn't he go home and finish the job by killing us? He must have stayed away all night yet the chances are he at least suspected we were at his place. Why, George?"

Bulman did not reply, and Scott had never seen him look so tense.

Chapter Ten

Connie Taylor found it difficult to act normally in front of Sealy. She had spied on him and it rankled that she had descended so low. The only person she felt she could tell was her friend Anna Brus in the United States Embassy, but on this particular issue she was blocked by the oath she had taken to uphold the Official Secrets Act. That she should feel guilty of spying in a building which existed on spying of one sort or another was lost on her, and she could not see the irony of her guilt. Her fundamentally decent nature could not make a connection.

She had not forgotten the shock of almost being caught putting the letter back in Sealy's family picture. Her colleague, Amanda Chapman, had merely seen her facing Sealy's desk and had been looking for nothing special. When she'd called out, Connie had almost jumped out of her skin. It could have been much worse, like Sealy himself returning, but it gave her a nasty jolt just the same.

Fortunately, any display of guilt she might show was lost on Sealy who seemed to have sunk further into his own problems, until at times they appeared to be his sole occupation. To see him so distracted and increasingly morose eased her feeling of guilt a little. She wanted to help him and did not know how.

Bulman rang a senior engineer in British Telecom who had helped him on a case a few years ago. As the engineer had played an instrumental part in supplying evidence in a particularly gory murder, he was not likely to forget the encounter; it had given him local fame and had kept him going on free beer months after the court case. Bulman's only concern was that the engineer might know he had left the Force. He gave the numbers he wanted investigated and insisted on secrecy between the two of them.

He then drove down to Oxford again to find Phill Marshall and to see what he could find out about the missing Wally McQueen. In truth he did not expect to discover anything spectacular but needed to get away from the possibility of Marvin Hayes wanting to see him. And he was still reeling from the death of the two women and almost certainly Julie Clarke, which had upset him more than he would admit to anyone. He had sent her to her death and could not escape the fact.

It was early evening before he ran Phill Marshall to earth and he liked the well-built undergrad on sight. Ginger hair canopied a pale freckled face and light, sometimes anxious, blue eyes. They met at Marshall's digs just as Marshall was about to go jogging in a well-worn track suit. They walked side by side and Bulman found it difficult to carry on a serious conversation so eventually suggested they went back to his car, which increasingly was becoming a mobile interrogation room.

Bulman went through the same routine he had used on the others without getting anywhere further. Marshall liked Don Hayes and it seemed that they might be particular friends. Marshall turned out to be a keep-fit fanatic, which induced Bulman to ask, "If you're so intent on keeping fit, how come you got so legless on the night of the finals?"

Marshall peered through the windscreen watching fine rain forming a faint mist on the glass. He leaned forward and rubbed a grease mark away with the side of his hand. "That could be distracting when driving." He sat staring ahead then turned to Bulman slowly. "You must have worked that one out by now, Mr Bulman. Some clever dick tinkered with the drinks. It could have killed us, we were so far gone."

"In the event it did kill one of you."

"Not exactly. But it might have provided the cover for it."

Bulman raised his brows. "So you've thought about it?"

"We'd have to be pretty damned callous not to think about it. We must all have thought about it. Paula was a nice girl, although it comes as something of a shock to discover she was a policewoman."

"But you have not discussed it with the others?"

"We haven't been encouraged to do so. In fact we've been warned, advised I think was the actual word used, to keep away from each other before the word conspiracy begins to wander the corridors. They don't want us concocting some universal answers for the police although I haven't seen sight of a copper since the day after the tragedy. In truth I don't think we want to see one another right now."

"Don't you think it curious the police haven't been round again?"

"Yes, I do, but I'd rather not see them." Marshall leaned back in the seat and was clearly disturbed at the recollection of Paula Smith. "Are you sure you don't want to jog? Only a few miles?" He smiled. "Get rid of some of your flab."

"It's not flab," Bulman explained. "I'm wearing badly fitting clothes. I'm a tailor's nightmare. It's just the shape I am. How did you get along with the others?"

Marshall shrugged. "We were a misfit party with one or two exceptions. Difficult to say how we finished up together. It didn't seem to matter. With the exception of Burke and McQueen I suppose we would have got on well enough. Those two are activists of one sort or another, staggering from cause to cause as long as there's a militant outlook. It's sad because both have brains on them but they seem to be warped, snarled up in some way. I don't think they even like each other."

Bulman nodded, watching Marshall closely, pleased with the apparently open replies. "So what's happened to McQueen?"

118

Marshall smiled grimly. "I suppose it would be too much to expect that he's been run over by a bus. The last I heard was that he was so juiced up he landed in hospital. There's a rumour floating around that he has developed liver trouble. It would not surprise me, he had a perpetual bad temper. I don't know how he gained entry."

"So you don't know which hospital he's in?"

"Good lord, no. That would presuppose that I cared."

"Do you think either he or Burke killed Paula?"

"That's not a fair question. Being nasty bits of work does not necessarily make them killers. A motive must have activated the shooting and I cannot begin to understand what that might be, unless someone found out she was police and close to finding something out."

Bulman smiled and tapped Marshall on the shoulder. "You'd have made a damn fine copper but I suppose you're destined for higher things."

"Is that why you are really here? To find out who killed Paula?"

"I'd certainly like to know. And so would her parents. Wouldn't you?"

Marshall gazed at Bulman with a sad expression. "There are times when I feel I would rather not know simply because it might turn out to be someone I would not want it to be. But basically, yes; it's the only way to clear the air."

"Could Don have done it?"

It was a question out of the blue and went straight under Marshall's guard. For a moment he was speechless as if the thought had never occurred to him. Now that it had he was faced with the possibility. "Because of that little drug blip at home?"

"Because of anything. What happened in America is hardly enough to justify a homicide over here, is it? Or is there something else?"

"How do you know about what he did in the States?"

"He told me. He seemed to me to be an honest lad. I just wanted your reaction as you seem to be close to him."

"That was below the belt. I just can't see Don carrying a gun, particularly at a party. He was certainly in no condition to use one long before we really freaked out."

"Someone was."

"Yes, indeed. But it might have been none of us. The state we were in anyone could have been hanging around without us knowing."

"Okay, fine. You've been very helpful. I don't think McQueen is in any hospital, by the way. I've checked around."

For the first time Marshall showed real surprise. "Then where is he?"

"He's either done a bunk or has been spirited away. If you hear anything, rumours, rubbish, anything at all, would you let me know? Here's my card."

"Have you asked the others to do the same?"

"No. You've got a copper's mind. I'd be grateful for any help."

"Okay." Marshall opened the door. "But tell me, Mr Bulman, who are you really working for? It's not Paula's parents, is it?"

Bulman almost told him but offered him a grin instead. "Work on it," he said. "It'll keep your mind off other things."

By the time he got back to London the late edition of the *Standard* carried the story of the two women shot dead in the DLA Agency. Bulman read the report when he got home. A professional hit-man was suspected and the place had been ransacked. There was a description of a man the police wanted to interview which bore no resemblance to himself or to Chernov, almost as though the police were either being clever or misled. He knew he would learn nothing of real value from the report but he did wonder why it had taken the news so long to break, bearing in mind he had reported the murders himself.

Mike Sealy and Stuart Wilson met in an apartment off St James's. It was a little-known small terraced building

120

with just a dozen service apartments for rental and was mainly used for foreign tourists who did not want an hotel. The top apartment was permanently rented by HM Government under a company name dreamed up by Sealy's predecessor. It was used mainly for visitors who needed a day or two's accommodation without drawing too much attention to themselves.

There was always a stock of liquor available and the two men poured themselves white wine. The rooms were just adequate, a small price to pay for being so centrally situated. They sat in opposite, slightly shabby armchairs, and Wilson showed his unease from the start. "This is getting a bit ridiculous," he complained.

Sealy raised his glass. "Because we're meeting here? We could hardly meet at the House. Now that might cause conjecture. And it's convenient here. What's on your mind, Stuart?" When forced to face his own crisis in the presence of others the complete professional came out in him and he could cope, even though it became increasingly difficult.

"I have the feeling it's becoming a mess. We have the murder of a young policewoman on our hands and nothing seems to be happening. And sooner or later the press are going to sniff around and all hell will be let loose. I think we should either arrest young Hayes or send him home to get him out of the way for good."

"And as soon as that's done the press really will go bananas. They will notice and wonder why and dig up any dirt they can – which means what has happened that side of the pond as well as this." Sealy's tone was quietly persuasive. "The object is surely to help the Ambassador, not to crucify him. We all know that the antics of his son almost cost Marvin Hayes his job. If it wasn't for his . . ." Sealy suddenly had trouble in breathing and this alarmed Wilson who rose from his seat, but Sealy waved him away and gradually steadied.

"Must be the dust in the room," Sealy explained, looking pale. "Hasn't been used for a while. Anyway, Hayes has a great reputation in Washington. He apparently did a really first class job with DEA and soon hooked his son away from trouble before it became a crisis. The whole thing was blown up too much and I must say I admire the President for standing by his old friend. There but for the grace of God, etc. But it could have cost him dearly."

"There has got to be a solution, Michael. Matters can't be left hanging in the air. I've lost sight of what you actually hope to gain by this. Perhaps it would be better if, after a reasonable time, we shipped the whole family back to the US. He can make a statement about ill health at the right time and we can then all forget it."

"And a murder goes unsolved. The police won't like that."

"But surely the bloody thing goes unsolved anyway?"

"That was never my intention. Look, I realise I have a time limit on this. But I'm convinced it's worth the wait. Give it two or three weeks."

Wilson leaned forward anxiously. "Now wait a minute. Are you saying you intend to have young Hayes indicted?"

"I said it was never my intention that the murder goes unsolved. Hayes' prints are on the gun. That is fact. And the police would be quite satisfied with that as evidence against him. I am not so satisfied. There are ways of getting prints on a gun. But it would be easy enough if Hayes was unconscious at the time and he seems to have done quite a lot of that on that particular night. It's just a matter of using the situation to our best ends."

"Which are?"

Sealy smiled slowly. "You've asked me that before. And I give you the same answer. It's much better that you do not know so that if anything blows up you can honestly plead ignorance. Trust me. You always have. It's not a bad thing to have the most senior foreign diplomat in the country in our pocket. Meanwhile we've told Marvin Hayes nothing but the truth."

"The poor man is suffering."

122

"Really! There are degrees of suffering." Sealy waved a hand. "I'm being uncharitable. I also know that you are under pressure from SB. Nothing's changed, still refer them to me. I'll know when it's time to opt out. Just a little more all-round patience and we'll be home and dry." And then at a seeming tangent, "By the way, do you know an ex-Yard man named Bulman? Used to be a detective superintendent."

"The name doesn't ring a bell. Why?"

"I'm surprised but I suppose it's because you haven't been at the Home Office all that long. I was thinking of using him, that's all. Well, I think that keeps us in touch, Stuart. You know where I am if you are worried about anything."

Wilson could not miss the condescending tone in Sealy's last remark and it irritated him. He rose, smiled and said, "It's true that I haven't been at the Home Office very long, but you, of course, know well where it is and will know your way there if I need to summon you. Don't keep us waiting too long."

When Wilson had gone, Sealy was angry with himself. He did not hold Wilson in high esteem but to show it as he had was foolhardy and he wondered what had happened for him to make such a stupid slip.

He poured himself another glass of wine, too warm by now, which made him wrinkle his nose. He wandered over to the window to face the back of a hotel across the narrow street. Some things had gone wrong, he reflected, but they always did. Few plans ran to perfection. The unforeseen was always lurking and Chernov had shown that all too clearly. There was nothing wrong with Chernov having a strong sexual appetite, and by going to what amounted to a call-girl agency, he had in fact acted quite sensibly. Bulman was the real cause and had become an increasing menace. It was clear that Bulman did not frighten easily.

As Sealy sat musing, occasionally sipping his wine, he felt the pressure build up in his head. He dreaded these moments. He put down his glass, moved over to a deeper chair and sat with his head right back and closed his eyes. By resting quietly he thought it would go. The pain lingered on and his own fears gradually increased the pressure. The more he tried to get back to normal the worse it became; it always did, and even knowing it made no difference because by then the fear had built up and when that happened the terror was not far behind.

He began to tremble and right on cue the sounds came like distant aircraft engines inexorably drawing nearer and his glasses began to mist up. Glasses? He was not wearing glasses and he put his hands to his face in desperation. He tried to shut out the vision that came with the sound as if he carried his own video replay in his head.

The sound of engines was now in the room, shaking the building like a jelly until he believed it would collapse. The pain was dreadful now, as though the pressure was from inside and out and would build up until his skull shattered. Then all too slowly the engine noise subsided and suddenly cut out altogether until there was only the rush of air and the dreadful sensation of sinking fast, gliding at sensational speed towards the mass of tree tops which formed the vast canopy of forest. And then silence.

There was no landing, just floating, until the flames burst up around him, consuming, searing, agonising, until the scorching heat was unbearable and the flesh curled back in ugly seared strips and the screams began. But the screams weren't his, they were disembodied and he was watching the flames burn somebody else to a cinder. The screams had reached an impossible peak which was mercifully bursting his eardrums, because he must shut out the sound of the excruciating agony of impossible suffering. Gradually the screams subsided, but in a dreadful, drawn-out way that produced with them the final whimpering of the living dead which tailed away so slowly, as though it continued long after all human suffering was possible.

At this point Sealy was a writhing, sweat-soaked mess, having slid from the chair and curled up against it, arms round knees, head buried into them while he whimpered like a mortally injured animal. It was some time before he could move at all and when he finally uncurled he was wet through, pale and quivering.

He shakily climbed to his feet. The pain had gone with the pressure but he felt as if he'd been swimming with his clothes on. Even his hair was wet through and when he wiped his face he was not surprised to find that he had been crying. That had been the worst attack yet and he dreaded the thought that it should ever happen in company. And yet, as he found the strength to strip and shower, he realised this was unlikely to happen. Other people were a distraction, it was when he was alone and his mind ran free that he became captive to the dreadful torture. He acknowledged that it was getting worse. And he knew why.

Although the apartment was not specifically allocated to him, Sealy seemed to make far more use of it than the others and he always kept a change of clothing there, including a dinner suit for unexpected functions. He began to recover fully once he had dressed and bundled his soiled clothes into a carrier bag. He finished his drink, sealed what was left of the wine and returned it to a hanging rack in the tiny kitchen, washed and dried the glasses and put them away.

He was quite sure that pressure from Wilson had provoked the attack; the man seemed to be losing his nerve, but it was why Wilson himself felt under pressure that concerned him most. Sealy was well used to the shadowy game he had played for so long with such good results, while men like Wilson were temporary spectators who would probably lose their seats at the next election. Just the same, he could not ignore the fact that Wilson was there and that he needed the minister's backing. And it was this that made him feel vulnerable.

Sealy felt washed out but much better by the time he was ready to leave the apartment. In a back-handed way Stuart Wilson had probably done him some good. He could see how pressure might be taken off himself and he would action that, but it was time to turn the screw in quite another direction. The timing was just about right and it might even reduce the screaming and terror that entered his head all too frequently these days.

Chapter Eleven

Bulman played back his answering machine about an hour after returning from Oxford. He hated the machine, constantly forgot to switch it on when going out, and on the occasions he did remember, invariably forgot to play it back on his return.

There were two calls, one from the BT engineer and another from Marvin Hayes who had apparently called from the Embassy but wanted him to make contact at his home after six. It was almost six now. Bulman rang the BT engineer to get no reply, relieved there was no answering machine the other end. He waited another few minutes before ringing Hayes. He was asked to get round at once and it was clear from Hayes' tone that something drastic had happened.

Bulman took a cab, and the door was already open when he arrived. The PC on duty saluted and told him he could go straight in, closing the door behind him. Hearing Bulman's arrival, Hayes came bustling out of his study, glanced furtively round the large hall and ushered Bulman into the study.

"What's going on?" asked Bulman as he sat in his usual chair. "It's a bit drastic using a police officer as butler, isn't it? Now that's something that could get around."

"I wanted to make sure that Zoë didn't answer the door. She's dying to get at you."

"There's nothing I'd tell her without your knowledge."

"She doesn't know that. I had to tell her what has happened. She's close to a breakdown."

"You told her all of it?"

"I didn't tell her that the dead girl was an undercover cop. That titbit might just have driven her over the edge."

Bulman took the proffered whisky. "Is that what you wanted to tell me?"

"I'd hardly call you over for that. No. I received this letter this morning. It came in the ordinary mail."

Bulman took the envelope that Hayes handed him. He did not handle it carefully, taking his cue from the Ambassador, whose prints would already be all over it. He took out a single sheet of folded paper, opened it to read a short typed message: "Your son should not go around killing young policewomen, particularly while they are on duty. Why has he not been arrested, Mr Ambassador?"

Bulman turned the sheet over; there was nothing on the other side. He examined the postmark and was not surprised to find it was Oxford. He read the letter again. The print was dark and even and had probably been done on an electric typewriter. He carefully put the letter back in the envelope and passed it over to Hayes.

"Don't you want to keep it?" asked Hayes in surprise.

"I'll keep it if you're afraid of your wife finding it but I don't think it will be helpful."

Hayes appeared to be irritated. "Goddamn, you're supposed to get information from things like that."

"If I had access to police resources, but I would guess they are being denied me at the moment." He pointed to the letter Hayes was still holding. "That wouldn't have been sent if there was anything to find from it, but I'll gladly take it from you." He took the letter back and put it in his pocket. "Don't let it rattle you."

"That's very easy for you to say, George. But I'm shattered. It must have been sent by one of the students who were with Don that night."

"For what reason? I've interviewed them all and I don't think any one of them, and they're not all saints, would have sent that. The only one resentful of Don and your position here is Burke but he's not stupid and wouldn't show himself in this way. This isn't a threat, nor a warning.

It's been sent to achieve exactly what it has done: to rattle you."

Hayes had no answer except to gaze at Bulman in puzzlement and mutely to ask by expression, "Why?"

"The emphasis is beginning to shift," Bulman explained. "And it raises a hell of a lot of questions. Motive, for one. Has Don made any enemies here that you know of?"

"I don't think so. He's hardly likely to run home to Daddy and tell me even if he had. Did you find something out at Oxford?"

"I would say Phill Marshall is a particular friend of Don's. And he's a nice lad. Tammy Rees has a crush on him. Neill Barker doesn't know him all that well but has nothing against him. Let's say he's indifferent. Jamie Burke hates his guts and his privileged position and is so vehement about it that he leaves himself chief suspect to anything that might happen to Don. That letter is not his style; he hasn't even called you or Don an American bastard. And the last thing he would want to do is to draw attention to himself: I don't think his past is open to too much examination. That leaves Wally McQueen and he seems to have done a runner."

"A runner?"

"He's walked. Disappeared. Vamoosed. Beat it. Vanished."

Hayes was forced to smile. "You're showing your age, George. You're out of touch with modern jargon. So where might he be?"

"The story was put about that he was so ill after the party that he went to hospital, but no local hospital knows of him. Then his college suggested that he was in a London hospital which specialises in drug cases. I think that's bullshit. I think he's either ducked out or has perhaps been taken out."

"Another killing? Surely not. That would make two."

"No," said Bulman soberly, "it would make five. But he might simply have been lifted."

"Five?" Hayes stared incredulously. "*Five*? Just what

129

the hell has been happening that you haven't told me about?"

"Look, the other three are not directly connected to Don but aimed against me. Just hold on and I'll tell you about them. Meanwhile your chief concern seems to be fear of your wife seeing the letter you've just given me. Okay, that's now not possible because I have it. But what if one is sent to her direct?"

Hayes did not move for a while. He seemed to be paralysed. Eventually he said in a tone so low Bulman barely caught the words, "That is my dread. How do I stop it happening? She's already a nervous wreck, the shock could kill her." He was still thinking about the dreadful possibility as he added, "Why would someone want to do that?"

"For the same reason that they've already done it. If Don has no enemies maybe it's you they don't like."

Hayes seemed to collapse in his chair but it was a move of exasperation. He did not really understand what Bulman was suggesting. "Are you saying that Paula Smith was killed to get at me? That's preposterous. And anyway, I've no enemies here or anywhere else for that matter who would go to such extreme."

"I'm not suggesting that at all. The girl might have been killed anyway. She was probably already targeted, waiting for the right moment which came the night of the finals. Everything was perfect. Big booze-up, a little help along the way with a 'micky' or two, or drugs, the weather was a backcloth that was God sent and the target was hit. The presence of Don could have been coincidental or organised. The question is, has the incident been opportunely used against you or Don? If so, why?"

Hayes struggled to grasp what Bulman was laying out for him. More than anything at the moment he was desperately worried about his wife's state of health, even more than the apparent danger to his son. Now Bulman seemed to be suggesting that he was as much involved as his son, and perhaps even more so. He had always accepted

130

that the British might seize the opportunity to demand a *quid pro quo* but was happy with his own limitations in that direction. Apart from trying to grasp a new implication he was still shocked by the letter he'd received and which Bulman did not seem to be concerned about.

Hayes did not answer immediately. When he did he seemed to be evading the main issue. "You'd never believe what this business is costing me in lost time and work. I am missing a function tonight, which means being discourteous to a friend and his country. We don't seem to be getting anywhere and now you're confusing things further."

"So you'd prefer to leave it as a simple case of murder against your son?"

"Don't be funny, George. I'm just finding it difficult at the moment to take everything on board. But if what you suggest is at all likely then the assertion that the prints on the gun are Don's is a downright lie."

"No. Whoever else may have told you, John Cordell would not begin to lie or even exaggerate about a thing so serious. If he says they are Don's prints then they are. You won't find a more honest copper. If he's gone bent you can have your money back and I'll pack it in."

Hayes closed his eyes, and the glass in his hand tilted slightly. "This is a nightmare. You've come up with nothing solid but have managed to raise far more questions than we started with. Where do we go from here?"

"We plod on. And you've been unfair. To my own satisfaction I've managed to eliminate a few people. That narrows the number of suspects. But I honestly believe that the real culprit in all this is not yet on the scene. We've had glasses trained on us all the time. My gut feeling is that we're getting nearer though."

"I wish I felt the same. I'm still worried about the letter."

"Of course you are. But that has come from the guy who has the glasses trained on us. Forget the Oxford postmark. That's just to confuse. My guess is that it started out right here in London."

"Okay." Hayes wearily rubbed eyes already bloodshot. "You'd better tell me about these other killings. Are you in danger?"

"Yes, I think I am. But I'm not alone. I've had friends helping me out with this case. One of them was a hooker. She's been killed because of it, and I find that very difficult to live with." Bulman felt himself getting maudlin and finished his drink quickly before continuing.

It was late by the time Bulman got back to his apartment, and he and Marvin Hayes had consumed some hefty drinks meanwhile. He staggered a little as he went up the stairs and used the wall on either side for support. He did not think the visit had done much good, having partially placated Hayes on the one hand and totally confused him on the other. He hated interim reports; they could never be conclusive and did little to help. He fiddled with his keys, chuckling to himself at his own clumsiness, well aware that he had drunk too much but relieved that it acted as an anaesthetic to the misery he felt about Julie Clarke. He unlocked the door and went in.

He switched on the lights as he went and found Chernov seated facing the door, in his hand a gun with a silencer attached. Bulman sobered fast and stood quite still. As Chernov did not fire immediately, Bulman, still unscrambling his mind, reasoned that the Russian had things to say first.

"Sit down," said Chernov. The gun did not move with the direction of the head.

Bulman sat down slowly. It was a long time since he had felt this kind of fear and he had no answers. Chernov was not a man who was open to reason. And then the burning anger came and Bulman glared hatred at the man whom he believed had killed Julie Clarke. For a moment his anger overcame his fear. "Nowhere to run, Aleksei?"

"You think I killed the two women?"

"Three."

"Three? Who was the other one? I know only of the two

132

in the agency. Why lose sleep over them? They run a dirty game so they take the risks."

Bulman was aware of his stupidity in arousing Chernov, whose purpose here was, at the moment, unclear. But he had to find out what he could while he could. "You dated a girl; what happened to her?"

"She didn't turn up. I never wait long, for safety reasons, but this time I waited longer than usual. Then I smell something wrong and get out fast. I think you set me up, Bulman. But before I kill you I need to know the rest."

Bulman sat there wishing he had drunk less. "Are you trying to tell me you didn't kill any of these women?"

"That is what I say. Tell me what happened." Chernov's gun did not waver and still pointed at Bulman's chest. The women had been shot in the head.

"But you're a professional assassin, for God's sake. Who the hell will believe you didn't do it? Your video information cassette was missing. Are you trying to tell me you didn't take it?"

"You know I didn't. Don't be too clever, Bulman, or I'll shoot your knees out. I want to know what happened. I know you've been round my apartment so just get on with it and don't play for time or I'll settle the score without waiting any longer."

Bulman gazed at the gun and then at Chernov's eyes; the Russian meant what he said, apart from which he had probably never bluffed in his life. "You're saying you did not kill any of these women and that you did not recover your registration details? Is that right?"

"I've told you not to stall. And I've already answered that question. I was set up. Now talk."

"Don't you think it could be whoever employs you? Isn't that a logical assumption?"

"It doesn't make sense."

"Have you been in touch with him since?"

"Don't try that. I never mentioned a him or a her or an it. It makes sense that you would want me out of the way. I impede you in your investigations. I warned you to stop.

You knew I would do something about it. You found a way to slow me down. You set up the date so that you could go back to my place and make a more thorough search and you fixed these executions against me."

Bulman noticed that Chernov had not used the word murder; it was not in his vocabulary. He took a chance. "You're off your rocker, Aleksei. I've never killed anyone in my life. I wouldn't know how. I can't use a gun. Even you couldn't teach me to do it."

Chernov sat quietly, thinking it through, keeping his gun up and his gaze stone cold. He was not confused but nor was he sure. He had lived so long in the shadows that truth was something difficult to recognise unless preceded by torture or extreme fear. He knew Bulman was afraid but equally he was not running scared. Chernov had seen all the emotions at one time or another at the end of a gun he had been holding.

He was silent for so long Bulman was forced to ask, "Why didn't you report back? Why did you think you were in danger if you'd done no killing?"

It was still some time before Chernov answered. At one stage he showed a flash of anger and Bulman thought it would be his last moment, but the phase passed and Bulman decided to say no more. He was in Chernov's hands and there was nothing he could do.

At last Chernov said, "It is none of your business."

"You came here to find out what happened. You think I set you up. Well, if I didn't, who the bloody hell did? Were you becoming an embarrassment to your employer? Your exposure might mean his. At the moment you're a wanted man; if not by the police then by the person who hired you. By removing risk of your identity coming out he covers himself as well. You'd better keep on the move."

"No." Chernov slowly shook his head. "You are deliberately confusing me. They would have tried to kill me if they wanted to get rid of me."

"You're not an easy bloke to kill, Aleksei. Whoever tries it has to be better than you and that would be difficult to achieve." But Bulman was thinking that the two women had been shot in the dead centre of their foreheads. Someone out there knew how to use a gun – unless Chernov was putting on a wonderful act, and Bulman did not think so. Chernov was worried not so much by the danger he was obviously in from one source or another, but because he was not sure of what was going on.

"Did you find anything of interest in my apartment?"

At that moment Bulman felt more under threat than since he first walked in. Chernov was vacillating, not sure of anything at the moment, and the easiest way to solve that sort of problem was to eliminate it. "Only the porno stuff. It led us to the agency but that was as far as we got. I don't expect you will tell me who you're answerable to? It might help me to help you."

Again there was a long brooding silence. Like badly kept explosive Chernov was becoming increasingly unstable. Bulman kept his eye on the trigger finger. He had done all he could, answered truthfully for the most part, but he knew that in the end it was a toss of a coin how Chernov reacted and he had come expecting to kill.

Bulman said quickly, "Have you any friends you can call upon? People you can trust?"

Chernov gave a thin humourless smile. "In my business? Friends? People I can trust? I know of nobody I can trust with my life and that is the only kind of trust that matters. I do not complain. I am well employed, but more vulnerable, I think. And right now I am thinking is it worth taking the risk of trusting you or should I take the safest route and blow your heart out? I quite like you but I have to live."

"Wait! Just a few seconds more. Do you know of anyone who executes by shooting through the head? I mean, it's a highly risky way of going about things. I believe our firearms people are taught to shoot at the biggest target, the body, and to pump as many rounds as possible in to make sure the enemy is dead."

"You're talking of your specialist army. Our work is

quite different and we work in different circumstances and on our own." He considered what Bulman had said then replied, "One or two prefer the head because of the increasing use of flack jackets for known targets. It would vary, depending on the range. It would also depend what part of the body was a ready target. I have used the head but not as a rule." For a few moments Chernov had been carried away by professionalism, talking about the subject he knew best.

"So the fact that the two agency girls were both hit in the head has no relevance, gives you no clue as to who did it?" Bulman was fighting for his life.

"How good was the grouping?"

"Just one shot each. Plumb in the centre. As accurate as if the gun had actually been placed on the forehead. There were no burn marks so the gun was fired at least a few feet away. Remarkable shooting."

"And you saw the result?"

"I have my instincts too. When I couldn't raise Julie, the girl you were supposed to see, I felt sick. I got round to the agency as fast as I could. The press got it almost right. Just one shot each. It was me who phoned the police." Bulman knew he had introduced a ghost, someone who might well operate better than Chernov, who some would consider a hasbeen.

"Guliyev. It might be."

"Guliyev? Do you know if he's over here?"

"Galina Guliyev. A woman. That would be how she got in so easily. A show-off. Has to prove she is better than the men. It's her kind of mark but I can't be sure."

"Just how many more of you are over here?"

"None that I know of. Some are scattered in Europe, and some went to America to work for the Company."

"Would she do something like that to you?"

Chernov grimaced. He was showing his weariness but the gun remained in position. "She would do something like that to anyone. Especially men, she likes devouring men."

"Then it's got to be her. You had a back-up you didn't know was there and who decided to take over the number one spot." He saw that he had made some sort of impact so added quickly, "They knew you used the agency, might even have recommended it to you."

"And they knew that you knew." Chernov was halfway to convincing himself.

Bulman had delivered a prime stroke under considerable pressure. He was not banking on it but for the first time he saw signs of Chernov relaxing. He wanted to shift his position but the situation was too finely balanced to distract Chernov now. His left leg was agonising with cramp but he held on, poker faced. He felt the sweat run down his temples and under his chin. And just as he thought Chernov was going to lower the gun the telephone rang and the Russian was on his feet, gun sweeping the room as if he had been trapped.

"It's only the phone." Bulman held up a hand and rose slowly.

"Sit down. Just what do you think you are doing?"

"I'm going to answer it, that's all." But the ringing had already cut out and his taped voice was telling someone he was unavailable and that he would contact them later if they left a message after the tone. He had left the answering machine on and cursed his luck.

Bulman's hand was outstretched and hovering over the telephone when Chernov snapped out, "Leave it."

As soon as the caller spoke Bulman despaired. "It's Rod, Mr Bulman. Those numbers you gave me are top secret. There's no way I can find out who they belong to. I can't help this time."

But Bulman was no longer listening. He felt rather than saw Chernov make his final decision.

Chernov said in a tone that told Bulman the worst, "So you only found the porno photos, eh! Goodbye, Bulman."

Chapter Twelve

Bulman dropped like a brick as he grabbed the phone. As he fell he turned and before he hit the ground the telephone, held before him, shattered in his hands as though some power source had tried to wrench it from him. He flung what was left of it as hard as he could at Chernov's head and rolled until he hit a chair, which moved but not far enough. He was fighting a crazy battle for survival which needed only one more shot to end it.

He dived behind the chair and emerged the other end to risk a quick look at where he had last seen Chernov. The Russian was still standing there with a hand to his bleeding face. The telephone had caught Chernov just above the bridge of his nose, and a jagged edge had cut him badly across the eye and on his forehead. The blood was still flowing freely as Chernov tried to wipe it out of his eye. The gun was still in his other hand, held out expertly by sheer instinct, for at that moment he could have seen little. The telephone cord hung over his shoulder and what was left of the instrument lay at his feet in a broken mess, traces of blood smeared over it where it had smashed into his face.

It took a split second for Bulman to assess the position and an equal time for Chernov to fire another shot at where he thought Bulman would be. And his blind firing shook Bulman badly as the shots flew dangerously close.

Bulman looked round for a weapon. There was a small bronze figure of a woman on the mantelpiece. He dived across the room. Chernov heard him and swung round to fire again but Bulman, coming up from behind, pushed him hard and the Russian stumbled and fell to his knees, but even then was professional enough to follow Bulman's heavy sound of movement and fire again.

His shot was wild and hit a glass cabinet, which shattered like a bomb. This more than anything spurred Bulman on. He grabbed the bronze as Chernov rose and instinctively turned towards the sound of danger.

Both Chernov's eyes were affected: one with blood oozing from it, the other filling with blood from the forehead wound. He could barely see, but Bulman had an outline difficult to miss. He fired as Bulman saw his own danger and jumped aside to crash against the settee and lose his balance. He was falling the wrong way and saw Chernov turn again.

The only part of Chernov Bulman could reach as he landed hard were his legs and he lashed out wildly to hit Chernov behind the knees and to see him sink slowly again. Chernov landed painfully as Bulman tried to rise. It was by accident that Chernov's fall spun him to face Bulman who was climbing unsteadily to his feet.

Bulman saw the gun come up, saw a hole in the barrel the size of a tunnel and could even smell the cordite from the last shot. Then in mad desperation he brought the bronze crashing down on Chernov's head just a fraction of a second before the gun was fired, the shot burying into the floor as Chernov collapsed again. Bulman scrambled forward for the gun and staggered to the nearest chair.

As he sat recovering, staring down at the bloody mess of Chernov, he was suddenly seized by a painful cramp in his right hand and realised he was still gripping the bronze as if welded to it. He had trouble prising his fingers open and had to lay the gun down beside him while he pulled his fingers back. When he could flex his hand he found the magazine catch on the gun and emptied it, slipping the rounds in his pocket, and then releasing the one in the breech. He picked up both gun and bronze as he rose to examine Chernov, not putting it past him to feign unconsciousness.

He stood well back at first. There was a huge bump on the back of Chernov's head and the skin had ruptured. "Turn over," he said. He knew it was an idiot request as soon as he spoke but as though heeding his words Chernov rolled partially on to his back.

The Russian's eyes were open but the usually bleak expression was hidden by the matted blood. His gaze seemed to focus on Bulman but it was difficult for him to see through the red mess. His lips moved and looked parched as if he needed a drink urgently. But Bulman was not willing to lay himself open to such a dangerous man: Chernov probably looked far worse than he was.

Bulman decided the best thing to do was to tie Chernov up and then treat his wounds. The Russian was trying to say something and Bulman leaned closer but not close enough for Chernov to grab him.

"If I don't get you the Firm will." The words came out in a slow painful wheeze. Chernov did not issue empty threats but at the moment was in no position to carry this one out.

Bulman did not respond. He did not care for the idea of going into the kitchen for string whilst leaving Chernov there. He looked around to see if there was anything with which he could tie the hands together as a temporary measure. Chernov gurgled and when Bulman looked at him again, the eyes, still open, were seeing nothing at all through the blood. He knew it at once.

Bulman bent on one knee, still not too close, reached forward to pull one of Chernov's arms towards him, and felt for the pulse. His own began to flutter when he could not find one. Even Chernov could not be that deceptive. Bulman tried the carotid artery to search frantically for a sign of life and failed to find one. Chernov was dead and he had killed him.

Bulman remained on one knee for some time. He was drained and still in shock. "Get up, you bastard." His voice shook but nothing was going to make a difference. There was blood on the carpet and it became a bigger worry than a dead assassin on his hands. He placed a hand on Chernov's chest as if about to give resuscitation but he was merely confused, not knowing what to do next.

He rose slowly and sat in the nearest chair, which happened to be the one Chernov had vacated. He could feel the slight warmth of the man. He sat there, hands between legs and fingers clasped, and stared at the body of the man who had tried to kill him. It had been self defence but his feeling was that there were strong influences about which might easily turn it to murder. And that was his problem: he did not know which way to turn or who to turn to. With the phone smashed he was isolated.

He could not remember how long he sat there but his fingers were painful where he clasped them too strongly and he tried to get circulation back in them. The action did not make his mind work any better. He was in a trap. His policeman's training made the issue quite clear: he should ring the police. But he saw that as a move to disaster. Somebody was waiting for just such a situation, God sent, to get him out the way.

By now it was after ten p.m. He was shut off and whatever he decided to do with the body he could not manage it all on his own. It gradually dawned on him that he must leave the body in the flat for the night. The idea made him feel sick.

He rose from the chair and stood still for a while, unable to tear his gaze from the dead Russian. He faced a nightmare. Increasingly he knew he must contact the police and that meant using someone else's phone or going to the nearest call box, and that fact gave him just that extra time to think and veer away from committing himself. He was quite certain it would not be a sensible thing to do. He had a reputation for eccentricity, so he would be eccentric and contact nobody until the next day.

He went round tidying up, moving the chairs back in position, picking up the scattered remnants of the telephone and throwing them in the bin after slipping out the disc with the number. He found a surprising amount of blood on the telephone pieces which he made no attempt to wash off. Whatever he did there would always be traces for a discerning forensic man to find.

He was stepping round the body as if there was a ruckle in the carpet, a sign of his increasing acceptance. The real shock was yet to come. He made coffee and sat in front of Chernov, drinking and wondering and thinking that the Russian was no loss to society and a lot of people would relish seeing him as he was, dead and vacant, having fired his last shot and killed his last victim. Bulman shivered. Chernov had come too close.

From time to time he gazed over at the glass cabinet smashed by one of Chernov's bullets and tears pricked his eyes. Never able to afford much he had built up a precious collection of eighteenth- and early nineteenth-century cups and saucers. They were all he could afford over the years and he had bought judiciously. He lacked the will to see the extent of the damage to his collection.

Bulman sat up all night. He could not face going to bed; he could not be that cold blooded, whatever Chernov had been. He sat in the living-room with the corpse, dozing in a chair, occasionally falling asleep only to have nightmares so horrific that they woke him instantly. In the middle of the night when he opened his weary eyes yet again he could not believe what he saw; the bile rose and he rushed to the bathroom to be sick.

By dawn he was in a terrible state but when he tried to rouse himself he found the body still there and realised for the nth time that Chernov was not going to get out of this one. He looked at himself in a mirror and was shocked by what he saw.

Showering and shaving got rid of the blood and the dried sweat of fear on him but did nothing for his state of mind. The terrible thing was that nothing was going to change. Chernov was not going to go away.

Bulman put on a complete change of clothes, went to his small antique bureau and fiddled with the secret compartment at the back and took out some cash. He took one last look at the body, went to the door and let himself out, locking the door behind him. He leaned against the wall for the moment, free of the body. He walked some distance from his home before searching for an early morning cab which took him to Tottenham Court Road. He bought a new combined phone and answering machine and some convenience foods to take back then returned to his apartment still half hoping that Chernov had made some miracle recovery and had gone. But the body was still there. He opened some windows.

He connected the phone to the point and rang Spider Scott at his office, hoping he would be there. When he got through to him he said in a tone Scott had never before heard from Bulman, "I need your help, Spider. I'm in deep trouble."

Scott arrived late morning full of apologies and not liking the way Bulman looked. He knew why the moment he entered the living-room. "Jesus Christ, this is the guy whose drum we cased. Is he . . . of course he is. My God, what the hell happened?"

Bulman told him while Scott sank into a chair, taking over Bulman's earlier role of not able to take his eyes off the dead Russian.

"Did you clean everything up?" asked Scott.

"The phone bits are in the bin. We can dump them."

"What about the bronze? Where the hell is that?"

Bulman was shocked at his own slackness, whatever the cause. They searched for the bronze and found it had rolled under a fringe of one of the armchairs. Scott picked it up with a handkerchief through force of habit and washed it thoroughly in the sink. He wiped it down, asked Bulman where it had come from and returned it to the mantelpiece.

"There's a lot of blood on the carpet," said Scott. "I doubt that you'll get it all out."

"I'll have to buy a cheap rug to cover the stains in the meantime." Bulman was immensely grateful for Scott's help and it had not gone unnoticed that the retired burglar

143

had not once suggested telephoning the police; it simply would not have occurred to him. Their friendship, forged during Scott's heyday in crime and founded on mutual respect, was probably unique. "You'll have to give me a hand, Spider."

Scott was gazing round professionally, looking for anything they had missed. "Any time," he responded. But he had misunderstood.

"We'll have to wait for dark before we move the body."

"You want me to help with that? Come on, George, you'll land me right in it."

"I can't manage him on my own. I'd have to drag him down the stairs, drag him to the car and do the same the other end. I need help."

"Just what had you in mind, George? Where were you thinking of dumping him?"

"Back to his place. It could be days or longer before he'd be discovered."

Scott was astounded. "You mean you want me to open up his place again while he waits outside? No way. The bloody corpse would be floating down the street by that time. He's already beginning to pong. You'd stand a better chance if you report it."

"I can't leave him here. How can I? We've got to shift him."

Scott sat down again. He knew he could not leave Bulman in the lurch but had a limit as to how far he would commit himself. "I'll help you get him outside but I'm not breaking into his place again just to dump him. He goes in the river or we just dump him in the street or something."

"Is that the best you can do?"

"It's the best I'm willing to do. I don't want to be caught up in this. Maggie would have a heart attack if she even knew we were talking like this. Otherwise you're on your own, George. After all, you killed him." He was sorry as soon as he said it; he knew Bulman had not set out or meant to kill. "I'm sorry," he said, "it came out the wrong way."

"No, you're right. We dump him. What's it matter? I'll dig out an old blanket."

"And make sure you cut off the maker's tag and any laundry marks. You must have had a helluva lot of luck solving cases when you were a copper."

The friendly jibe brought a faint smile to Bulman's lips; he was just grateful to have Scott around. "I'm hardly myself," he said. "I've been up all night with that thing. He spoke for a while with difficulty, but he was lucid; the bastard threatened me." Bulman stared at Scott in a fixed sort of way, his eyes suddenly bright. "He's given me direction. I don't know the person but I do know the organisation who's behind all this. I had my suspicions but it could have been one of about three. I now know it's the Firm. I'll sort out that blanket."

Scott was not so pleased to hear what Bulman had said; he'd had too many brushes with the Firm including when working for them. While Bulman was out of the room Scott cast a professional eye around. He saw the damage to the glass-fronted cabinet and then saw the mass of broken glass at its foot. He could not understand how he had missed it before. He eased out the loose glass from the frame and piled it carefully and then went into the kitchen to get a dustpan and brush.

As he worked painstakingly to clear up the mess he heard Bulman cursing in the bedroom as he tried to find an old blanket. Scott put the glass in the bin and brushed out slivers of glass from inside the Cabinet. With the fragments out of the frame the Cabinet appeared to be quite normal except for a broken cup and saucer which he carefully removed. Bulman had been lucky in that he had lost only one set, but he would be devastated to find that it was his prize Dr Wall, blue and white Worcester. Scott put it in the bin with the glass, for it was way beyond restoration. Bulman would have to find out in his own time.

Scott moved the other cups around to cover the gap and then saw the bullet lodged in the wooden back of the Cabinet. He prized it out with a clasp knife and slipped it in his pocket. He then went to find out why Bulman was taking so long. Apparently Bulman kept his spare sheets and blankets in a chest under the bed; he was just packing them away when Scott entered the room. A ragged old blanket lay on top of the bed.

Twenty minutes later Chernov was wrapped in the blanket, thick sealing tape keeping the folded ends in place and several pieces wound round the body. They now had time to kill and that was going to be the worst part.

Bulman remembered the BT engineer whose call had started the events leading to the killing and rang him. "Rod? Sorry about last night, the phone crashed out and I had to get a new one this morning. Wasn't worth repairing, too old fashioned. So what's the news?"

"You're lucky to find me in. No joy. I dunno where you got those numbers from but they're red hot, top secret stuff. Unlisted to the likes of me. They're not only ex-directory but they don't even officially exist. Sorry, guv, but you'll have to go over my head for this lot."

"Haven't you tried any of them?" asked Scott when Bulman put the phone down.

"I thought it would be more useful if I knew who I was calling before I did. These numbers nearly cost me my life." Bulman pulled out Scott's original list from a pocket while Scott could only reflect his incredulity at Bulman's seeming lack of security.

Bulman seemed to be untouched by Scott's unspoken criticism, his earlier trauma gone now that Chernov was covered up. He fixed the recorder on the answering machine and dialled the first number. It simply pealed until it cut out.

"At least it's connected," observed Bulman drily. "I'll try it from time to time." He tried the second number. A recorded male voice said, "Leave your name and number and we'll get back to you. State any priority code."

Bulman hung up and stared at Scott. "I think we have a bearing. Let's try the last one." The recording was the same but a different voice, still male, and without the coding message.

The mood in the room changed. At first there had been near panic, fear and trauma. Then the arrival of Scott had calmed Bulman down more than he cared to admit. Scott had been in so many tight situations in his life that it had always seemed to Bulman that he could cope with anything. If that was completely true Scott would never have gone to jail, but Scott was expert at his old job and did not panic. His presence gave Bulman reassurance. Bulman had killed a man and there was no easy way out of that; Scott being there made the difference.

However disastrous it might seem, they could cope with the situation given a modicum of luck. But now a new element had entered the arena, and one they had both come to detest. The negative response from the telephone calls conveyed far more menace than anything. To them it represented danger, deceit, treachery, the unknown. It had not always been like that, there had been times when they'd been only too grateful for help from the grey men, but they had never been a real part of that establishment and were therefore useable and expendable. A temporary membership was like an acting rank, it was not the real thing.

Scott said, "There's been a lot of tightening up, you know. They can't get away with it like they used to. Attitudes are different."

Bulman glanced at the shrouded body. "Take another look at him and tell me that. There are still some of the old boys about and they are very good at their jobs. I'm not criticising the need to defend the flag, but some can't handle it. They are not a perfect combination, any more than in any other field. There are rogues amongst them who abuse their power and I think we've landed one. And it only needs one."

"So where does the American Ambassador come in? He, or his son seems to be the target and your attempts to

147

help him are not entirely appreciated. Don't lose perspective, George. Chernov wasn't sent round to kill you but to put the frighteners on you. The women were killed to cut off his tail, not yours. And he came here the second time to find out what he could because he was not going to be enlightened by his employer. If he took you out along the way, jolly good show chaps, but he wasn't instructed to do it. Any dirty work against you is to stop you stopping dirty work against the Yanks."

"That was a long speech for you, Spider."

"Yeah. Like a detective inspector promoted to superintendent, these days I just sit on my arse and growl. But I'm right and you know it."

Bulman did not answer; he was trying to think up a way of plucking out Chernov's contact. Darkness came all too slowly and they microwaved convenience food but it was difficult for them to eat with the body still there. They washed up – Bulman did not have a dishwasher – and an edginess crept back into the room.

"We can't take him down the stairs," said Scott. "It only needs one person to come out of one of the other flats or to come back late and we've had it. What's at the back?"

They should have discussed it hours ago but neither had been willing to broach it. Now the time was near it was suddenly urgent and no longer straight-forward.

"I'll go get the car," said Bulman, leaving the problem of disposal to Scott who made no effort to move.

When Bulman had gone, Scott turned the lights out and went round the rear windows, opening them and peering down. As far as he could see there was a communal garden at the rear; the house was in one of the numerous old squares and the garden formed a mini-park. Three sides were flanked by railings with streets running alongside. The fourth side of the square comprised the building itself, late Victorian and solid. There must be at least one gate from the street leading to the garden.

Scott was nervous. They should have spent time thinking it through instead of leaving everything to the last moment.

It seemed to be hours before Bulman returned and when he did it was obvious that the operation was now so near that he was a bundle of nerves. Scott said straight away, "We'll have to lower him out the back and then go round to collect him."

"The gardens are shared by the people in the ground-floor flats. I've no key to the gates."

Scott, who had put the lights back on was getting angry. "You're a bit bloody late in coming out with that. You've been sitting there all day without even thinking about it. We've got to get this bloody corpse out of the way. We'll spring the locks. Go get some rope to lower him with."

Bulman stared numbly. "Rope? I've got no rope."

Scott could not believe it. He had come to help a friend, a onetime top detective, who was slipping up on the most elementary of issues. He was about to blast off when he realised that the whole murderous business had shocked Bulman far more than he had outwardly shown. Bulman simply was not capable of sorting it out at this moment. In any other circumstances it might have been comic but there was a corpse to get rid of and suddenly the task was monumental and the whole world was waiting outside for them to bring it on view.

"Okay, we wait until three and then we push him out."

"There's a narrow passage between the building and the railed gardens; it's where they keep their dustbins and each ground-floor tenant has his own gate and key. We can't afford to drop him this side of the railings."

"You're testing me to the limit, George. I've had to spin one hell of a story to Maggie to justify staying out most of the night and now you put up obstruction after obstruction. You don't deserve any bloody help. Have you got a ball of string?"

Bulman went to the kitchen and came back with several loosely rolled bundles of variable-sized string. "I'm sorry, Spider. I don't seem to be able to snap out of it. It's knocked me up a bit."

"Well, let's hope the string holds. Come on, let's bind him top and tail."

It was a crude arrangement but they used most of the string Bulman had produced and sat back uneasily to wait another two hours. They pulled Chernov into position under the open bedroom window and returned to the sitting-room. At least the corpse was no longer in view but that comfort was nullified when Scott turned out all the lights. They sat in the dark listening to the faint noises that floated through the open window.

Conversation died as the time approached. The room felt like an ice block as an early morning chill crept into the apartment, but much of the coldness arose from their own disquiet.

When the clock on the mantelpiece struck three they rose without a word and groped their way into the bed-room. Scott leaned over the sill and peered down into the darkness. There was nothing he could see, little judgement he could make. "How wide did you say the passage is?"

"About three feet, maybe four."

"It's not going to work," said Scott. "We can lower him down but we won't be able to get sufficient swing for him to clear the railings."

It was so dark now that the two men could barely see each other. Outside it seemed to be absolutely dead.

"What more can go wrong?"

"We're just not used to disposing of corpses. Lift him up on to the sill."

Bulman did not move.

"Lift him, George, or I'm leaving you to it."

Between them they managed to get Chernov on to the sill where he was finely balanced but held firmly by the two men.

"Let go of him," said Scott. "I've got a grip."

Chernov hung feet first and Scott held him by the shoulders. Bulman knew what Scott intended to do but had no more will to object. He stood beside the window with his back to the wall and closed his eyes; he was better

150

at facing personal danger than coping with breaking the law he had been taught to uphold.

Scott changed his grip, let Chernov's trunk dip towards the floor, bent his knees then gave a massive heave and the corpse arced out into the night. Scott leaned out to hear the sickening crunch which somehow did not sound right.

Chapter Thirteen

"Take the car round to the back of the gardens." Scott closed the window quickly. "I'll foot it."

Now that Chernov had finally left the flat Bulman sprung into action and hurried out. Scott wanted to give a last look round to make sure all trace of Chernov had gone with him but he resisted putting the lights on and hurried after Bulman.

Bulman was still trying to get the car started when Scott reached the street. He strode over, bent down to the open window and snarled, "That's right, wake the whole bloody neighbourhood." The engine caught as he spoke and he sprinted away. He still reached the rear of the gardens before Bulman, who had to warm the engine for fear of stalling, and located the heavy gate easily.

He fiddled with his keys and sprung the lock, leaving the gate ajar for Bulman. The gardens were mostly laid to grass but there was the odd central flower bed which he was just able to pick out. He crossed swiftly to the point below Bulman's flat to find Chernov partially caught up in the railings just on the garden side. Chernov was hanging head down with the end of the blanket ripped and caught between the spikes of the railings.

Scott tried to release him but it was not until Bulman arrived to help that they managed to get the body free. They then carried it to Bulman's car and bundled it in the boot. Scott locked the gate and sat next to Bulman who said, "Where to?"

"Head for outer London. We want to get as far away

from here as possible. And stick to the minor roads. Don't go anywhere near a main street."

Bulman drove on with headlights dipped, still trying to come to terms with what he was doing. The streets were dead, it now being close to four a.m., but it would not be long before the early workers started out. There was a sense of relief between the two men – they had at least got the corpse out of the building – but increasingly Scott was turning in his seat to look back. After a while he said, "We've got company."

"That's impossible. There are no lights behind us."

"I've followed without lights. It isn't easy and should be left to experts. Pull up round the next corner and move over to my seat."

"I'm Hendon trained. I can cope."

"I don't care if you came first in the Indycar, this is my territory and you're not chasing, you're running, mate. Turn here, and pull up sharp."

Bulman turned, braked, put her in neutral and awkwardly climbed over the central column.

Scott was out of the car before he actually stopped. He raced to the other side, climbed in and was off, jerking Bulman back in his seat. The years fell away, the feel of the steering wheel therapeutic under his relaxed control. He could not recall the last time he had raced the streets at the dead of night, but it seemed like yesterday.

As he concentrated on his driving he barely heard the increasing shouts from Bulman as he took corner after corner in controlled skids. He was enjoying himself but not to the point of recklessness, as Bulman believed.

The journey was uncanny as Bulman quietened down and the only sound was the engine and the occasional whine of tyres. As Bulman finally came to terms with Scott's driving skills a sense of self disgust assailed him. He was being saved by an old lag.

He glanced at Scott, saw the total concentration of the man and knew it would be pointless trying to say anything anyway; Scott was unaware of him just then. He did as

Scott had done and looked back to see headlights come on: nobody could follow Scott's speed and skill without them.

During the hectic race – the swerving, the bursts of acceleration, the following lights sometimes falling behind, sometimes catching up – Bulman could not lose sight of the fact that they had a corpse in the boot and if a chance police car signalled them, God knew what would happen.

"I'm sorry," he said. "I should be tougher. But I've never killed before." But he was speaking to himself, hunched in his seat without the seatbelt fixed.

Without taking his gaze from the road Scott said, "This guy's good, but he's living on his luck." As if to prove the point Scott took a particularly awkward bend on two wheels, kept on track and then behind them came the horrendous sound of tearing metal and a great lump appeared in the rear-view mirror like a flying meteorite. Headlights shot upwards like searchlights, probing the sky in wild movements before dipping as the car crashed down, overturned, screamed along on its side and crashed into a row of cars, bouncing from one to the other before the lights suddenly snapped out.

Scott did not see the final result because he took another turn and slowed right down, pumping the brake until they were back to normal speed. Only then did he blow his cheeks out with relief.

Bulman said, "Someone might need help back there."

"Tough," Scott replied tersely. "Now let's get out of town."

They didn't get as far out as they wanted. Very gradually the early traffic started to appear and whilst this in itself posed no danger, they did not want the car seen or remembered by anyone. A passing patrol car reminded them that they were still highly vulnerable. Scott pulled up in a small square with a central garden, not unlike the one they had just left, on the outskirts of north London.

It was already too light for comfort but they had to make a move. Without even discussing it, they climbed out, Bulman opened the boot, they took a long good look up and down that side of the square, and with some difficulty heaved Chernov over the railings. They climbed back into the car and pulled away.

It was some time before they spoke, they were so tensed up at finally ditching the body. Bulman, who had taken over the driving again, was not conscious of direction. A huge cloud had been lifted but another was on the way down.

Scott said, "You'll have to get rid of the car, George."

Bulman nodded. "Yes, I know I should. Someone may remember it. Maybe I could sell it in part exchange."

"You might have done but for the bullet hole in the offside rear window."

"Bullet hole?" Bulman turned quickly and got the merest glance of the hole just behind him, not knowing whether it had been caused by a bullet but absolutely certain that it had not been there when they started out. "I never heard it," he said feebly.

"We'll have to take the car out into the country, remove the plates, file off the engine number, and set fire to it. Then report it stolen unless you want to replace it at your own expense."

"No. I can only go so far with this. I'm not burning the car. I'll keep it garaged."

"You'll be making a mistake. This is a distinctive car; it might be remembered by someone. If it's found so will traces of Chernov's blanket in the boot."

"I'll take my chances. I'm not burning her."

Scott dropped off a short walk from his home. Bulman drove back to his lock-up and put the car away. By the time he reached his apartment he was drained. Chernov had gone but his aura remained everywhere. He was far from happy in the empty apartment and brooded over the way they had finally felt forced to dump Chernov. All that could be said was that the Russian had finished up a good distance from where he had died, but it should have been further still.

After he had cooked himself a scratch meal he took

155

stock of the living-room, saw the various blood stains and doubted that any amount of washing would remove them completely; there would always be traces left for forensic to pick out. He took a couple of small rugs from each side of his bed and placed them over the stains. It might fool nobody but it did remove the blood from sight.

He switched on satellite TV news plus the local radio station hoping to pick up news of the car crash and Chernov. Car crashes were too common for normal mention but the driver who had followed them had been armed. It would be remarkable if anyone had walked away from a crash like that.

It was some time later that he pricked up his ears and turned up the volume of the radio and turned down the TV. The car crash details were being reported, having been held back pending identification of the dead driver. Several cars had been damaged in the crash. The woman driver had been armed and the police were still investigating the accident.

Bulman knew the form: she was probably so badly mangled that they could not take a satisfactory photograph of her or they would have shown one on screen if not sure of identity. They probably had no idea who she was. She had to be the one who had chased them. A woman. Galina Guliyev?

There was still no news of Chernov. Corpses wrapped in blankets could not be that common. It was possible that he just lay behind some shrubs and nobody had yet found him.

He slept intermittently throughout the day and at eight p.m. rang the number from which he had received no reply.

A voice said, "Yes?"

Bulman stiffened. "Is Bob there? Bob Clifford?"

"What number are you ringing?" The man's voice was cultured and full of suspicion.

Bulman gave the number, transposing the first and last digits.

"I'm afraid you have the wrong number." The man hung up and Bulman removed the tape and replaced it. He had not recognised the voice at all. He sat staring at the phone knowing it was important to identify the person he had called. After a while he rang Scotland Yard and asked to speak to Assistant Commissioner John Cordell. He did not expect him to be there but he did find out that he was expected at nine the following morning. He declined to leave a message. He rang the other two numbers again and got the same result as before. He was now satisfied that the numbers connected to the answering machines were purely message machines to take incoming calls only, to record in order to give sufficient time for the caller to be vetted.

There was nothing more he could do until morning. He switched the TV volume up and wished Scott was still there. Scott was a rare character and his word was his bond, a fact many found difficult to swallow about an ex-cat burglar. He watched the ITN news at ten with his mind not really on it, and became all attention when news of Chernov at last surfaced.

The shrouded corpse had been found in north London by a woman exercising her dog in the railed gardens. Examination showed that the man had been viciously bludgeoned to death. As yet the man remained unidentified. Bulman switched off. The news item brought Chernov back into the room and brought the nightmare back with it.

Michael Sealy put the phone down and was worried about the wrong number. If he had suffered pressure of late there was still nothing wrong with his retentive memory. He jotted down the number Bulman had said he thought he had rung and rang it. A titled lady answered and she certainly knew nothing of a Bob Clifford. Sealy apologised and hung up.

Sealy was angry with himself. He should never have used someone like Chernov but he really had no choice. It was impossible for him to use his own people without eventual doubt spreading and questions being asked. He was really lucky to have cast-offs like Chernov available. They were well trained in what they did, and they were expendable. But their ways were not his and their code of conduct was different. He knew that Chernov secretly despised the lack of ruthlessness his Russian masters would have insisted upon. Warnings were a weak form of deterrent, non effective unless followed through. Had he let Chernov have his head in the first place there would be no Bulman and, therefore, no problem.

Now Chernov was dead and so, he had just learned, was Galina Guliyev, who had grossly exceeded her orders in order to impress and had paid the price. It was true that he had told Galina to deal with the call-girls because they pointed the finger at Chernov who had become high profile, but she had to be flashy and show off with the single shot business when she could have killed them by seemingly natural means. And she could not keep away from Chernov, as if he presented a personal challenge and she hated him and had to prove herself better. It was a stupid mess – childish, if the results had not been so horrific. It would be easy to say that the two Russians should never have been taken on, but they had had their uses. And they were easily replaceable.

Meanwhile Bulman had employed someone much more effective. Sealy had checked the records and Willie "Spider" Scott had come out strong. Years ago he had broken into the Chinese Legation in Portland Place and had got away with it, doing a job for Stuart Halliman who headed DI5 in those days. Scott had been blackmailed into doing it and had survived. Bulman was lucky to have such friends in times of crisis. And it was Bulman who had just made the telephone call. He was certain of it. And he must have raised the number from Chernov's flat in the safe block, using Scott's expertise. Perhaps it was as well Chernov, and certainly the unstable Galina, were dead. But it still left the problem of Bulman, who was still ferreting and whose police records suggested he would do until stopped.

*   *   *

158

Bulman rang John Cordell at nine thirty next morning and gave his name. He was surprised when he was put through almost straight away.

"George! It's been years. What's new?"

It was true that they had worked together for a time, and for a period Bulman held the senior rank, but they had never been close friends in a true sense and the affability surprised Bulman; even being put through at all was something he had hoped for but about which he was far from confident. So instead of being pleased he was suddenly suspicious.

"I manage to buy a crust now and then. I'm glad you've done so well, John. I wondered if we could meet some time. Lunch or something like that. I know you must be up to your eyeballs but a quick meeting would do. There is something important I want to talk to you about."

Cordell, still with an air of friendliness, said, "Look, I've a crummy luncheon fixed for today but I can wriggle out of that. You know that place off Victoria Street? The small one with the artificial onions and leeks and the real ale? It's still there. Twelve thirty? I'll be delighted to see you again."

"Me too. I'll be there."

It had all been too easy and Bulman, who needed the meeting badly, was now unsure of his tactic. He could see no other opening.

Cordell was already there when Bulman entered the cramped reception. He was expected and was ushered forward in a great flurry as if he was VIP for the day. The seated Cordell rose to greet him so effusively that Bulman began to wonder if they had been better friends than he recalled.

"Whisky and water, I remember," said Cordell and Bulman thought that at least that was right, but then his taste for drink had been well recorded.

Cordell was dressed in a smart grey suit with a pale red tie and his silvering hair was brushed back and as

thick on top as Bulman remembered. They had an isolated cubicle to themselves and Bulman was quite sure
that Cordell would have insisted on that kind of privacy.

They sat and chatted about old times and they certainly
had a good few to remember. Cordell insisted that everything was on the expense account: "I'd rather spend it
on an old copper like you than leave it in the slush
fund. You were always special, George. A bloody good
copper. Never really understood why you resigned. You
could have had my rank."

Bulman accepted the magnanimity with surprise. "I
could never see myself as Assistant Commissioner. Look
at me. I don't like wearing a suit, let alone a uniform.
That's why I plumped for CID; I could wear rags and get
away with it. This food is good. Better than I remember,
but then I could only afford it now and then."

"Well, I wasn't going to bring you to a doss house. So
what's your problem, George?"

Bulman had repeatedly mulled over what to say and
Cordell was making it easy for him. He decided to accept
from the start that Cordell knew he was acting for Marvin
Hayes. If he had not found out directly he would by
now have found out from the Home Office or SIS. "I
thought hard and long before deciding to contact you.
It's reached a point where I really had no option and
yours was the only sane opinion I might get. It's about
the murder of Paula Smith, the SP girl who was at Oxford.
I understand the American Ambassador's son, Don, is
under suspicion."

"Who told you that? You're on *subjudice* ground there,
George." The friendliness was still there but there was now
a cutting edge to the voice which warned Bulman not to go
too far.

"His Excellency Marvin Hayes, United States Ambassador to the Court of St James."

"That's a mouthful. Go on."

"I'm trying to point out the importance of this matter;

we're not dealing with petty politicians, always assuming you can find some who are not."

"He got in touch with you and told you that?"

"He employed me. And the reason he did that is because he thinks something stinks about the whole business. Is there anything you can tell me?"

Cordell dabbed his lips. "If I don't tell you you're going to stir it up anyway. I know very little indeed, actually. If you're employed by the Ambassador he will no doubt have told you that we met in the presence of Stuart Wilson, a junior Home Office Minister, and we did tell him that the fingerprints on the gun that killed Paula Smith belonged to the Ambassador's son. That's a fact."

"And are his prints actually on the gun?"

"That's impertinent, George. Of course they are."

"Then why wasn't he arrested?"

Cordell pushed his plate away. He was cautious now but a residue of friendliness remained. "You've just entered the political arena which is beyond your brief. Even I don't know the answers to that."

Bulman gazed miserably at his empty glass and decided Cordell's expense account must have dried up or had suddenly been curtailed. "The only brief I have is to get at the truth."

"You've just been given the truth, George. I think the powers that be are just trying to give the Ambassador a break and not mess up a valuable international friendship."

"Bullshit. You're crucifying the guy. Marvin Hayes and his wife are in a terrible state, not to mention their son. Is someone trying to get the youngster back on drugs? Or just bust up the family? And what about Paula Smith? The SB must be fuming. You must think it bloody queer, John. Have the police been side-shifted on this? Because if they have they had better stand their ground for once. Who in SIS is handling this?"

"I never mentioned SIS and you are abusing my hospitality."

"I did ask to meet you and I did say it was important. I understand that you can't tell me certain things but if I give you a tape can you get the voice identified for me?"

Cordell gave it some thought. "It would be easy to say yes but in the end I suppose it depends on whose voice it is. If indeed we recognise it at all."

"Are you willing to try?" And before Cordell could answer Bulman leaned across the table and said earnestly, "Look, John, you've a reputation for being as straight as a die. That's how I remember you and I can't believe anything has changed. But I do understand when the security services get involved they highjack everybody else's principles and manage to get the ranking politicians on their side. I'm willing to gamble that you're no more happy about this situation than I am."

"You never used to be this loquacious, George. Never used four words when an effective two would do or even an expletive in sign language." He smiled and so did Bulman. "I can't add to what I've said, whether or not I'm happy about it. But I'm willing to take the tape, play it, and if at all possible tell you whose voice I think it is. You obviously think it's someone I know. But, if I am unable to identify or am able but unwilling to disclose who it might be, then I'll let you have it back."

"Can I be there when you play it?"

"No. That would mean coming to the Yard and tongues might wag."

"Would you come to my place and let me play it? It's only a snippet."

"No. What you are saying is that you don't trust me to return it. You should have made copies if you're that unsure."

"I know I should. But I'm only an out-of-work ex-copper and can't afford the luxury of that kind of equipment. And I don't want strangers in on the act."

"It's up to you. I might refuse to give you information but I wouldn't do the dirty on you."

Bulman slid the tiny cassette across the table. "You might have to play it a few times there's so little there. On the other hand you might get it in one."

Cordell looked round for the waiter and to Bulman's relief ordered more drinks. "Is that it, George? Nothing else?"

"One more thing. You probably know I've interviewed the students at Oxford who were involved in this business. The one I can't find is a guy called Walter McQueen. He's disappeared. Do you know where he is?"

"No. I understand we're looking for him." Cordell swallowed his coffee and said, "I think I should explain that I am not directly involved at any level with this murder enquiry. I was brought in because the Home Office considered that the Ambassador would only believe his son's involvement on the say-so of a senior police officer. So as I was not willing to be a puppet I had to acquaint myself with the case first. I read what little evidence there was, the police interviews with the students, and I spoke to one or two coppers at Oxford who were handling the case. But that is as far as it goes."

"Could you give me the names of the coppers at Oxford?"

"It won't help, George. Paula Smith was a Special Branch officer. The moment they were informed of the murder it was taken from the hands of the locals whether or not they liked it. And it seems to me that in no time at all SB in turn handed it over to whoever pulls their strings on occasion, and there it rests. There must have been some pretty swift action. Someone had their ear to the ground and didn't waste a second. That's as much as I can tell you."

"Do you know what Paula Smith was doing there?"

"If I did I wouldn't tell you. She was undercover." Cordell shrugged. "There is a general drug problem. Universities are far from being detached from it."

163

"Drugs? Special Branch? Surely that would be left to the Anti-Drug Squad."

"Not if related to terrorism. Terrorists raise an increasing amount of money from drug deals. And it's not unknown for sections of the security services to take the weed. But you know all this."

"Do you think they'll find McQueen?"

Cordell gazed impassively at Bulman. "How long is a piece of string? I did check his record out of curiosity. Apart from latching on to any militant and violent cause, he has a lot of suspicion hanging over him in some very nasty quarters. Never been to jail, though, but a seeming nut case. He's one big question mark of the kind that makes us nervous. It makes you wonder how he ever got entry into Oxford, but then I don't suppose they ask to see police records, and I suppose if they did in his case there would be little if any hard evidence." And then Cordell seemed to fall into a kind of reverie with eyes closed, hands quite still on the table. It was a while before he spoke again, with Bulman unwilling to interrupt the silence as he realised that Cordell was grappling with a problem. Cordell's eyes opened and he said, "You know you're being monitored?"

"Oh, yes. I've known almost from the start and I've also been warned off." And as Cordell showed his surprise, added, "By freelance Soviet discards." He stopped in time from adding they were dead. The police were doing their own investigations.

This seemed to worry Cordell much more than Bulman expected. For a while he made small talk as if the serious discussion was over but Bulman could see he was mulling something over and could not make up his mind. Bulman played his part in keeping the small talk going, hoping Cordell would make a useful decision. When he did it took Bulman by surprise.

Cordell said, "I'm retiring in August. I've been offered a good job. I wouldn't want to make life difficult for myself before I leave." He smiled. "That does not mean that I will shirk anything meanwhile. Even so, what I am about to say I would immediately deny should I later be challenged on it. You understand?"

Bulman nodded. "You are going to tell me something on trust. I wouldn't let you down, John. Nobody would find out from me."

"I don't think we will find McQueen. I think he's already been found."

Bulman whistled softly. "Killed?"

"Tucked away. This is what I believe, not what I know. I don't know the reason and I've no idea of what might happen to him. And I could be hopelessly wrong. And, no, I don't know where. If I knew that I'd know for a certainty what had happened to him. McQueen's been plucked out of the game, George. Find out why and you might come up with the other answers. Be very careful."

Chapter Fourteen

When Bulman left Cordell he was more worried than when he had arrived. He went home feeling depressed because he could not see a solution. His timing of the meeting had been impeccable. Cordell was more concerned than he dared admit and had said more than Bulman had hoped for. He was satisfied about the general source of his problems but could not determine whether he was up against the whole organisation or one individual playing a solitary game.

Bulman was quite sure that Cordell was not at all happy about matters or he would not have said a word. At one point he considered asking to see Stuart Wilson, the junior Home Office Minister, but concluded that he knew no more than Cordell and had been deceived just as much. Even so, by now he must be worried about where it was all leading.

Bulman reached home, saw the blinking green light on the answering machine and ran it back. Spider Scott had rung to ask how he was. And then there was another message: a muffled voice said, "Bulman, this is Bob Clifford. Just returning your call."

It was no surprise that the person who had answered the number he had called should know who he was, bearing in mind the attention he had attracted and the number of people who had been killed as a result. What concerned him was that whoever he had so briefly spoken to had not accepted the wrong number story and had then followed it through and made sure Bulman knew his degree of disadvantage. There was a chill about the crude message, an uncompromising warning to him that there was little he did that was not recorded. It made him wonder when he might join the Chernov ranks of the great expendables. At the same time it did mean he was getting closer.

"That was marvellous. You Brits seem to have taken over the musicals."

The two women stood to one side of the exodus streaming from the theatre in Shaftesbury Avenue. Once on the street the mass of people slowed down as if their main purpose was to free themselves from the confines of the theatre and then take their time and get in each other's way.

It was a warm night and attire was light. Anna Brus and Connie Taylor made quite a striking couple and attracted many a male eye, but each having suffered in their own way, for the moment at any rate, they preferred each other's company. The hired mini cab eventually arrived and the two went back to Anna's flat off the Gloucester Road.

Over coffee Connie said, "I've been trying to get my boss to go to a show, have even offered to take him. I don't know what's happened but it's the anniversary of losing his son and his wife and I'm worried about him."

"Did they die at the same time, then?" Anna already knew they were dead.

"Almost the same day but two years apart. The son went first. My boss seems to be disapppearing into a personal trough of misery. His concentration is going."

Anna could understand the concern of her friend, but she could see it was something more than that and this intrigued her. "Then he should retire."

Connie crossed her long legs. "He won't do that."

"And you wouldn't want him to, right?"

"That sounds awful." Connie felt she had shown too much of her feelings. She shook her head. "I think he's far from well. He needs to get away for a while. But if anyone suggested that, he'd hang on just to prove them wrong."

Anna eyed Connie over her coffee cup. "Well, you're not alone. The Ambassador is all doom and gloom these days. He sure is worried about something. And it's something he's keeping me well clear of. But I am concerned." She suddenly smiled and when Anna did that the room lit up. "Maybe it's just the season for men." And then with a frown, "There couldn't be a connection, could there?"

Connie looked up. "You mean they might have the same problem? That's stretching it a bit."

"All men have the same problem, honey. It was just a thought."

"I don't see how they could have. I don't think they've even met."

"Come on. They've met all right. It's my boss's job to meet everybody who is anybody, and it's your boss's job to make sure he's one of them." It was the nearest she had come to indicating that she knew where Connie actually worked.

Earlier that same evening John Cordell took home the cassette Bulman had given him. His wife had gone to a Women's Institute meeting and had left his dinner in the micro for him to give it a few minutes' blast. It was ironic that this was one of the few evenings he had managed to leave the Yard early and his wife was away.

He went into his den and produced his own mini-recorder, and slipped Bulman's cassette in and played it. The reproduction was poor but good enough. As Bulman had said there was little there, but one word from that voice would have been enough. He played it again to make sure then went into the kitchen to heat his dinner.

The ping of the micro cut through his reverie and he found himself by the kitchen window looking out into the garden and the shrubs enclosing it. With the warmer weather the Koi were already jumping in the large ornamental pond and the aquatic plants were beginning to bloom. He did not remember going to the window or even leaving the micro.

He had expected the voice to be the one he recognised but that made it worse. He had hoped it would turn out to be someone else, someone he did not know so that he could give an easy answer to Bulman. Now he could not give one at all.

He barely tasted his dinner and in the end it got cold and he threw it away. A usually decisive man, he was now faced with indecision and this alone annoyed him. He was not the type to sit on the fence but now he could see no alternative. Unless he did a little probing himself, and in his position that could be self-destructive. It would be better if he could consult the Commissioner next morning, but his senior was in Frankfurt for the next three days for an Interpol conference. He was on his own in a no-win situation. Sod's Law.

He rang Bulman to find the line engaged and sat in a chair staring into space waiting for a few minutes to pass so that he could try again. His mind had numbed because meeting Bulman had forced him to face certain issues that had been worrying him from the start. Recent developments had not eased those worries. It was lucky that Bulman had been hired because most others would have taken a chance and released what they had to the press whether or not it damaged the Ambassador; it would not have damaged their pockets. He briefly wondered how the Ambassador had got hold of Bulman in the first place, but quickly recalled that Bulman had a lot of friends, home and away.

He rang Bulman again and this time the phone rang out but clicked into the answering service. He was just about to hang up when Bulman's voice cut in, "Bulman."

"It's Johnny. Johnny Cordell. I played your tape. No luck, George. The reception wasn't good but it was nobody I recognised. I played it a couple of times but as you said there's not an awful lot there. Perhaps had it been longer I might have come up with something. Sorry, but there it goes."

"Thanks for trying, anyway. Can I have the tape back?"

"Of course. I'll put it in tomorrow's post."

"I'd like to get hold of it sooner. Couldn't a messenger bring it round? If I'm not in, it can be slipped through the letter box."

"You always were pushy. Okay, I'll use the taxpayer's money. Sorry I couldn't help."

Cordell returned to his chair wondering just why he had started lying to old friends. Ironically, Bulman would have understood his dilemma had he known, and might have done the same himself.

After speaking to Cordell Bulman rang Marvin Hayes at home and was relieved the butler answered the phone. Hayes quickly came on. "Yes, George," which indicated that Hayes was alone.

"Can I pop round?"

"It's late. I'm just back from one of your sports dinners: stag and dirty. Be as quick as you can."

Bulman had more questions to ask than news to report, but there were a couple of items that could not wait. Nothing could wait any more. He was full of a foreboding that a crisis was not far off.

He locked up. He would have to get a cab, as he wanted to keep his car out of sight. At the bottom of the stairs he opened the heavy front door, stepped out and took a deep gulp of fresh air, then exhaled immediately in a massive gasp as someone hit him in the stomach with some sort of weapon. He doubled forward and sensed someone else come up alongside. He tried to straighten but was in too much pain and could only stumble sideways. Something hit him on the back of the head and he fell to his knees, barely conscious.

Another blow came from behind and he felt himself falling forward and he crashed down the shallow steps, whereupon it seemed that the whole street started to kick him to death. The pain carried through into unconsciousness and there was no fight he could put up. He lay spread out, arms and legs splayed and his bloodied head hanging down into the street. The last thing he heard was someone call out, "Don't forget his wallet." He did not hear the running feet moving away from him or the scream of a distant witness. It had all happened on his own doorstep.

He regained consciousness five hours later and could barely move. Whoever had hit him on the back of the head was still doing it and his ribs felt as if they were in a tightening vice. It was some time later before he could open his eyes and even then he delayed doing it for fear of what he might see.

A soft hand closed over his wrist and through the pain he wondered what was happening. He opened his eyes. In the subdued light he saw a perfectly oval face hovering over him. It was black and young and the eyes were bright and smiling. "You're back with us, then. Just lie there."

Bulman thought that a fatuous remark and tried to smile, discovering that his face hurt too. He tried to speak but nothing came out and it seemed that his lips were glued together. He tried moving his eyes and even that was an effort but he saw enough to know that he was in a private ward on his own and that he could not afford such luxury. At that point he realised he was far from dead if he was already worrying about money. But he was in a very bad way.

"You're tough," said the nurse. "Don't make them like you any more." She smiled cheekily but Bulman could not respond. If he was alive it must be by accident; he realised the beating he'd suffered might have killed a lot of people.

"Did they get them?" He managed to get his first words out and he could barely hear them himself.

"The muggers? I don't know."

"Did they take my wallet?"

"There's no wallet in your kit. Stop asking questions and rest."

The missing wallet was cosmetic, just to make it look like a mugging. He never carried much cash but his credit

171

cards were in a separate leather holder. He was beginning to think but the pain was difficult to contend with. His arms were already on top of the sheets and he had a drip in either arm and he was wired up on his chest to monitor his heart. Was he that bad? He carefully raised a hand to his head to find it heavily bandaged. It was difficult to explore his body with the drips in the way. He was disgusted with himself. "I'm too bloody old for this," he muttered.

The nurse heard him and said, "Only if it happens again."

Bulman began to develop a great liking for the nurse who had his kind of humour.

Bulman had never been a good patient. Within an hour of reaching consciousness he was restless, wanting to get out. When he tried to sit up he paid the price and collapsed back in pain. The nurse, now out of sight, scolded him and told him not to try again. From then on he drifted in and out of sleep aided by painkillers and sleeping pills. The next time he was really aware of where he was it was daylight and a different nurse was with him, more formal and militant.

They brought him breakfast and he realised just how hungry he was and that he could not be that bad if he could eat. It was not until the door opened again that he saw a policeman standing outside and wondered if he had been there all night. The three people who entered this time were a doctor, ward sister and a nurse he hadn't seen before.

He was given a thorough if painful examination and was assured that nothing was actually broken; they had X-rayed him on arrival. But he was massively bruised both internally and externally and there was a gash in his head. They had shaved part of his cranium while he was still unconscious in order to treat and dress the wound. He had lost some blood but nothing to worry about. He was disconnected from the heart monitor and one of the drips.

"Which hospital am I in? I need a phone. Certain people need to know where I am."

"You're in St Peter's. The phone is level with your head. Dial nine and you'll get an outside line. There's the panic button if you need a nurse. There's the radio control and the TV remote control is on the other table. But you should take it easy for some time yet. Just rest, Mr Bulman." The doctor had already gone by the time the ward sister gave this information.

"How did I get a private ward? These places cost more than the Ritz, pills more than caviar."

"I'll check the admission records but I'm sure it's been taken care of." In fact it was four hours after admission that Bulman was shifted from a public ward to a private.

As the day drifted on Bulman accepted that he had been badly beaten up and that they would hang on to him here longer than he wanted. He had not telephoned anyone because his detective's mind wanted to see who would find out where he was and what would happen next. He was surprised that the police, who still maintained a presence outside his door, had not questioned him. It would have been normal practice, and as soon as possible. The answer came about mid-afternoon when he was dozing again.

John Cordell must have been standing by his bed for some minutes before Bulman was fully awake. "I thought you'd like these." Cordell put down a beautifully prepared basket of fruit.

"Thanks," said Bulman. "I'd have preferred a bottle of Scotch."

Cordell grinned and pulled up a chair. "If you're allowed to have it and if you're still here tomorrow I'll bring a bottle of malt."

Bulman tried to struggle up and a nurse bustled in to help him with another pillow. "It might be worth staying in for that, Johnny," said Bulman. "How did you get to know I was here?"

"I'm a policeman," said Cordell drily. "Keeping a distant eye on things."

"You must have known very quickly, because the wooden tops outside have made no effort to question me."

"After I phoned you last night I had a sense of obligation. I passed it down the line that if anything happened to you I was to be informed. Although your wallet was taken you still had your driving licence and credit cards in a separate little pack so identification was easy. Hospital authorities are obliged to report any serious injuries through violence to the police. The system worked and I was advised. I wanted to question you myself."

"That doesn't help the pain go away, Johnny. And I don't suppose the questions will be any different. Supposing I tell you what happened and we'll leave it at that?"

Cordell removed the cellophane from the basket and selected an apple. "Go on."

"Hardly anything to tell. I was on my way to see my client and they were waiting for me in the porch. Bang, bang, wallop, I was on the deck imitating the Pope kissing the good earth."

"That's all you remember? Seems like a straightforward mugging."

"What, waiting for me like that? Everybody who knows me will know that I carry very little cash around. I live on plastic except in pubs."

"But they did take your wallet."

"As an afterthought. Apart from them running away, the last thing I heard was one of them calling out, 'Don't forget to take his wallet.' With a mugger it would have been the first thing they'd have thought of."

"So who do you think it was?"

"Whoever is on that tape I gave you. Not personally, but he was the one who organised it. He must know I saw you and he's getting a little out of hand. I'm beginning to be a nuisance. I just wish I knew how much of a nuisance, because I know I'm near but can't see how." Bulman looked around in despair. "Did you fix this ward?"

"No." Cordell appeared vaguely uneasy. "I let your client know what had happened and where you were. I thought he should know. It will be difficult for him to visit you but I would guess he arranged this room." Seeing Bulman struggling to come to terms with what he had just heard, Cordell added, "No, I did not tell him who was ringing. It was an anonymous call. I used a Scottish accent. You'd have been impressed."

"You? Going under the counter? Why? You've always been as straight as a die."

"There is little about this business that is straight. All I did was let him know. There was no need for me to announce myself and had I done so he would have thought it very odd indeed. I did it for you, I felt I owed you that much."

"That suggests a guilty conscience, Johnny. Have you been playing straight with me?"

"You don't ask questions like that of the Assistant Commissioner of Police, even if we did once serve together."

"So you haven't. That disappoints me because you were always one of the few who could be believed. Don't go bent on me, Johnny."

Cordell winced, but he said, "I'll not go bent on you or anyone but some things I must handle my own way. We are old friends and colleagues but you chose to be a civilian. I'm still a copper. Trust me."

"You knew that voice, didn't you? You bloody well know who had me clobbered. For chrissake, Johnny, the bastards could have killed me. And they still can. This bashing won't stop me."

"I know it won't, which is why I haven't bothered to ask you to lay off. I'll handle things my way. Anyone you want to be informed of where you are?"

Bulman was about to say, "Spider Scott", then realised it was better for Scott to be left out of it. While he was still mulling over the point, Cordell added, "No wife yet?"

"Who'd be crazy enough to have me? I'd be no good at it. Came close a couple of times, though." Bulman looked whimsical. "Almost came off." And then in a different voice altogether, "If this happens again, Johnny, they will kill me. What will happen to your keep-it-in-the-family

175

outlook then? And I don't want to be buried. The spare parts might come in handy for someone else, the rest can go on the compost heap. But whatever he's up to, whatever his purpose, this maniac has got to be stopped before he drags everybody down with him. You know who it is, go to it."

Cordell rose, carefully wrapping the apple core into a paper napkin. "There are more powerful people than top coppers, George. And they are unaccountable. They can lie their heads off and justify anything they do as long as there's some sort of result at the end of it and even that can be exaggerated. They can make themselves look good simply by saying nothing and acting superior. It only takes one to land us all in it. I'll do my best."

And just when Bulman thought Cordell was about to give a lecture about staying out of it and not to confuse things, he said, "We need you out of that bed, George. Get yourself well first, but keep up the good work. I can't give you official protection, you must know that, because I have no proof of conspiracy. Move away for a few days. Operate from somewhere else." He nodded and smiled. "Cheers, George. Don't choke on the fruit."

John Cordell returned to Scotland Yard and changed into uniform. He dealt with a few urgent matters, and then at five p.m. left for Century House for an appointment with Michael Sealy he had arranged before going to see Bulman. It was late for an appointment but he had insisted and had got his way.

They gave him his identity disc and he was escorted up by lift to find Connie Taylor waiting for him on the upper floor. She introduced herself and led him to Sealy's room where she knocked on the door.

Cordell had elected to wear uniform with its impressive braid to bring home the full importance of what he represented and that it was at the highest level. He was greeted warmly by Sealy, whom Cordell thought had developed a sort of wild look since they last met.

They shook hands and sat down, the door closed behind them.

Cordell noticed the family photograph on the desk, although he could see it only obliquely; he knew a little about the tragedy.

"Would you like tea or coffee?" asked Sealy, noticing the direction of Cordell's gaze and feeling unreasonable resentment.

"No, thanks. I've just come from seeing George Bulman in hospital. He was lucky to survive."

"Who's George Bulman and what has happened to him? You speak as if I should know him."

"I should think you know of him very well indeed. He's rather a thorn in your side just now."

"Is he now? But shouldn't I know about it?" Sealy pushed his chair back so that he could comfortably cross his legs.

Cordell knew that Sealy could be hard, one-tracked, dedicated, all in the course of duty, but now he was seeing something else, as if Sealy had put up a shield he knew to be impenetrable and was inviting Cordell to try to break it down. He had come up against many hardened criminals in his day, some prolific and expert liars, especially the con men, but he knew that in Sealy he was up against something rather special. With Sealy having already shown which way he intended to play, Cordell was immensely confident.

"Come on, John, what's this about this Bulman fellow?" Sealy got in before Cordell could reply. "It's not like you to mess around."

"Okay. Let's do it your way. George Bulman, an ex-copper, one of the best and whose reputation alone I am surprised has apparently passed you by, has been employed by Marvin Hayes to look into the question of the accusation of murder against his son. I take it you have heard of Marvin Hayes, United States Ambassador? Since it was your idea to protect him against his son's misdeeds?"

177

"Don't be funny, John. It's Bulman you were talking about."

"Are you saying that you've distanced yourself so much from the affairs of Marvin Hayes that you are unaware he employed Bulman? Do you think I would put Bulman at risk by mentioning this at all if I didn't know full well that you already know?" He unbuttoned his tunic pocket and removed the cassette, tossing it on to the desk. "There are two voices on there; one is Bulman's, the other is yours. And you still claim not to know him?"

Cordell had expected some reaction but was not prepared for what followed.

Chapter Fifteen

Sealy stared at the cassette without moving. A series of subtle changes swept over his face as if revealing in turn every facet of his character. It was like watching dissolving and overlapping scenes on film. Each part was struggling for dominance and then, the most subtle change of all, he was suddenly relaxed as if nothing had happened, and the internal struggles had been some kind of act. He smiled quite warmly. "I'm on that? Really?" He leaned forward and picked up the cassette.

"I had copies made," Cordell said drily.

"Of course you did. And quite proper too." Sealy opened the central door in his desk and took out a hand recorder. He flipped it open, removed the tape and inserted the one Cordell had produced. He placed the recorder between them on the desk and switched it on. There was no mistaking the gravel tones of Bulman asking to speak to Bob Clifford. The second voice was brusque and dismissive and, to Cordell, clearly Sealy's.

"That's supposed to be me?" asked Sealy in total surprise. "Do I really speak like that? And if it is me, am I supposed to know who called? What game are you playing, John?"

Cordell was unaware of the call back to Bulman in the name of Bob Clifford – Bulman had been attacked just after – but he knew that Sealy knew who had called on the present tape. "Okay," he said, "let's get a voice expert on the job. There is no doubt in my mind that that is your voice and the other one is Bulman's. It seems rather childish to

179

me to deny knowing of the man. I never suggested that you have met him."

Sealy appeared to be aggrieved. "What's the point of all this? We're wasting a good deal of time. What does it matter one way or the other?"

Cordell had reached the point of no return. He was fully aware of taking a terrible risk and that he could fall down on it. He had to stick to what he believed, but making that decision against Sealy's plausibility was increasingly difficult. None of this was a normal police matter and Sealy could be so devious that Cordell began to wonder about his own judgement. "I think you had Bulman duffed up, almost killed."

Sealy burst out laughing but Cordell did not miss the strange, bright flecks in his eyes he had not before noticed. "You're talking of the man as if you were once lovers. God forbid, John. What on earth has happened to you?"

Cordell remained calm. Sealy could keep this sort of dialogue up all day, he lived by it, but it was still not the kind of reaction he had expected. No anger, shock, just scathing recrimination. His control was excellent and now he was quietly mocking.

"John, really. It's difficult to believe I am addressing the Assistant Commissioner of Police. Of course, our game can be most devious at times but you are suggesting I almost murdered a man. Why would I want to do that anyway?" Cordell reached for the small tape recorder but Sealy grabbed it first and sprung the cassette loose. He tossed it contemptuously across the desk. "Play it again, Sam. I really should report this little episode. But that might ruin your pension prospects."

Cordell watched carefully, waiting for Sealy to become over confident but Sealy suddenly realised he was going over the top with the ridicule. "Look, John. I know we work in strange ways but I ask you to be patient for just a little longer when all will make sense. I do understand your concern but you don't have to jolt me with this sort of stuff to get me mobile. Things are very much on the move. I hope the meeting has been of some use to you."

"Oh, yes." Cordell smiled. "I've learned a good deal by just listening to you."

For the first time Sealy appeared worried, not sure how to take the remark. "You must remember I am a member of the Joint Intelligence Staff. Whether that particular appointment exceeds that of Assistant Commissioner of the Metropolitan Police I am not sure, but I imagine it would when the chips are down. This is a political exercise we are following and our informing you is a matter of courtesy and not obligation."

"Balls. There has been a murder and this, in the final event, is a police matter. My inclination is to have Don Hayes pulled in for murder and to take it from there. And there is nothing you can do to stop me."

Sealy's alarm was obvious. He sat staring at Cordell and had difficulty in getting out his words. "For God's sake don't do that or you'll ruin everything. We must have more time."

"Ruin what? I've never understood what. We've co-operated against our better judgement all along the line. All we've had in return, judging by this meeting, is contempt." Cordell rose quite slowly, and carefully put his cap on. "You should never have had George Bulman beaten up because he's prodding around your little schemes. You could have come to me and I would have spoken to him."

"Would it have made a difference to such a man?"

"Probably not. But I find that an interesting remark: I thought you didn't know him or of him."

Sealy rose. "It's getting out of hand, John. Okay, we've played it close to the chest but that's the way we have to do it. I think you know that only too well. Nothing has changed in that respect except that the thing is drawing to a head and then we'll all be happier."

Cordell did not see Sealy press a buzzer but the door behind him opened and a smiling Connie Taylor was waiting to escort him back to the lift. The two men did not shake hands. Sealy was smiling politely and Cordell made a dignified figure as he crossed the floor towards Connie.

Cordell deliberately slowed the pace to the lift. He had taken a calculated risk in coming here and was now about to take another for there was unlikely to be a second chance. As Connie was about to ring for the lift he placed his hand over the button.

"It's all right," he said. "I'm going down. But there is something I would like to ask you and I can't do it here. You know who I am?"

"Yes, of course. Assistant Commissioner of Police, Mr Cordell."

Cordell nodded. "How long have you been with Mr Sealy?"

"Five years or so."

"Then you must like him to have served him so well for so long." Cordell did not miss the eyes lighting up and he wondered if he should continue. "You would do anything to help him?"

"Of course. He's been very good to me."

"I would like to help him too. Is it possible for us to meet somewhere? To have dinner, perhaps? I think it would be useful all round. But you'd have to be willing to keep it to yourself. If you find that a difficult condition then say no now."

Connie was uncertain. At first suspicious, she quickly ruled that out. But why did he want to see her? There was only one way to find out and she did not have to say a thing if she did not want to.

As she was slow to reply Cordell added, "Please don't feel obligated. You don't have to do it but if you do I won't be in uniform. I wouldn't want people to think you were under arrest." Cordell was at his most charming and produced a laugh from Connie.

"All right, then. Where and when?"

Bulman was making himself a nuisance all round. The aches and pains were still bad but he found he was able to move and that was all he wanted. He could think too and he'd had plenty of time for that without getting too far.

Spider Scott arrived during the evening having heard on the grapevine that somebody had tried to break George Bulman's skull. He sat on the edge of the bed, a huge grin on his impossibly honest face and said, "I only came to see if someone had managed it at last. You're so thick headed that I couldn't believe anyone would be stupid enough to try to crack it."

"Very funny, Spider. Look, I've got to get out of here and I'd better not go home. Can you lend me a few quid and do you know anyone who can give me a billet for a while? I know you haven't got the space but I don't want to stay in a doss house; I must have freedom."

"I'll ask around. Give you a bell here." Scott produced his wallet and pulled out some notes. "That's a loan," he said. "I want it back. I don't want any crap about loss of memory."

"Thanks, Spider. I want out of here. I don't think I can manage another night."

"Don't push your luck, George. That sort of damage takes time. You need another few days at least. Maybe longer."

"Stop winding me up, Spider. Go find me somewhere."

At six thirty there was a telephone call for him and he recognised the North Atlantic tones at once. "What happened?" asked Marvin Hayes.

Bulman told him and that he would be leaving shortly and for Hayes not to worry. "You must have wondered why I didn't turn up at your place."

"I was angry at first then realised you weren't the type to stand someone up. Then I became worried, yet there was nothing I could do until I knew what had happened and where you were. I had a tip-off."

"Thanks for the private room. A luxury."

"It was the least I could do. Look, I can't come to the hospital in case I'm recognised but we should try to sort something out. You wouldn't have wanted to see me unless it was important. Presumably you have made some progress."

"Some. But I'm not going to discuss it over the phone. I could have done that from my own place and avoided being duffed up. I'm trying to sort out a temporary home. I can't go back to my own, they were right on my doorstep. I've got someone working on it."

"Then tell him to stop. I've got a place for you. A friend of mine who's in Washington at the moment. I have access. Have you got a pen handy?"

When John Cordell had left, Sealy sat back in his chair and broke into a cold sweat. He knew he had handled it well enough, confused the issue, admitted nothing, kept within the nature of his job, which allowed for quirks of motive and misleading explanations. He knew that and so did Cordell. But he had far from convinced Cordell and that annoyed rather than worried him. He had expected questions about Walter McQueen and was relieved that they had not been asked but was not fooled by their absence.

Cordell had been fishing expertly, letting Sealy do all the work and patiently listening as all good policemen can. But Cordell must have given the continued absence of the student some thought. As he sat back he began to think that perhaps the wrong people were suffering. Bulman was a pain in the neck and had to be got out of the way one way or the other, because although he had no facilities other than his own expertise and sharp instincts, he was more of a risk than Cordell and his whole police force because he was not bogged down.

Cordell was hampered by red tape, protocol, effete politicians and the need for the secrecy surrounding the SIS in all their wisdom. Cordell was far from being the first senior policeman to be frustrated and angered by the intelligence services. But he knew how to play it and that was a danger.

Sealy considered he was being successful in what he was

doing but it was taking longer than he had wished. In any event there was no way back now. He had gone too far, particularly with Bulman. He had to go on and the fever started to inflame him again, stronger and stronger each time until it sometimes scared him.

Don Hayes was having consistently bad nights. The results of the finals were not yet through and increasingly they became less important. The threat of a murder charge hanging over his head became a strengthening nightmare. As things were, he tried to keep in daily touch with his father but the diplomatic rounds kept him busy and he was reluctant to ring the Embassy. So he had to wait for his father to call him and there was no set time he could expect a call. When the calls did come it was clear that no progress was being made to prove his innocence and he found that ominous.

The situation could not stay like this for ever. Either he would be arrested or sent back home. To him, one was almost as bad as the other, for being sent back meant disgrace and a problem for his father. Knowing him as he did, he thought that if either one of those possibilities happened, his father would resign at once and the effect on his mother would be devastating. She would be unable to face her friends. The family would be ruined.

It was because so much was at stake that Don himself was beginning to crack up. Everything was hanging on his shoulders and the weight of responsibility was increasingly unbearable. What made it worse was that he was sure that he had shot nobody. He could not conceive that he could do such a thing, drunk or sober. The worrying aspect was that he, and it seemed most of the others, had been totally freaked out and nobody seemed to know what anyone had done.

And then there were the fingerprints. He could not understand why no one had raised the point that if he was so bombed out of his mind, how had he made such an accurate shot? If it had been just an unlucky shot then it wasn't murder anyway. Yet the fingerprints seemed to be damning.

Whatever the outcome, and something had to give some time, he was meanwhile under unbearable pressure and was beginning to crave for something to steady him. And this made him more afraid than anything. To lapse into the old habit, no matter how briefly it had lasted, would finish his highly sensitive, but very loving, mother. He just tried to hang on, knowing it to be more difficult by the day.

Bulman found his clothes, dressed, and discharged himself from the hospital. He did not do this officially. He used the phone in his room to order a taxi, waited for the night staff to take over and for the hospital to quieten down, then left. He raised a few eyebrows, for late evening was hardly the time for patients to be discharged, but he brazened it out, limped through Reception and waited on the gravel drive in the cool air outside, hoping the taxi would not be late.

It arrived, and Bulman climbed in and instructed the driver just as white-coated figures appeared behind the glass panels of the hospital entrance. He sat back in relief and pain.

The apartment was in Mayfair. The cabbie pulled up, eyed Bulman with suspicion, took the fare and expected the change to be a tip but Bulman was waiting with his hand out. Bulman walked unsteadily across the pavement to the huge glass doors covered by a network of wrought iron. He pulled out a piece of paper, studied the code, then punched it out on the bank of buttons by the door. He went into the vast, marble-floored vestibule with a sparkling central chandelier. He was having difficulty in moving at all and for the first time wondered at his wisdom in leaving the hospital prematurely.

Bulman slowly crossed the floor to the curved reception desk and the uniformed custodian watched him approach with increasing suspicion. Bulman seldom managed to look smart even in a new suit but his clothes still had signs of the attack and were crumpled and soiled.

"I'm George Bulman." It even hurt to smile but he got an instant response as suspicion turned to a beaming welcome from the man behind the counter.

"Didn't expect you for a day or two, sir." He groped under the counter. "Here are the keys. Would you like me to take you up? You seem to be having difficulties."

"I was mugged," said Bulman cheerfully. "I can manage, thank you. Which floor?"

"Top. Penthouse suite."

Bulman shuffled to the lift with its hidden lighting and luxury carpeting. He reached the penthouse level. There was only one door, which gave no indication of what to expect behind it. He went in and almost collapsed behind it. He stood there supported by the door until he felt he could go on. Corniced lights sprung on as he progressed and he realised he was actioning them by his own body heat.

He reached the spacious drawing-room, the far end of which began to haze over. He almost fell but grabbed the back of a chair and managed to hold on. He was surrounded by comfort and luxury but right now he was having difficulty in standing. His head throbbed and suddenly he did not feel so clever in discharging himself so soon. He looked into the nearest gilded mirror and saw a middle-aged tramp with a drawn face and a white turban on his head. The unlikely image in surroundings like these brought a smile to his lips. He sat in the nearest chair and passed out. The phone pealed out, a genteel buzzing and a flashing red light, but did not penetrate Bulman's unconsciousness. He lay in a most awkward position but he was free and his sleep was healthily deep, for the moment shutting out the pain.

The following day Connie Taylor went to the office as usual. Inevitably she had to spend time with Sealy and noticed his preoccupation had deepened only from yesterday. The visit of the Assistant Commissioner seemed to have had an adverse effect on him and she was so concerned for Sealy that she considered cancelling her meeting with Cordell. She had the sense to keep the arrangement to herself, for only that way could she discover how yesterday's meeting between the two men could have had such effect.

There were times when she thought that Sealy did not realise she was in the room, giving the impression of talking to a machine, surprised when it answered back. This hurt her deeply. But it worried her too. Sealy left mid-morning without explaining why or telling her when he would be back. She had no idea he was off to see McQueen, who was being held illegally and about whom there would be a public outcry if the truth were known.

When she stole glances across the desk, almost afraid to look at him in case he caught the deep concern in her expression, she noticed the tremor in his hands; hands that until quite recently were as steady as a rock. And when she did brave it out to look him in the face she was alarmed by some of his expressions and the occasional cold hardness as he reflected on God knew what.

It was becoming difficult for Connie to act naturally herself but she was saved from his curiosity by his almost total absorption with his own demons. She developed a knack of just saying enough to get a job done and ceased to be conversational; it was easier to cope that way.

Bulman had just climbed out of the sumptuous bath when the doorbell rang. He quickly dried off, slipped on a dressing-gown and went to the door to peep through the spy hole. He opened the door at once. "Sorry to keep you," he said to Marvin Hayes.

Hayes entered the penthouse and said, "I guessed you'd be here. Thought you might still be asleep. But look at the state of you. You should have stayed in hospital. I'm sorry, George. I'm sorry this should happen to you." He slumped into a chair.

"You don't look so good yourself." Bulman pulled the gown around him and sat opposite. "This is bloody marvellous comfort. Much better than hospital and no bloody pills to take."

"What about painkillers?"

"I'm trying to give them up. I ache a bit. I have two heads and they both hurt, but have you seen the array of Scotch in here? Rare malts I've never heard of. Beats the pills hands down."

"I can't stay long, George. I had to reschedule a meeting in order to come here. I'm cancelling our arrangement."

At first Bulman did not understand. He could see that Hayes was tired – more than tired, worn out – and his hands were restless, but he was late to grasp the meaning. "You can't do that."

"I'll see that you are fully compensated. You'll be taken care of, don't worry about that. But I can't ask anyone to endure the beating you've just had."

Bulman could hardly believe it. "I don't want compensation. This isn't about money. I like to scrounge a drink or two, it's my way, and friends would worry about me if I didn't. It provides a talking point, someone to call a mean bastard. But they know if the chips are down there is nothing I wouldn't do to help. It's all a joke. But don't insult me by talking about taking care of me. You think money is the only reason I took it on? I'd have taken it on on an expenses only basis once I got the hang of it. Mr Ambassador, you can't do this to me. I've never been taken off a case in my life."

Hayes had started to smile as he listened to Bulman's indignation. "It's your life I'm worried about. And don't you think it's time to call me Marv?"

"No. It would spoil the employer – client relationship. How can I haggle about terms if I call you Marv? You'd expect me to act as a friend and provide cut prices. You can't sack me now." Bulman knew he was contradicting what he had just said about money but was trying to ridicule the seriousness of the situation. He put a hand to his bandaged head and winced. "We've got the bastard on the run."

"Bastard? Just one?"

"I think so. The rest have been misled. Cleverly, but it can't last for ever."

"I still can't allow you to be exposed to danger any more. It's got too dangerous."

Bulman wondered what Hayes would say if he knew exactly what had happened to Chernov and Galina and the hookers. He still felt low about Julie Clarke. "I'm the one to judge the danger. I got careless. If you sack me, or fire me, whichever you prefer, I'll take it to tribunal for unfair dismissal. That'll drag your name through the news-sheets."

"That's blatant blackmail, George."

"Yep. Something else I'm good at. Let's cut the blarney and get down to it. Once I met young Don, I never really believed he had murdered anyone. There are several reasons which we don't need to go into. The prints on the gun are real and that's still their hold but that is all it is. Have you got any enemies in the SIS?"

Hayes glanced at his watch, clearly worried about the time, but he was intrigued. "How could I know that without having a list of them? I know a few, men and women, who I would guess work for the SIS, one or two I'm absolutely sure do, but know none who I would consider an enemy. Are you saying that this business is aimed at me? Someone wants to harm me?"

"Perhaps the whole family."

"Are you sure?"

"No. But of all the alternatives this is coming out strongest."

"You know who?"

"I haven't a clue. But it's someone powerful enough to influence politicians and the police. For a short time anyway, and perhaps he believes he only needs a short time."

"Then it's time to take it straight to the Prime Minister."

"And tell him what? On the face of it someone is trying to help you by protecting your son. We're up against a clever sod. I want to know why – and when we know that, we know who."

"Is there anything I can tell Don? He's suffering hell and I worry about him."

"Nothing absolutely positive. You can tell him I believe he didn't do it. We're up against those damned prints all the time, but you can try to reassure him. The trouble is that whoever's doing this has left himself with the final option of getting the police to pull Don in. The threat is there all the time. He's a cunning, evil bastard."

"And you've still no idea who the son-of-a-bitch might be?"

"I'm working on it. I have a little help in odd quarters. But he's certainly not going to declare himself."

"A cornered rat is highly dangerous, George. I still think we should call it off."

"Even if we do he won't believe it, not now. What I'm afraid of is that he'll do something really stupid by speeding up the process. Have any of the Company boys over here any knowledge of our safe houses? I bet they know one or two."

"It's a difficult thing for me to ask them. I'm the senior representative of the United States of America in this country. I'm supposed to be above all that stuff, and mostly I am. It could raise more questions than I would want to answer. And although I went to the FBI in the first place, the way this thing is going, the fewer Americans involved the better. The whole business is getting very tacky. What's in your mind?"

"We've two options. We can try to flush out the guy behind all this or we can try to find McQueen and kick his treacherous brains out. I think the guy in the first option knows bloody fine where McQueen is."

"So you think McQueen is still alive?"

"At the moment. But when he's served his purpose I wouldn't fancy his chances. I need your continued backing. Don't desert me now or we all lose and then we've lost the war, jobs and perhaps even sanity. I think this bloke

191

intends to go all the way. There is no sign of a backdown. If you want your family to survive you'd better keep me on the payroll. If I fail then at least we tried. For Zoë's sake, eh?"

Hayes winced. "There are times when I think you're as big a bastard as the guy you're looking for."

"I hope so. It takes one to know one."

Later that day Connie left her office at the usual time, went home and took time over preparing herself for her meeting with Cordell. She was far from easy about it but was willing to do anything that might help Mike Sealy, who was fast disappearing as the man she had known over the last few years. At seven thirty she took a cab to the Chelsea address Cordell had given her, rang the bell and announced herself on the speaker and entered when the buzzer released the door. She went two flights up in the lift and Cordell was waiting for her as the doors opened.

"The least I could do," he smiled. "You did it for me." He led the way to his front door.

Connie was suddenly reluctant. "Are we eating here? I thought you were taking me on somewhere."

"And take the risk of being recognised? You'll be perfectly safe here. My wife has arranged a meal for us and no she won't be here. She's gone out with a friend."

"She must be very understanding," said Connie as she entered the pleasant apartment.

"A gem," Cordell agreed. "May I take your coat, and what would you like to drink?"

When they were seated Cordell was aware that Connie was still uneasy. "Look," he said brightly, "shall we get the official stuff out of the way first and then relax over a meal?"

"I'd rather get it over with."

"Right." Cordell slipped off his jacket and adjusted his tie. "It's warm in here." He gazed at the young woman a few feet from him and considered she was far too attractive to be unattached. He had done his checking and knew about her ex-husband and had seen her reaction to Sealy. If she was not in love with him she certainly had an attachment to him and he would have to be careful. "I'm concerned about Mike Sealy's health and I wondered if you could throw some light on it. Now, before you ask what the hell business is it of mine rather than Sir Maxwell Swain at Century House, we are engaged in a project together, which was why I was there yesterday. I am not normally involved with the SIS at all. It's just one of those things I've been dragged into and which you would not expect me to discuss. Help me. I don't think he's well."

Connie was quite composed and more at ease now but still not sure she should talk about her boss. She wanted to say something but the words stuck.

"Some say," said Cordell with a smile, "I'm arguably the second most important copper in the country. Most Chief Constables would dispute that vigorously and I would agree with them, but I'm sufficiently high enough up the tree for you to stop worrying about my credentials. I understand your reluctance and admire your loyalty but you have to decide where that loyalty lies: to the man or the more important broader picture? Your oath was to protect the country not the man. Connie, if you feel there is something wrong you must say so, if not to me then to someone else you can trust."

"I do understand. I've understood for the last few days but I'm still not happy about it. It's like a betrayal. Whether or not it needs to be done it will still feel like that."

"Then why are you here?"

"I hoped I might learn something from you, something that would help me understand why he is deteriorating." She gazed firmly at Cordell. "That wasn't a slip. I know what I'm saying."

"So you've noticed a change in him?"

"Oh, yes. The last few days have been worrying."

Cordell noticed Connie's distress. "Have you kept this to yourself? Bottled it up?"

"Yes." There was a slight hesitation as she considered Anna Brus, but that had been in general terms.

Cordell did not miss the blip. "Have you tried to find out what is wrong? Overwork? Anything like that?"

"I think it's personal."

Cordell said cautiously, "What makes you think that?"

Connie dropped her gaze. Did she or didn't she? Her feeling was that she would have to tell someone some time, if only it were Sealy himself. But she could not do that without explaining how she knew and she could never do that to him.

The watching Cordell made no attempt to rush her. He could see something of the internal struggle. Connie Taylor was an intelligent girl with old-fashioned loyalties who had held down a highly responsible job for some years. She was poised to break all the rules to help a man who these days barely knew she was there.

Connie glanced at her drink; she had not touched it. She now drained half the contents of the glass in one gulp. "There's a letter he keeps reading. He keeps it in the back of a family photograph which is on his desk and which he takes home every night and brings back the next day."

"I know the photograph. Has he always done this?"

"If he has I haven't noticed but he certainly has the last few days. He takes it out and reads it at odd times and each time he does he goes to pieces and it takes him time to recover."

Cordell casually reached for his glass. Without looking at her and in a soft tone he asked, "Have you had opportunity to read it?"

Connie was well aware it was all leading to this. "Yes. He carelessly left it on his desk while going to lunch." She believed she was entitled to one lie to protect herself. "And before you ask me what is in it I'll tell you. And I've told nobody else at any time. I'm doing it now because I'm out of my mind with worry."

He listened to her faltering account of the letter and was almost as shocked as Connie had been when she first read

194

it. Without twitching a nerve or muscle he asked quietly, "Do you think you can get it for me? Or a copy?"

Her composure froze as if she was suddenly posing for a picture. Then it began to crumble as her hands shook. Her face had paled and he could see that her lips were trying to move. Connie was deeply afraid.

Chapter Sixteen

Cordell at once thought he had asked too much of her. He had not quite believed her story of how she had found the letter on Sealy's desk. He did not think it had been that easy or that Sealy had been so careless. The experience had probably scared the wits out of her and here he was asking her to do it again; worse, to make a copy. If he said the wrong thing now it would be over. He must leave it to her.

Connie shuddered, recalling her fear of the last time. She shook her head slowly. "That's asking an awful lot of me. It's very risky."

"Of course it is. I'm sorry. I've obviously misjudged your degree of concern for Mike Sealy. It was very silly of me."

"I am concerned for him. Deeply. It's just that I don't think I could go through that again. It's scary."

"Don't give it another thought." He refilled her glass. "Don't think I'm trying to get you sloshed so that you'll change your mind; that would be a stupid thing to do. It needs dedication and nerve to do something like that and it can't be done with the aid of a bottle."

Cordell smiled. "We'll have dinner in a minute. Maybe I can think of another way to get sight of that letter. It seems to me to be the key to his deterioration. If he goes on like that he'll be asked to resign because he'll become a danger to himself and the SIS. That should not be allowed to happen to a man with his track record."

Connie sipped her drink thoughtfully. "Of course, if I knew for certain that he would be away for a set

time it would be easier, but his movements are errat-
ic."

Cordell smiled. "You're not still thinking about it?
Forget it. He'll have to take his chances."

"Could you make an appointment with him? Take him
to lunch or something?"

Cordell chuckled. "At the moment I don't think we are
on lunching terms. We covered what we had to say to each
other yesterday. Don't torture yourself, Connie. You've
helped a lot by coming here." And then as if her idea had
spurred him, he said, "You've given me a thought, though.
I might be able to convince a Home Office Minister to take
him to lunch or give him strawberries and cream at the
House of Commons or something. Would you like me to
look into it for you?"

So far George Bulman had told nobody where he was, not
even Spider Scott, and this had its disadvantages. The
day after dining Connie Taylor, John Cordell had been
phoning him in an attempt to find out where he was.

Eventually Bulman realised that he could not carry on
without some help so he telephoned Scott at his office.

"I've been trying to get hold of you," Scott complained.
"What the hell did you do a runner for with a hole in your
head?"

"To prevent me getting another. I'll give you this
number and address but don't tell a soul. I'm okay,
right? Ribs kicked in and a coconut on my bonce but
parts of me are working. I want you to go to my pad
and pick up a small cassette. It might have been slipped
through the letter box. And then remove the tape from the
answering machine and bring them both here. It's not safe
for me to go back there, Spider."

"What about me going back there? I don't want my head
bashed in."

"It's not you they're after. Anyway, you're better
equipped to look after yourself and you'll be doing it in
broad daylight."

"Will I? I have a business to run, George. I can't keep dropping everything."

"If you're worried take Knocker Roberts with you if he's still around. His mashed-up face would scare the daylights out of anyone. I'll meet all costs." He hung up before Scott could put up further objections.

Bulman was lonely and felt out of touch in his luxury penthouse. At first he enjoyed the comforts but decided it was not for him. Even the malt whisky was wearing thin; it was a great drink but he was more used to Bell's and was sorry he hadn't asked Scott to bring some. He played music, watched television, operated the remote control curtains and lights but he wanted to get out and knew he was not yet fit enough to go. He could tolerate the pain, but the frustration of inactivity was building up. He was at last willing to admit that he should have stayed in hospital longer.

Scott called at lunchtime. He stood in the middle of the drawing-room and pivoted slowly, blowing out his cheeks and whistling. "How the hell did you get this? I used to screw drums like this. There's some *objets d'art* here that tempt me."

"Did you get the tapes?"

"No. There was no tape on the doormat and the one in the answering machine has been removed. You've been done over, George. Fairly neat job but not to the trained eye. There were a couple of bills." Scott handed them over.

Bulman sat quietly, looking rather ridiculous in his rewound head bandage. He was fully dressed but his suit was still crumpled and there were blood stains on it which Scott quickly noticed.

"You look as if your house burned down after your insurance lapsed," said Scott. "Cheer up, mate, it can't be that bad."

"It can. I've just lost two pieces of evidence, dodgy but the only ones I had."

"They obviously weren't dodgy to the bloke who nicked them or he wouldn't have bothered."

"Well at least it shows I was right not to go back." Bulman rang Scotland Yard, gave his name and asked for Cordell.

Scott, wide eyed, backed away from just the mention of so high a rank.

Cordell answered and echoed Scott's earlier words. "You've just caught me. I'm already late for a late lunch appointment. Tell me where you are, George. I need to know."

Bulman made a quick decision and gave him the address, but Scott was surprised to see he was not happy about it. And then hurriedly, "Did you have that cassette sent round?"

"Yes. A messenger delivered it. I didn't know at the time that you were about to be mugged."

"Someone's done the place. The cassette has gone and so has the tape in the machine containing the message the guy couldn't resist leaving when he called back under the name I gave."

"You haven't been back to your place?"

"No. A friend looked into it for me."

"I've got a copy of the first one. But the second one would have been useful."

"Why? If you didn't recognise the voice on the first?"

"Look, I'm running very late. Stay indoors and don't go entering any marathons until you're fit. I'll be in touch."

"What was that all about?" asked Scott who did not like the proximity of serving policemen of such high rank, if only down a telephone wire.

Bulman was clearly worried. "I wish I knew. I'm not sure what's going on."

"I've got to go," said Scott. He gazed at Bulman, a pathetic, forlorn figure at the moment, and said, "Jot down a list of what clothes you need and I'll bring them over some time tonight."

Connie Taylor was not at all happy about agreeing to

copying Sealy's letter. Now back in her own office nothing appeared simple. She was petrified of the prospect, the deep feeling of disloyalty constantly cluttering her thoughts. She did not believe she was being disloyal, quite the contrary, but her conscience kept getting in the way of logic. She convinced herself that she would do it in the best interests of a man for whom she had increasingly deep feelings and concern. Had she known that when Sealy went out at lunchtime she would never have a better opportunity, she could have put herself out of her misery and done the job. She continued to wait to hear from Cordell.

Meanwhile Sealy had gone to see Walter McQueen in his rather special cell. Tommy Wise was on duty and was as bored as McQueen but not nearly so worried. This time he made sure his automatic pistol was clean and in its waist holster where it should be.

They went through the same security procedure before Sealy entered the cell. McQueen stood at the far end of the cell as he had before but a good deal of his earlier defiance was missing. He was becoming an increasingly worried man.

Wise stood gun in hand with his back to the door and Sealy sat on the end of the bed and told McQueen to stay exactly where he was. Sealy allowed an uncomfortable silence to build up until McQueen showed signs of twitchiness, his gaze darting between the two men and often to the gun.

"Fancy your chances, Wally?" challenged Sealy. "It would save us all a lot of trouble if you did. But we couldn't guarantee to return your body to Scotland. Not that you would mind."

"I was born in England. I'm not a Scot any more than all the Murphys are Irish. What's your game?"

"It's confession time. We'd like a written statement from you."

"Confess to what? Getting pissed? Being kidnapped by a bunch of uppity bastards? Get stuffed."

"To the murder of Paula Smith."

"Murder? You're out of your mind. And who the hell is Paula Smith anyway?"

"One of the undergrads in your party the night of the finals in Oxford. As if you didn't know."

"I remember the party. Just about. But I didn't know all those who took part. What are you trying to pull?"

"So you have no idea who Paula Smith was?"

"I think there were a couple of birds with us. Maybe more. But what happened as we went along, God knows. We were gone, stoned out of our minds. And I bet so were a lot of others. I vaguely remember one of the girls hitting the deck but had no idea who she was or what had happened to her. I passed out and the next I knew I was here."

Sealy shook his head slowly. "You're leaving big chunks out, Wally. Like you were stone cold sober and knew perfectly well what was happening all along the line. And in view of the atrocious weather you fired a damned fine shot, although Special Branch won't see it that way. Then you took advantage of a couple of incidents which fell right into your lap. Quick thinking for a man who was supposed to be bombed out of his mind."

"You're trying to fit me up. You won't get away with it."

"So you don't remember the struggle just outside your lodgings? That was quite a good touch of yours to lay low for most of the night, which would give an impression that you were crashed out. Had you dashed back home straight away you'd have given the game away. But that move also gave us time to muster and we went straight for you. You put up a hell of a fight, so they tell me: broke a nose and raised quite a few bruises and they had to put you out before they could get you into the car."

"I seem to remember a fight. It was bucketing down and I vaguely thought some of the others had pitched up. And then I was clobbered. It's all a hazy recollection. I was tanked up, I tell you."

"You didn't even smell of booze, Wally; not even from the others."

"You'll be crucified in court and you bloody well know it."

In a quiet tone which startled McQueen and alarmed the silent Wise, Sealy said, "You will never reach court, Wally. Don't think that will save you. Nothing will."

For once McQueen was incapable of reply. Wise appeared to be worried and glanced uneasily at Sealy who added with a slight smile, "Where did you get the gun?"

"Don't try that. I've never had a gun. I've only your word for it that someone is dead." McQueen felt he was recovering.

"You realise your prints are on the gun?" Sealy was mocking.

McQueen was about to burst out a denial when his jaw clamped shut.

Sealy openly derided him now. "You were just about to say that is impossible, but that would have given the game away, wouldn't it? You shouldn't have killed her, Wally. In the event she had uncovered very little about the drug ring with its tenuous terrorist connections. There weren't as many of you as was first thought. She was young of necessity, to pass as an undergrad, and it followed that she was relatively inexperienced. Her job should have been safe from maniacs like you. I suppose you panicked when you discovered who she was and you convinced yourself you are a great opportunist. You're a loser, Wally. You're not a fraction as good as you think you are. You're a smalltime, gun-toting pratt and will pay the price."

McQueen gave no warning, no sign of any kind. He hurled himself down the cell straight at Wise in order to get hold of the gun. Wise, who had been fascinated by what Sealy had been saying and not a little worried by it, had lost concentration and McQueen got a grip on the gun before he could do anything.

Sealy rose to his feet as he watched the two men struggle and tried to ease away from them in the restricted confines of the cell. When it was clear that McQueen's brute force was more than Wise could cope with, Sealy side-handed McQueen at the base of his skull and again as he fell.

"Let's get outside while he's still groggy," Sealy snapped at Wise who was still recovering from his tussle. Wise glanced down at the crumpled form of McQueen and hastily opened the door. He was badly shaken but relieved that he was still holding the gun.

Wise locked the door and quickly checked the monitors. McQueen was still down. Sealy went into the duty room to continue to watch the monitors; he wanted to be sure McQueen recovered. Wise went into the wash room to bathe some blood from his face where McQueen had headbutted him, and to generally tidy himself up. He felt wretched and dreaded joining Sealy.

"You were slack," accused Sealy when Wise eventually joined him. "You were watching me instead of McQueen. Just who the hell vetted you for this job?"

"You were saying some pretty drastic things, sir. I was beginning to believe we would have a corpse on our hands."

"Don't believe all you hear, Wise. The man is on the verge of breaking and the only finger we've laid on him was in self defence."

"Apart from when he was originally picked up, sir." Wise was pushing his luck but he knew he had a point.

Sealy unexpectedly smiled. "There's hope for you yet. I'm staying just long enough to make sure McQueen is still with us, then I'll push off. He's stirring now."

They watched McQueen move and then slowly rise. He staggered against the bed and held on, then without warning he bawled at the mikes, "You bastard! I demand a lawyer and a phone call."

"He's always on about that," Wise commented, relieved that McQueen was all right. "How much longer can we hold him?"

"Just as long as we need. Don't feel sympathy for McQueen. That would be totally misplaced. He has a gifted intellect and he's chosen to squander it on the dark side of his mind. He'll always be trouble because he's anti everything and tackles it in the crudest possible way. He thrives on violence of one kind or another and like all bullies squeals when confronted with his own kind of treatment. He's bad and will always be bad. He'll be no loss to anyone."

Sealy put on a light coat and prepared to leave. "I know this is not the best kind of work for you. But it is experience and one day you'll find it useful. I'll be in touch."

Bulman dozed most of the afternoon and when he awoke he had a headache, a nasty taste in his mouth and knew that his head needed dressing; he could feel the pull against the stitches. He made himself some tea, watched children's hour on television, thinking some of it was better than the adult programmes, and decided he would start walking the following day.

He had buried himself in studying some of the fine *objets d'art* which had so interested Scott, when the doorbell rang. Scott had brought him a suitcase of clothes.

"Thanks, Spider. Were you followed?"

"Yep. Very good too. I was hampered by the case so it took me a little longer than usual to leave them chasing their tails."

"So they've got a stake-out on my old place?"

"Looks like it. They wouldn't dream of looking in Mayfair. You have friends in high places."

"Yes, well, it's the ones in low places who are the real help. Have some tea."

"By the way, I found this in the hall." Scott handed over an old buff envelope, unsealed and empty.

"Must have fallen out from somewhere."

"No. It was at the foot of the letter box."

"But there's nothing in it." Bulman looked inside again, then turned it over. Someone had pencilled something on the address side. Then, when he could read the faint print, he saw that it was a name. He looked at it closely. Scott had already seen it so he read out, "Michael Sealy." And then to Scott directly, "Does that mean anything to you?"

"No." Scott had flung himself down in a deep chair, his legs overhanging one of the arms. "Michael Sealy. I thought about it as soon as I saw it. Nobody I know. You want me to ask around?"

"*No.*"

That was sharp for Bulman and Scott was surprised. "Okay. Don't get shirty."

"Let me put it this way. I'm sorry you've seen it. Keep it to yourself."

Scott was silent for a while then said, "You think someone is trying to be helpful?"

"Possibly. It's a strange thing to happen."

"Maybe it's been lying around all the time and a draught from the door has blown it out from somewhere. I mean, if it's to help why not do it openly?" And then, "I've lost touch. That was a dumb question. Where are the telephone directories?"

They looked through and found nothing. They had a name but no address or telephone number and then suddenly Bulman was saying he did not feel so well and had better lay down and would Scott excuse him.

Scott gave a slow understanding grin. "If you want to get rid of me just come out with it. You've had an idea, haven't you? Okay, I can take a hint. I'll see if there's a stake-out on the way out." Just before he closed the door he called out, "Be careful, George. You remember what happened the last time you were working alone; they'd make sure the next time."

"Don't worry. And thanks for the clothes. That was really good of you." When Scott had gone Bulman studied the envelope; it was the buff, cheaper kind used for bills. There was a name and no phone number because he already had the number and now he knew who had delivered the note and why so secretly. He picked up the phone and punched out a number and spoke into the answering machine and said, "I really must speak to

Wally McQueen. If he's still alive." He put down the phone and thought that there must be better ways of committing suicide if his enemy knew where he was. He had to hope that he did not. But the call might draw him out from the woodwork, for he would now know that Bulman knew who he was. And that would have to be actioned as a matter of urgency.

Later he thought he might have been too clever. It was too late now; he had announced that he was still in business in spite of the beating, but was in no condition to suffer anything like the same, and he was on his own now. He was playing a dangerous game.

Chapter Seventeen

Sealy went back to his office feeling shaken. He had eaten no lunch, having been too preoccupied with McQueen. He was used to dealing with difficult people but McQueen was exceptionally important and a strong reaction had set in. He buzzed Connie and told her he wanted no calls or interruptions until he said otherwise. He sat behind his desk and trembled, sweat bursting from his pores.

He opened his central desk drawer and took out a bottle of co-codamol. He chewed two of them up and swallowed. He sat back with closed eyes and hoped the attack would pass. It did not. He felt vibration all round him and the sound of aircraft engines hammering away, one of them missing now and again and ejecting black smoke. The jungle passed below, just under the wing tips like a replay from a badly held camera as the image became more fuzzed and confused. The landing was rough but miraculously did no real damage and then there was blank and a false tranquillity and his headache began to diminish.

The fire brought back the pain, a huge roaring of flames from the mouth of the crude bakery and then the screams, screams such as he had never heard before nor wanted to again, but was trapped by their recurrence, and increasingly the vision of twisting, flailing human remains as the screams gradually died with the charred, black remnants like chunks of burned wood.

Everything went black. Recollection was dead as the blanket of terror provided its own cloak of safety against fear and pain. Sealy passed out and when he came to he was on the floor, having slipped down from his chair into the kneehole of his desk.

When Connie tapped softly on the door to give him an urgent message which she was reluctant to buzz through in view of his orders to her, and received no reaction, she opened the door just a little to peep through. There was no sign of Sealy and she imagined that he must have left the office. She crossed to his desk, scribbled the message on his pad, and left.

Sealy was just coming round when Connie entered the office. Instinct warned him to stay where he was. He vaguely saw her legs cross towards him but was unable to move. Then he could see not much more than her ankles as she bent over the desk. And finally her legs were retreating again. The door closed and he was still unable to move. But before he did he realised that she had not seen him. His head was resting on the edge of his seat and the rest of him tucked into the cavity of the kneehole.

As he gradually stilled the shakes he realised it was a wonder that Connie hadn't seen something of his legs. Quite obviously she had not. He should have locked the door.

It took Sealy some time to come round and even when he managed to pull himself on to his chair he still felt drained. He rubbed his face; it felt bloodless and dry. He placed his elbows on the desk and buried his face in his hands. He could not go on like this, it was taking far too much out of him. When he got home that night he must bring things to a head.

He tried desperately hard to get back to something like normal and remembered Connie's entry. He found her note and cursed. He saw no point in having lunch the next day with Stuart Wilson. He knew Wilson would whine, he always did. But he needed his support and so must make the effort.

When Sealy reached home that night he dug out his typewriter as a matter of urgency and typed the brief note, addressed an envelope and stuck the note inside.

He felt better then. He felt the time was right for drawing the strings of the net together.

His mood was buoyant, the attack during the afternoon now pushed aside. He searched for a ready-cooked meal to microwave, saw the green light flashing on the answering machine and pressed the replay switch. Bulman's voice came like a physical blow. He recoiled because he had not expected it. For a moment he thought he was going to have another attack, quickly recovered but still felt shaken.

He calmed down, heated his meal and ate in reflective silence. He poured himself wine as a matter of ritual, not sure whether or not he liked it, but needing a drink of some kind. After eating what became a tasteless meal he sat down and glanced towards the framed family group he had brought home with him as usual, noticing he had put it on top of the small piano instead of its usual place, the mantel piece. He resisted the strong urge to take it down. If he read the letter much more it would fall apart. He ought to make a copy. Perhaps he would the next day.

Evenings were the worst time for him. He usually worked but tonight he lacked the mental energy; the earlier attack had taken its toll. To occupy his mind, to fight off the demons was becoming increasingly difficult. He was all too aware of his encroaching madness, and in moments of clarity was almost able to fight it off, to rethink the whole problem. But fate had served the cards into his hands and there was no denying the pattern they took. It had all been offered to him and he had always been quick to act and, so far as he knew, had never been guilty of missing an opportunity.

Yet that was not quite true. He had lost an opportunity with George Bulman, a name he was beginning to hate. And it was now a matter of some priority to find out where Bulman was hiding.

Bulman had tried to get the address through the telephone company, having given them the name and telephone number. He had tried before without success but he believed different operators did different things. It did not work. There was a block on the number or name or both. Once he got the address he hoped he could persuade Scott to break in with him.

He believed he now had the name of the man causing the havoc, but what he sorely needed was a motive and it had to be a strong one. He had long since kicked out the idea of the threat overhanging Marvin Hayes and his family as providing some sort of diplomatic advantage. It could be argued that it was useful for a country to have a senior foreign ambassador in its pocket, but to him the argument was no longer strong enough. And he now knew Marvin Hayes well enough to know that the American would not sell himself to the devil so easily; he might to save his wife Zoë's sanity, and for his love of her, but he somehow did not think he would do it for his son, who he would consider must fight his own battles.

At a time when Bulman considered Hayes might be home he rang and got the butler. He heard the click of the extension being lifted and knew that someone else was listening. He asked for Hayes and was told he was out and was not expected back until late.

"How late?"

"It's impossible to say, sir, but it's sometimes after midnight when he returns from some of these functions. May I take a message?"

"No. You don't think I can raise him anywhere? I just want to ask him a quick question."

"I don't think he would care for that, sir. He's the main speaker."

Bulman hung up. He rang Scott just for someone to talk to but nobody answered. They were all out enjoying themselves while he was confined to an ultra luxurious prison of ridiculous size and incredible loneliness. He felt more comfortable in his own modest apartment and for a while he was very homesick and felt extremely vulnerable. He was not feeling sorry for himself, he was frustrated and wanted to get on with solving his problems. It was not enough that he had made some sort of breakthrough; that was useless unless he could follow it up. Bulman had never been good at waiting once he had the bit between his teeth.

He found some sleeping pills amongst the array of bottles in one of the bathroom cabinets and took two to get him through the night.

Connie was a bundle of nerves the next day. Michael Sealy had agreed to have lunch with Stuart Wilson, and she knew what Cordell expected of her. The more she thought about it the more edgy she became and that was made worse by the obvious moodiness of Sealy. They were both committed to doing something they did not want to do.

Sealy left late, whether out of pique or deliberate policy Connie could not determine. She had hoped he would have left earlier.

Sealy called up one of the staff cars to make it official and was driven to the House of Commons where an agitated Wilson was already waiting in the foyer. They shook hands.

"Do you mind if we go straight in?" asked Wilson. "We're running late and the police bill is coming up this afternoon."

They went into the visitor's restaurant, familiar figures entertaining friends, smiles, nods of recognition, and Sealy forced himself into a near normal state. They sat down and ordered and it became clear to Sealy that Wilson was almost as reluctant as he to have the lunch. And he was right about the whining.

They went over familiar ground and Sealy gave the same answers and arguments and in the end it came down to the usual problem of how much time he could have to see through what he wanted to do. Everything was beginning to sound hollow although Sealy put up a good and convincing fight out of sheer necessity. He needed just a little extra time. But whereas before there

211

had been a good deal of understanding, the tolerance was now wearing thin and resentment was setting in.

Sealy achieved the extra time but there was now clearly a time barrier. Towards the end of the lunch a certain friction crept in between the two and rather recklessly Sealy declared in icy tones that he must get back to get on with the job in hand. As it turned out it was the right way to handle Wilson who said he understood. But the rot had set in between the two and Sealy recognised it before Wilson.

Sealy wanted to get back as soon as possible to shake off the political threads that were threatening to bind him.

Connie waited a while to make sure it was absolutely safe before going into Sealy's office. She left his door partially open so that she would hear anyone approaching. Her hands trembled as she fiddled with the clasps on the frame but she got the letter out, more flimsy and delicate than she remembered. She carefully tucked the two sheets into the top of her shirt and just as carefully replaced the back on the frame; it was more work but safer if seen by other eyes.

She went downstairs to the copying room to find the smaller machine had broken down; the giant which did all the work was in use and the pile to be copied was formidable. She knew the fair-haired girl who was operating and said, "When have they got to be done, Susan?"

"Like now. I haven't had lunch yet but they want these back. Why, have you got something to do?"

"Just two sheets both sides."

"Well, that's no problem. Hand them over and I'll slip them in now." Susan's eyes were searching to see where they were and was curious when she could see nothing.

"They're upstairs. I just came down to see if the copier was free." Connie was aware that she sounded ridiculous. She was acting like a young girl caught with her hand in the petty cash box. "How long will those take?"

"About forty-five minutes at full pelt. Maybe longer. But once it's on a run I won't want to stop it."

"That's okay. I'll be back."

Connie skirted a shredder ironically close to the copier and went back to her own office and sat down behind her desk. She did not know what to do. Her inclination was to put the letter back in the frame. Then she thought of faxing it; who to? She couldn't send it to Cordell at Scotland Yard so openly and she thought that there was some accountability to faxes: they could be traced. Anyway, she had no idea of the number. She kept glancing at her watch. She was sure that Cordell would be away for at least two hours but time was passing. She waited thirty-five minutes and could hang on no longer. She went back to the copying room and Susan was still there, studying her nails as the sheets piled out.

"I had a couple of jams so it's taking longer than I thought," said Susan. "You should have let me do it when I offered. Have you brought it down?" She gazed curiously at Connie, wondering why she had nothing on view. But as Connie was far more senior she made no further comment.

There were two choices for Connie: to give up or wait. She waited, the room gradually filling up as personnel returned from lunch. Eventually the machine was free for use and Connie waited until Susan had collected her pile of sheets, moving them on to a side trolley to wheel away.

Connie produced the letter. It had been next to her skin for so long that she wondered if the ink had run. She ran off two copies, hid the original between them and went back upstairs. She took the copies into her office, hid them under some papers in her desk drawer and went to Sealy's office. When she tried to unlock the door she found it already unlocked.

She leaned against the wall and tried to compose herself. She was holding Sealy's letter in her hand and she quickly returned it to inside her shirt. She gathered her nerve, tapped briefly on the door and went in.

Sealy was sitting behind his desk studying some papers. He looked up. "Hello, Connie. Was that you who tried the door just now?"

She was fighting off an impulse to glance at the photo frame and had immense difficulty in keeping her gaze on Sealy. "Yes. I was hoping you'd be out. I'd forgotten to remind you about your luncheon date today. I was going to check your appointment book. I did give you a note yesterday, didn't I?"

Sealy managed a brief smile. "You did. I've been. And I'm back."

"It doesn't sound as if you enjoyed it."

"I didn't. Was there something else?"

"No." In spite of all attempts to stop herself her gaze drifted to the frame and then as quickly back to Sealy. "I'll have the Malta stuff ready for you by morning."

She was not sure how her legs got her back to her own room. In the event she had appeared much more composed than she realised. But she still had the letter and could only hope for an opportunity to return it.

The rest of the day was an agony of waiting. Sealy buzzed her on occasion and each time she went in she stole a glance at the frame. Her job was one at which she sometimes worked late but the official time for leaving was five.

At five past five Connie went to Sealy's office to see if there was anything more he wanted her for before she left; that in itself was unusual because he always buzzed through to say he was off. His door was locked. She knocked and then went back for the key to unlock the door. Sealy had gone. And so had the family group.

Bulman had been trying to raise Cordell all day but the Assistant Commissioner was out, according to his secretary, and might be back early evening. He kept ringing at intervals until he reached him at after six p.m.

It was no time to complain; Bulman came straight to the point. "Thanks for dropping in that name. Is there an address to go with it?"

"What name? Look, George, I've been up to my eye-balls all day. I can't continue to give you this sort of time."

"You didn't drop a name through the letter box? Are you serious?"

"I don't know who you're talking about. If it's about what you're working on I wouldn't dare to give you names. I'd be out without a pension."

"I see. Well, do you think you can give me an address you are not allowed to give to match the name you never gave?"

"How did you reach Chief Superintendent? You're bent. Maybe that's why you left."

"Okay. You've made it difficult for me but thank you for what you haven't already done."

"Sarcasm won't get you anywhere. It's more than my job is worth to give that sort of information, even if I had it, which I haven't. I'm sorry I can't help you but I think I know someone who might just possibly be of use. Tony Cooper. Used to work in dark corners but had a personality clash with the establishment. Don't know whether he's still in the country. Used to live in East Dulwich. Hold on, I might have an old number of his but it's the best I can do. Pen ready?"

Bulman rang the number straight away, got a ringing tone but no answer. He rang later, reflecting he had been on the end of the telephone all day with little result.

"Cooper!"

"My name is George Bulman and a mutual friend told me you might be able to help me."

"I know of you. The Yard. A long time ago though."

"When you were with the SIS?"

"That sounds like an airline. I was never a pilot. What is it you want?"

"An address." Bulman wondered if Cooper had already been warned that he might call; he did not seem too surprised. "A bloke called Michael Sealy."

There was a long silence before, "You realise these

airlines hold you to the Official Secrets Act for life? That's a bloody long time, I hope."

"I'm not after secrets. I just want an address to send a bloke a Christmas card."

"It's only just June. That must be some Christmas list if you start now. But anyway, anyone can call me and say they are George Bulman whom I recall had a reputation for integrity. Give me your number and I'll ring back."

"No bloody fear. I've gone to earth. Maybe things aren't the same since you left. I'm willing to meet you. Anywhere you say."

"Oh God, I'm too bone idle for that kind of palaver. Is there someone I can check with? Give me a name and number."

"I don't intend to land anyone in trouble. I can give you the names of a few villains who might swear by me."

Cooper laughed. "I like your style, George. You haven't changed much. You won't remember but years ago we were on the same caper, just briefly. But my name wasn't Cooper then. I like to change it with the fashion. What else can you offer me?"

"A bloody great telephone bill. This is costing me a fortune. Can you help me?"

"Cheaper than meeting somewhere. Do you mean him harm?"

The question seemed innocuous but Bulman suddenly realised it was a trap. How should he play it? "I want to kill the bastard. He's causing me a lot of aggro." He said it humorously so that it could be taken either way.

There was no humour about the reply. "I hope you mean it, George. The last address I had for him," there was a pause, "was an apartment off Sloane Square." Cooper gave the address. "He lived there even when his wife was alive."

"Did you know her?"

"Oh yes, I knew her." There was something odd about the way it was said it but before Bulman could raise it Cooper added, "Keep in touch if you can. Good luck."

Bulman sat back with a smile. It had not been a wasted day after all.

When Anna Brus rang Connie Taylor that evening she found her to be in a strange mood, agitated and wanting to get her off the line. Realising she would get nowhere she offered her help in any way possible and hung up. Something had clearly gone wrong and Anna suspected it was something to do with her job. She had suffered from her own boss lately, who suddenly did not seem to know which day it was or what appointments he had.

Meanwhile Connie had been trying to get John Cordell, without success. At a time when she needed complete support she found herself deserted. She wondered if Sealy had discovered his precious letter was missing and the thought turned her to jelly. She was not hungry but made a scratch meal just to pass the time. She was sorry she had upset Anna but it was not something that could be explained to anyone not involved.

The door bell rang at eight thirty that evening and the peephole revealed a distorted image of Cordell. She fumbled as she undid the chain to let him in.

As he entered the living-room he saw at once she was in a highly nervous state and said, "What went wrong?"

She went to pour him a drink and he said, "Never mind the drink, Connie. Just tell me what happened."

She poured herself a gin and the bottle rattled on the glass.

"Calm down. Now sit down and tell me about it."

Before she did she went to a bureau, pulled out a copy of Sealy's letter and handed it over, saying bitterly, "This is what you want, isn't it?"

He did not read it at once, more concerned for her. "Out with it. If you can't tell me, who can you tell?"

"I didn't get a chance to return the letter." Connie shrugged. "He keeps it in the back of a family photo group. He'd returned from lunch before I could put it back. I got held up and he came back earlier than I expected."

"Then wait your chance. It shouldn't take you long."

"You don't understand. He has a daily ritual of taking it from the frame and reading it; it sort of depresses and hypes him up at the same time. And he takes it home with him each night. I'm dreading going in tomorrow. I'm not sure I can face him."

"Wait till tomorrow and play it the way you see it. If it's all gone wrong you'll have to tell him the truth."

"That you asked me to do it?"

"Absolutely. He'll have to take it up with me, then."

"I'll still be guilty. He won't understand. The least that will happen is that I'll lose my job. He means a lot to me. I'm sorry I ever did it."

"You won't lose your job, Connie. With him maybe, but not with SIS. Trust me."

"I do. But I've still got to face him. And I'm dreading it." Connie went back to the bureau and returned with the letter. "That's the original. The copy is easier to read."

Cordell held one in each hand, put down the original and read the copy as suggested. It made grim reading and his lips tightened as he read. He put each page down after he read it. When he had finished he put the two pages together and folded them along the dark lines the copier had reproduced of the original folds. He put them in his pocket then picked up the original again, examining each sheet both sides. He put them down.

"You say it has a disastrous effect on him when he reads this?"

"Terrible. He goes to pieces, but there's more to it I can't describe."

"I'm not surprised. It's gruesome. As you know, there's a pretty graphic description of how his son was thrown into a furnace alive. It made me shudder just reading about it." He glanced at the letter beside him. "Belize. Used to be British Honduras before they got their independence. I think there's still a British Army presence there because the locals were afraid of a takeover from the Paraguayans. But he was apparently murdered in Colombia, which is a different proposition altogether. What well-meaning, insensitive, stupid bastard would send a letter like that? No date, no decipherable name, no full address. It's enough to derange anyone. And maybe that's what it's done. But is it true?" Cordell looked up. He smiled painfully. "I'll join you in that drink now. And don't worry: you did the right thing."

"Maybe. But I'm the one who's still got to face him."

The next morning at breakfast Zoë and Marvin Hayes sat each end of the breakfast table and went through the motions of eating. The strain between them had not improved and it was difficult to see how it might until the issue of Don was resolved, and that seemed to be as unlikely as ever.

Conversation was difficult for there was only one issue in the back of each of their minds. It was easy to say, as Hayes had said to her so often, "Put it out of your mind until we are sure." How was she to do that? Their son Don was the only son they had left and all the love she had nurtured for both sons was now concentrated on the survivor.

Zoë had suffered from the absences of her husband, often on dangerous missions, and the loss of a son and the lapse of her younger son had affected her considerably, but now this. And this one would not go away. No matter how many reassurances Hayes gave her she saw them as all empty because nothing had changed except that she was nearer to a breakdown than ever. For how long was she supposed to take this kind of strain?

"That man Bulman rang up last night. I was listening on the extension. No doubt he wanted to report another no-go and to take your money."

"That man Bulman was almost killed and rushed to hospital on our behalf. I think he's earned his money."

She clutched the table, pale faced. "I'm so sorry. Why didn't you tell me?"

"Because I didn't want you upset. But I can't let that kind of remark go by, so now you know."

They had almost finished their second coffee when the butler brought the mail; it was the only time he was allowed to intrude at this one time of day when they preferred to be alone. Most of the mail was for Hayes but Zoë enjoyed her share of circulars and letters from friends.

Hayes was looking through his mail when there was a terrible sigh from Zoë. She was deathly white, clutching a letter with one hand and the table with the other when she emitted another dreadful sound and fell sideways, still clutching the tablecloth. The crockery went with her as Hayes dashed round the table to see what had happened.

Chapter Eighteen

Bulman felt worse the next morning, perhaps reacting to leaving the hospital so soon. He shaved and showered, wearing an available shower cap to keep his stitches dry, and felt a little better after making himself a strong espresso. He dressed in some of the casual clothes Scott had brought him and decided to ring Hayes again, disappointed that he had not been contacted by now.

The butler answered the phone and said Hayes was out and the time of his return was unknown. Bulman had struck up a mild rapport with the butler and was surprised at the stiffness of tone. He needed to go out to exercise but felt he really wanted to speak to Hayes first. He hung on until eleven a.m. and then rang the Embassy, which he hated doing because it brought matters too much under the microscope. The Ambassador would not be in today.

Bulman guessed something was wrong and felt utterly detached and helpless. Frustration had played a big part in the case since he first took it on. At eleven fifteen the bell rang and he was relieved to see the Ambassador on the other side of the door.

A grim-faced Hayes came in, heavy strain incised on his features. The man looked ill. He sat down and Bulman remained standing, worried by what he saw.

"You'd better tell me about it," Bulman said as he sat nearby.

Hayes pulled out a note, passed it across and said, "Zoë received this through the post this morning."

It had been screwed into a ball and Bulman smoothed it out. He read: "Did your husband tell you your son is a murderer? His prints are on the gun which killed a Special Branch policewoman. He can't be protected for ever."

"Bloody hell. What was her reaction?"

"I've just left her at the London Clinic. She's in a state of shock and just now nobody can get through to her. There's nothing I can do. I came to you because you are the only one who knows what's happening. And I consider you a friend, George. But we're not getting anywhere, are we?"

Bulman felt that Hayes himself was not far from a breakdown. "Will she be all right? What's the prognosis?"

"It's far too early to say. I'll go round again this afternoon but I think this will be a long job; it's history repeating itself. Why is someone doing this?"

"To ruin you. You, Zoë, the family. But the suffering must come first. I have a name at last. Does Michael Sealy mean anything to you? Give it some thought."

Hayes shook his head slowly but gave it more time before saying, "It doesn't mean anything to me."

"Well, we can't try Zoë. I'll bounce it off Don and see what his reaction is."

"Is Sealy the guy who's doing this to us?"

"He might be. I'm following it up."

"Then why can't we go for his throat? Stop him in his tracks?"

"Because we have absolutely no kind of proof. None. It's a conviction, no more. But also because he's in an occupation that thrives on misinformation, lies, half lies, innuendo, you name it. He is a highly respected, highly placed official whose word is accepted, as it has been over so many years. He will be Mr Plausibility himself. That he is grossly abusing his power is yet to be established. We have a name to work on, now we need a motive. Is all this aimed against you and your family, or is it against the USA, you being its senior representative in this country and therefore an object of hate?"

"How would I know? With all due respect, George, don't you think it's time we called in your big guns at

Scotland Yard? You've done your job, you've come up with a suspect and provided an angle."

Bulman shrugged. "By all means. But we've been through this. It depends on how quickly you want it solved and what more damage can be done to you and yours. If all this is aimed at your country, your family are the ones who will still take the flack." Bulman stood up and stood squarely in front of Hayes.

"This guy is very powerful and has undoubted influence over issues of law and order when it matters to him. He can plug the gaps and obstruct and claim not only the right to do so but the actual necessity. He and men like him are unaccountable. You know bloody well what it's like: your lot are worse than ours.

"He can be broken down but at first there will be an official reluctance, particularly if he is convincing, and as sure as hell he's obviously been that so far. SIS don't like interference against their own; they would rather accept a cock-up and sweep it under the carpet. He can hold things up until his objective is achieved, and it seems he's well on the way to that. Once he's done what he set out to do he may not give a damn what happens next, to him or anybody. Bring the police in, but they will have to move extremely carefully and it will slow things down. Now me, I don't give a sod. He's already had a go at me. I'm close, Marvin. And he bloody knows it."

Hayes was torn. He had complete faith in Bulman but was thinking in an American way. Bring on the power, the sheer weight of numbers. There was someone now to aim at. Crush him. The British were too apt to think with their feet on the table and send a man in to have a look-see. But he was on British soil and when he looked up at Bulman – the crusty face still showing bruises, the roughly applied bandage that looked like last year's fashion – the chin and eyes told him Bulman would never let go, even if he worked on his own for nothing.

Hayes gradually relaxed and even managed a self-deprecating smile.

223

Bulman said, "You were thinking of bringing in the bloody cavalry, weren't you?" He grinned. "In your position I'd have done the same. But why use an army when one man will do?" He sat down. "I've got official help on an extremely unofficial level. There's a limit to how much my contact can help me without landing himself in the mire. I want to contact him before I make my next move. But there's something you can do: get in touch with your friends across the pond and see if they have anything on Sealy."

"I'll contact the Company and the FBI."

"Good. But more particularly your old mates in the DEA."

Hayes, puzzled, gazed silently for a while, then rose. "Okay. I'll let you know." As he moved to the door he said, "I'm worried sick about Zoë, George. She's a highly sensitive lady. All I've brought her is trouble. She deserves better."

Connie Taylor went to the office next day in a highly nervous state. Sealy was already in because her green intercom light was on and it had been cleared the previous evening. She had two lights, one green and one red, the former summoning her to Sealy's office, the latter telling her he wanted to speak to her on the intercom. She put her things away and buzzed him. When he came on she did not know how she kept her voice steady.

"Good morning. Is there anything you want me to bring in?"

"Just yourself, Connie. Something's cropped up."

She steeled herself for the worst, straightened her skirt and left the office. Sealy's letter was tucked back into her shirt. She tapped his door and went in.

Sealy did not look up for a while as he rustled through some reports. He then took two reports from the pile and handed them to her. "Fairly urgent. Can you get copies off to the respective stations and let me have the originals back?"

The reports shook in her grasp as she took them but Sealy appeared not to notice. He even smiled at her, something he had hardly done for days.

"Is that all?"

Sealy looked surprised. "Of course. Unless you have something to tell me. By the way, my lunch might be protracted today."

"There's nothing in your book." She was beginning to feel more confident.

"I know. Something's cropped up."

He was almost normal, unlike his manner of the last few days, but there was still something in his gaze, as if he was quietly deriding her. He was exercising a great deal of control.

Connie returned to her office and started to tremble. The photo frame had been on his desk. She knew he had taken it the previous evening. Had he tried to take the letter out? Or was he about to do so now? She worked through the morning in a daze. She had yet to return the letter which seemed to be burning her skin.

Connie was not sure how she got through the morning, nor whether Sealy was playing cruel games with her, but she did know she could not continue like this; if she tried she would become a nervous wreck. She worked hard on the reports and returned the first batch well before lunch, to Sealy's seeming amusement and copious thanks.

He buzzed through just before he went to lunch to advise her he did not know when he would be back but would probably be late. She had waited all morning for him to leave and now he had she could hardly stand upright.

Connie left her office about fifteen minutes after Sealy had gone and went to his office carrying the second batch of reports so that her excuse was ready if she was walking into a trap. She unlocked the door and went in.

Now she was in she worked fast. She put the reports down on his blotter and immediately set about removing the back from the photo frame. Her hands were steady as she carefully returned the letter and fastened the clasps.

She put the frame back exactly where it had been, glanced round to make sure everything was as she had found it, left the office and returned to her own where she locked the door behind her, stood against it and broke into a fit of trembling.

Her nerves gradually eased as the day wore on. The job was done; she could get back to normal and put the whole unsettling episode behind her.

She saw no further sign of Sealy and was not sure whether he was back until he buzzed her at ten minutes before five. She almost collapsed as she went in and saw the frame face downwards, the back off and the still-folded letter set to one side.

"Would you prefer to sit down, Connie?"

She knew he was playing with her. She sank on to the nearest chair, groping for arms that were not there. Her eyes were riveted on the letter for she simply could not face Sealy.

"When did you put it back?" he asked reasonably.

She could not reply. She sat transfixed, her mouth dry.

"Speak up, Connie, I can't hear you."

"I was worried about you," she at last blurted out. "Worried sick. I've seen the change in you, the dreadful effect that damned letter has had on you." The volume and pace of her reply gave it steadiness.

"If you were so worried why didn't you take it up with me? Why act behind my back? Who have you discussed this with, for you took it home with you last night?"

There was no point in lying. She took Cordell's advice, wishing fervently she had something to hold on to. "The Assistant Commissioner of Police, John Cordell."

"Yes, I thought as much. You've betrayed me, Connie. You've betrayed a trust and broken an oath of allegiance. I suppose you took copies?"

"Yes." What point was there in denying it now? And then with conviction, "Whatever I did I thought it was in your best interests. It was impossible to approach you, you've changed. I thought we were rather close but for some time now I've been pushed further away." She could feel the tears at last. "I suppose I will have to resign?"

"Resign?" Sealy gazed across the desk and she could see again the expression which he had subdued all day, waiting for this moment. To Connie, it seemed that he was looking at her as if she was some sort of insect whose shape and form he could just make out.

"Resign? You should have done that at the outset. No, Connie, you are suspended pending an enquiry into your actions and for breaking just about every rule in the book. What you have done is subject to prosecution and imprisonment. Go home and take nothing more than your personal belongings. Do not try to move from your address or I'll have you arrested. If you play up in any way I'll have you taken into custody. And don't go anywhere near the Assistant Commissioner."

As she shakily rose from the chair he added brutally, "I've had my doubts about you for some time. I believed if I gave you enough rope you would hang yourself." He smiled, a thin satisfied smile. "And you have. Not very bright of you. Goodbye."

Connie somehow got back to her office and slumped into her own chair. Gradually the tears came, not in force but seeping out as she wondered where she first went wrong. Her life would never be the same again for she had been tainted with dishonesty and disloyalty.

John Cordell had arranged to meet Stuart Wilson at the Home Office that same day. The meeting was late at four thirty because Wilson had a lunch appointment and was not sure how long it would take. Cordell was there at four twenty and was still waiting half an hour later. When he was eventually shown in Wilson was full of apologies but cool with them. Affability had been suspended, though they shook hands.

When they were seated Wilson said, "The reason I was so late had nothing to do with the lunch. Something cropped up with the Home Secretary . . ."

"That's okay. I'll save your time and tell you why I am here. A delicate matter." Cordell well knew that Wilson was recognised for his waffle and wanted to get the meeting over with. He was about to start when Wilson held up a restraining hand.

"Before you tell me anything," said Wilson, "there is something I must tell you. The Chief Constable on instructions from the Home Secretary would normally conduct this interview but he's out of the country. On his return I am sure he will confirm to you what I am about to say."

Cordell was restless; so far Wilson had said nothing that led anywhere. He kept quiet because it was the only way that Wilson might finish what he had to say. So he sat back and waited without warning for the bombshell to come.

Wilson was uncomfortable but had adopted the image of competence some politicians are able to adorn during moments of great uncertainty. "I don't know any other way to say this except straight out, and believe me, John, it causes me a lot of pain. I am instructed to say that you are forthwith suspended from duty on full pay pending an enquiry into certain aspects of your behaviour."

Whatever Cordell had expected it was not this, but when he reflected more he supposed he had been slow not to. It took a time to sink in, during which he lost no composure. He gazed at Wilson who was obviously relieved that he had done what he had to do. "That's a bombshell," he said at last. "May I ask the charges against me?"

Wilson referred to a note in front of him. "There are no charges, certainly not as yet. But there are allegations against you that need to be investigated. It is normal practice to suspend officers in these circumstances."

"I am not an officer, I'm the bloody Assistant Commissioner of Police. Now tell me what the allegations are."

"There's no need to be personal. I like it no more than you. If I'm . . ."

"For God's sake get on with it, man."

"You are accused of seducing a female member of the

SIS, thereby enticing her to steal for you top secret information relating to an overseas operation, of copying such information so that you continue to possess it while the original is returned." Wilson looked up. "Very serious accusations, John. We have no choice but to suspend you."

Cordell was getting his second wind and even saw the funny side. "Well, at least I seem to have seduced a woman. God knows what you might have said if it had been a man. You'd better listen to what I have to say."

"No." Wilson was shaking his head vigorously. "I don't want to know and it would do no good. You can have your say at the enquiry."

"Then I demand to see the Home Secretary, and damned quick."

"I am sure he will see you. He might have been doing so now but for an impossible number of commitments. But it will make no difference to the need of an enquiry. The accusations have been made by a senior civil servant, they must be investigated. That is all I can tell you. If things turn in your favour no one will be happier than me but until then we are bound by procedure."

"So you don't like him either?"

"I beg your pardon?"

"You were almost wishing me good luck. You realise, don't you, that the person who should be suspended is Michael Sealy? He's gone over the top and must be stopped." Cordell put his hand in his inside jacket pocket and added, "I can show you . . ."

But Wilson was half out of his seat, hand held out as if to ward off a blow. "I don't want to know. Put it away or you'll implicate me too. Anything you have to show must be made available to the enquiry. I mustn't see it. And you know it."

"I'm trying to cut through the bullshit. When will the enquiry be?"

"God knows. It takes time. Weeks. Months. But you'll be on full pay."

"That's exactly what he wants, Stuart. Time. And you're making sure that he gets it. He just wants enough time to do whatever his sick mind needs to ruin a few lives and bring about a situation with our strongest ally. He knew you would go by the rules to protect your skin. Now sit back and listen to me."

"No. I cannot do that. I've done my job, the rest is up to procedure. I must ask you to leave."

Cordell returned to Scotland Yard, advised his deputy that he would be away for a few days and that he should take immediate command. He apologised for the workload he was leaving but it couldn't be helped. He realised that if he did not give some explanation his sudden departure would be open to speculation and rumours would fly, so he said, "I've had a run-in with the SIS. They have a rogue amongst them and the only way he can cover himself is to get me out of the way for a spell. But I'll be back. Just keep it under your hat. You're the only one who knows, other than me. Good luck, Sam."

It was a good precaution, for his deputy would want no brush with the SIS himself; they could be trouble and the police invariably finished on the losing end.

When Cordell returned to his apartment he explained as best he could to his wife and realised that no matter how much he told her not to worry, she would do exactly that.

He rang Connie Taylor and was not surprised to hear her say that she had been waiting for his call. She was tearful but calm. He said, "Don't be alarmed, but this call is probably being monitored. We could devise a complicated method of communication but I don't think it's worth it. I suppose you've been suspended? Well, so have I. Don't let it get you down, Connie. By the way, they'll shoot at you that I obtained information from you by seducing you. And they'll press home that we have been alone. Just so you are prepared. Is there anything I can do for you pending the enquiry?"

"I'm just scared. Whatever happens, I've lost my job.

They'll say I should have reported it to Sir Maxwell Swain, for there is no one else senior enough to cope with it that I know. But where do you think that would have got me?"

"You'll get another job, Connie. Just hold on. Anyway, you might be able to screw some compensation out of them. I just wanted you to know that you are not alone in this. He's got us out of the way for a spell and he's hoping red tape will hold things up long enough for him to finish whatever he's doing. Did you meet his wife or son?"

"No. Apart from the photograph on his desk he kept his private life very private. May I ring you if I feel desperate?"

"Of course. And if I'm not here speak to my wife. You'll find her very understanding and I'll fill her in meanwhile."

Cordell felt frustrated because if his own phone was tapped it would not be safe to ring Bulman or to visit him.

Cordell was not the only one suffering the pangs of lack of communication. Don Hayes had been trying to raise his father all day and when that drew a blank he reluctantly tried his mother, not really wanting to worry her but to find out where his father was. She, too, was not available. Don tried to break the butler down but all he got was that his mother was away for a few days and that his father was at a prolonged meeting and the butler was not sure whether, in fact, he was still in London.

This worried Don a good deal. For the last two days he had been followed: quite carelessly, otherwise he would not have noticed. Whether this was deliberately obvious he did not know. But he did know that the experience was thoroughly unnerving at a time when his nerves were already in shreds.

There was little he could do. It was impossible for him to go to the police; they were the last people he wanted to see. It could even be the police trying to break him down for a crime they believed he committed. If he tried to lose himself with groups of other students, which at this time he did not want to do anyway, two men were always there, but not always the same two.

If the idea was to wear him down it was succeeding. He was already as low as he could be. He needed some sort of support to get him through, for there was nobody he could turn to except Tammy Rees. She could be a comfort when she was with him but she was not always there and the loneliness magnified his problems. He was hanging by a nervous thread. He continued to ring his father at intervals. Had the butler acted unwisely and told him where his mother was he would have probably cracked.

Bulman, too, was suffering from lack of knowledge. He had not seen Hayes again since his visit and could not raise him on the phone. For the moment he had nothing more to say to Cordell, accepting that however the policeman helped him it would have to be unofficially and, therefore, of limited use. He did not know of Cordell's suspension and there was no likelihood of it appearing in the press. And he did not know that Connie Taylor existed. He had as safe a house as was possible and had no intention of letting others know where he was. The only people who knew, outside Hayes who had provided the penthouse, were Scott and Cordell.

He had one source he could readily tackle and instinct warned him against phoning first. It was eight p.m. when he decided to visit Tony Cooper in East Dulwich. He rang down to the porter to get him a cab and ten minutes later he was on his way.

It was his first time out since leaving the hospital; the fresh air made him woozy and his legs weren't as strong as he had hoped. But he was out and that in itself was an achievement. It was a reasonable time to travel and the streets were fairly clear, so he arrived at Cooper's house before nine.

Bulman had discarded his head bandage as too conspicuous but the night air played on the bald patch where his hair had been cut away for the stitches. He opened the gate. The house was well detached at the expensive end of Dulwich and there was a deep porch from the centre of which hung a wrought-iron lamp. He rang the bell.

An attractive woman in her late forties opened the door and Bulman asked amiably, "Have I got the right house for Tony Cooper?"

"You've also got the right house for Nancy Cooper. And who might you be?"

"I'm George Bulman. I spoke to him on the phone yesterday. Can I come in?"

"Not without some form of identity. But you'd be wasting your time. He's at the Swan, up the road and first left. Tall, good looking, fair hair, blue roving eyes. He says he knows you so he's likely to see you first. He was expecting you." Nancy Cooper was quietly laughing at him.

"He couldn't know I'd call."

"He thought you might. Some time. He was right, wasn't he? Do you want me to take you?"

"You've done enough. Thanks for your help. Up the road and first left. The Swan."

The Swan was a blaze of light and laughter. The local was full and Bulman suddenly realised it was a Friday night. The days had meant little to him. He went in, the warm air rushing at him, the ceiling smoke a cloud above the turmoil. He stood by the door sponging up the atmosphere of what he saw as a yuppie pub, although there was plenty of beer evident among the small drinks. He gazed round the L-shaped lounge bar looking for a tall, fair-haired, middle-aged, blue-eyed man with roving eyes when a voice at his side said, "George? George Bulman?"

Bulman turned and recognised Cooper at once, though he had been called Thomas the last time he had seen him some years ago. "Your wife is still looking at you through rose-tinted glasses," Bulman said with a smile. "You've put on weight, but she's almost right about what's left of the hair and the blue eyes just about get through." He held out a hand. "How are you? Fred, wasn't it? So is it Fred or Tony?"

"Don't talk to me about weight. And it really is Tony." Cooper grinned, eyeing Bulman's own waistline. "Let me get you a drink." He called out, "Vince," to the barman above the heads of the others and squeezed his way through telling Bulman to stay where he was. He returned with two large whiskies. "I remembered yours because we drink the same."

It was difficult to find a quiet spot so they went outside in spite of the cooling air. They shivered at first but Cooper said, "I guess you would not want what you have to say overheard. Besides, it's easier to pick out listeners out here. Cheers," he said.

"Cheers. You haven't lost the need for caution, then?"

"I'm even more cautious since I left the Firm. I don't think I can add to what I told you, although I half expected you to call some time."

"So I gathered." Bulman shivered. "It's chilly out here. I'm noticing it because I've been cooped up. I believe your man Sealy had a go at me the other day. A few odd-job men duffed me up on my own doorstep and cracked my skull. A brief hospital job. I was lucky."

"That's all he can use: odd-job men, redundant foreign agents looking for work and a quick doublecross for their old masters. There are plenty around just now if you know where to look and he knew before they were redundant. He can't use the MI5 people and they'd have a fit if they knew what he was getting away with on their patch. So he takes casual labour."

"Can you tell me anything about him?"

"No. What I've just said is common sense: there is limited cheap labour around and he knows where to find them and how to dump them. But I can't tell you what he's up to because I don't know. Tell me why you didn't phone me first before coming?"

"You're an old boy. I'm looking for information and you are a likely candidate."

"You haven't answered."

"If he thinks I might approach you he might have your line tapped."

"You haven't changed, have you?" Cooper took a large sip of whisky. "That's precisely why I can't tell you anything. I've not been safe since the day I left. Nay, that's a lie, I was kicked out. But, George, in all sincerity I haven't the slightest idea what he might be up to now. You're much more likely to know. Whatever it is, I wish you luck. You'll need a hell of a lot because he's a crafty sod. Marvellous agent not so long ago."

"So why were you kicked out?"

"You can't have the full story until he's dead or discredited." Cooper eyed Bulman in the light reflected from the pub. "I'm serious when I say that."

"I can see that you are. Do you need another drink first? I'll go get one."

"No." Cooper caught Bulman's arm as he moved towards the door. "We'll have the drink later. It almost bust up our marriage. Sealy's wife made a play for me. I'm not kidding myself. I was far from being the first, but I was the nearest to him, worked with him daily."

"And did you?"

"Yes I did. I could blame booze, a weak moment, but the truth was she wanted another scalp and made it pretty impossible for me to resist. Of course I should have done for security reasons if for no other. But she was a very determined, very sexy, and very passionate lady. She usually got her way."

"And he found out?"

Cooper's bitter smile could just be seen in the bad light. "It's more likely that she told him. The way she spoke about him to me it was clear she loved to see him squirm."

"You've told me quite a lot, in the event." Bulman finished his drink.

"I've told you nothing but a personal affair. That's the reason I left and that's the extent of my help."

Bulman gazed at the sky and went giddy. He steadied himself against the wall. "It's this bloody head wound," he explained. "I should avoid sudden head movement. Anyway, that's quite a turn-up. Was she like that all the time?"

Cooper thought long and seriously. "She was big trouble. But he doted on her. Really doted. She was a scrubber and he must have known. Perhaps he could black it out."

"Well he didn't over you, did he?"

"No. But I sometimes thought she was punishing him for something he had done."

Chapter Nineteen

Cordell, so used to getting hold of staff when he needed them, was finding it difficult coming to terms with being unable to raise anybody of real importance. He had phoned Marvin Hayes several times but he was always out and Cordell was reluctant to leave his name with the butler. He stuck at it and got a response just before midnight. He now accepted that he would have to leave his name.

"Tell the Ambassador that this is Assistant Commissioner of Police, John Cordell, that I've been trying to raise him all day, and that it's a matter of urgency that I speak to him."

"He came home a few minutes ago. I'll tell him, sir."

Hayes came on. "Mr Cordell, I've had a tough day, but you wouldn't be calling at this time of night to say hello. What can I do for you?"

"Stay up a little longer, Ambassador. I don't trust the phone. I can be round there quite quickly."

Cordell was as good as his word and took his own car. There was no point in taking evasive action if his calls were being monitored. He arrived well after midnight and Hayes, who had told his butler to go to bed, opened the door himself.

The two men briefly shook hands and went into the study where two balloons of cognac were already waiting. Hayes passed one over and as they sat down Cordell remarked, "You don't look well, has something happened?"

"Someone with a twisted mind sent my wife a note telling her that my son murdered the policewoman. Up to that point I have managed to shield her from the worst. It's blown her mind. She's now in the London Clinic under psychiatric care. At the moment she's so drugged up that she doesn't know me. What is it you wanted, Mr Cordell?"

Cordell reached down over the arm of the chair to place his glass on the carpet. "I have today been suspended from all duty on full pay. I am not in a position to tell you who's involved in this, but I am sure George Bulman might, if indeed you don't already know."

"He's given me the name of Michael Sealy. I'm doing my own check in the States. But George was careful to make no direct accusation. Why are you suspended?"

"For the same reason George was cracked over the head."

"So we are getting close. But it must be someone of immense power to get so high a ranking police officer suspended."

"It's simpler than you think. An accusation is made against the officer. Even if it was from a villain it would have to be investigated. But from someone of long service and high appointment, it has to be actioned as a matter of routine."

"Are you saying this guy Sealy has done this to you?"

"I'm saying nothing. I still have a responsibility to my masters and am under oath. I haven't given you a name, you've given me one, although you might ponder on how George got it to give to you. I have to be extremely careful, which is why if I need to contact George I can operate through you. I'll be watched. You are less likely to be followed because all hell would break loose if it was discovered that you were under surveillance. I just don't want to lead the way to George's front door."

"As best I can I'll act for you. But tell me, do you still believe my son killed the girl?"

"No. I've never been happy about it but the evidence was there. It still is. I think I know who did it but he's missing and again I think I know who knows where he is.

Why else would I be suspended? I'm not the only one to get a sideways push, by the way, but that's another story."

Hayes wearily closed his eyes. "If you know who is doing all this I can't understand why nothing can be done."

"Oh, it can be done, all right. It is being done, but apart from George, who has always had his own way of working, we have to act within the law and there will always be those who know how to use the law against us. We've actually come a long way."

"Meanwhile my family is being ruined around me. If something doesn't happen soon this guy will have achieved his object. God knows what other damage he's done."

"That's why I need a link with George. I'm now reluctant to phone or call on him."

Hayes looked washed out and his hand trembled as he lifted his glass. Then he said, "I've already agreed to act for you. But contacting me might be difficult."

"Could you see that he gets this?" Cordell pulled out a copy of Sealy's letter. "The envelope is sealed." Cordell handed it over.

Hayes stared coldy. "Do you imagine I would read it?"

"No, sir. I did not mean to imply that. I'd better get back. My wife is wondering what the hell is happening to her."

"The repercussions from this thing go on and on. My wife has passed that stage into coma."

Bulman played back the answering machine. He had not returned to the penthouse until almost one a.m. He had stayed with Tony Cooper until the pub closed and then Cooper took him to a small club which never seemed to close. But drunk or sober, Cooper had come up with nothing more. Marvin Hayes had phoned and wanted him to phone back whatever the time.

Bulman phoned and Hayes answered, "I hope that is you, George. I've been waiting up."

"I'm returning your call."

"Cordell has been to see me. He's been suspended from

duty and believes he'll have a tail from now on. I'm acting for him. He seems to think his phone might be bugged. Do you think mine is?"

"The temptation must be there, but officially, at any rate, Home Office permission has to be obtained although the reasons given for the necessity might not be all that honest. I think it's more than they dare do – someone would get to know about it and word would fly round. Imagine how your people would react if they found that out."

"Cordell gave me a letter to give to you. It's sealed so I can't say what's in it. The best thing is for you to collect it as and when. I'll leave it with Harry the butler."

"Will you be around if I need you?"

"I've had to reschedule my meetings. I won't be around officially for the next day or two. If I'm not at home call me at the London Clinic."

"Any news from the US yet?"

"I'd have told you. It's too soon."

"Chin up. We're bloody close now. Which will be the reason Cordell was sidelined. They are trying to isolate me and they've pretty well done it. We've almost got the buggers."

"George, you keep talking in the plural. How many are there?"

"Probably one. The plural was just sloppy English. But we are close."

"I believe you. What worries me is just how much damage can be done meanwhile? How many lives can be wrecked?"

At eight thirty that same morning Bulman caught a cab and went to Regent's Park to collect the letter. He did not ask whether or not the Ambassador was around, he simply told the butler what he wanted and the letter was handed over. He took the same cab back.

In the massive penthouse kitchen he cooked a huge breakfast and did not open the letter until he was on his second cup of coffee, which he took into the drawing-room, then sat in his favourite chair and tore open the plain envelope. He read the letter, and then again more slowly. It had the same impact on all those who read it: it deeply shocked and repulsed, and he sat staring into space with the letter in his hand while his coffee went cold.

Is that what had happened to Scaly's son? Had he really been thrown into a furnace alive? Had it deranged Sealy to the extent he was making others suffer? Indiscriminately? The address at the top of the well-worn page merely stated Belize. No date, no address. The handwriting was quite clear and the copying machine had enhanced the print. Belize.

Bulman phoned Hayes but the Ambassador had already left. He phoned the London Clinic but he was not there and was presumably somewhere between home and the clinic. He felt inclined to ring Cordell but decided against it just in case Cordell was bugged. He waited until midday, to give Scott an opportunity to do some work first, then rang him at his agency.

"Any chance of you coming round this evening, Spider? Something's cropped up which will interest you. If you can drop everything and come now that would be even better. I'll wait here for you. And, Spider, I know I am teaching my grandmother to suck eggs, but make absolutely sure that you bring nobody with you. Things are desperate and the knives are out."

As he put down the phone Bulman folded the letter along the dark imprints of the original folds as if it would fall apart if he did not. He was just beginning to realise what an immense risk John Cordell had taken. What was left of his career was already at stake but if he was disgraced he would also lose the job he was retiring for. It could ruin his life. And that seemed to be the name of the game all round as far as Bulman could see. But burned alive in a furnace! It was not difficult to produce a mental image and if that was what Sealy had been doing, the man must by

241

now be a nutter. But who was he actually blaming and had he real cause?

Sealy was satisfied about suspending Connie Taylor. It got her out of the way at a time he needed to be unhampered. There had been a time when he thought of her too often. He had detected a long time ago that she had some sort of a crush on him and he might well have responded given time, but then Marvin Hayes was appointed Ambassador to Britain and that changed things. The event brought back into focus that which he had forced out along the years. And he had given more and more time to it as the days passed, and Connie had been pushed to the back of his mind, further and further until she was no longer in it at all except as an occasional nuisance. It had all been a mistake anyway because nobody could possibly replace Meg.

Tommy Wise was on duty when Sealy arrived at the mews. It seemed to Wise that nursemaiding McQueen was his sole function and he was beginning to rebel. He tackled Sealy as soon as he checked the monitors.

"Is this to be my main occupation, sir? I didn't sign on to be a Government Custodian. Couldn't someone else at least share the work with me?"

"Of course you didn't, Tommy. And neither did I. But you've increasingly won the confidence of McQueen and that is terribly important. You've done an exceedingly difficult job well and I appreciate it. Anyway, it won't be for much longer. Not long at all now."

There was a way Sealy had developed of looking at people which made them uneasy. And Wise had also learned that when Sealy, usually so formal a man, called him Tommy, he was about to be misled in some way. The truth was that during the time Wise had spent looking after McQueen he had learned far more about Sealy himself than about the prisoner. And what he learned was very unsettling. He had begun to feel as much a prisoner as McQueen, for he was now obliged to live in all the time, on the promise of just a few more days' duty followed by a long leave. There were times when he thought neither would happen.

"It's unnatural for me to be cooped up like this, sir."

"I know it's very difficult, but you have comfort all around you. How would you like to be in the SAS buried in a filthy bolthole in a field for days on end, in all kinds of weather, living with your own mess, stink, and dogs and foxes sniffing around to betray you. *That's* unnatural, Tommy. And that's dedication. Which is why I chose you; I knew I could rely on you and your discretion. Very little longer, dear boy."

Wise knew he would get nowhere with Sealy but he had one last shot; "If I had wanted the SAS I'd have put in an application, sir. I don't think I can stand this much longer."

"Nor will you have to. Let's have a look at McQueen."

McQueen was strangely subdued. When they went in he glowered at the far end of the cell and it was obvious that every time Sealy came his mind was activated into planning an escape. He was still sore from the last attempt.

Sealy said, "I suppose you're worried about coming to trial for the murder of the policewoman."

McQueen had squeezed himself into a corner as if he needed propping up. "You think you're so clever. In the first place I've killed nobody so don't keep trying to hang it on me. In the second we both know I will never go to trial. You'll either kill me or let me go."

"Which do you think it will be, Wally?"

During these exchanges Tommy Wise became increasingly uneasy. He accepted that Sealy was a master of bluff and interrogation but a new dimension was creeping in which concerned him a good deal. He was beginning to think that what happened to McQueen might influence what happened to him and this worried him.

"Well, Wally?"

"It could go either way. I don't think you've made up your mind yet. Only you know why I'm here at all. I bet *he* doesn't know." He glanced at Wise. "And I bet he's not so happy about it either. You're a mad bastard."

"Coming from you, that's ripe. You could have done something better with your life instead of latching on to mad causes and drugs and violence and killing police-women. You are really very stupid and this is where it has landed you."

"Get stuffed."

"Profound for you. Well, you'll be out of your misery quite soon. If you've got a God you'd better try to get in touch. He's the only one who might help you. There is one other possible source of help." Sealy glanced at Wise who was po-faced and anxious to get out of the cell. "Your guardian will give you pen and paper and you can make a confession about the girl. You've had plenty of time to think it over; now is the time to cleanse your soul. It could make a big difference to you."

McQueen's lids flickered. He was losing cohesion of thought because he recognised that much more lay behind his abduction than what had happened to the girl. This was not a police cell, and he was convinced he would not see one. "I'd prefer a typewriter," he said as an act of defiance. "But you still wouldn't get a confession for what someone else did, if it was ever done at all. Now piss off and see a shrink."

Sealy blinked, aware that he was being closely watched by Wise. He smiled. "Goodbye, McQueen. Sleep well."

Bulman rang the hospital where he had been taken, located one of the nurses who had attended him and asked when he should return to have his stitches out; they were beginning to irritate.

Scott called at twelve thirty with two Chinese takeaways and Bulman made the coffee. They ate first before the meal got cold and then Bulman handed over the letter.

Scott, softer at heart than Bulman, showed revulsion on his open face. "This is sick," he said.

Bulman brought him up to date on all he knew, and

finished, "The guy in the letter must be Sealy's son. He has to be."

"Or his boyfriend. That could upset him."

Bulman did not give the idea too much thought. "No. It was his son. Look, I need to contact John Cordell but he might be staked out and his phone tapped."

"What about the Ambassador? Supposing he's followed?"

"He has an armed police bodyguard, a man trained to look for trouble and for tails. Sealy wouldn't be that stupid."

"Sealy could tap into the Diplomatic Protection Group."

"He could, but if he did MI5 or SB would almost certainly get to hear of it and then there'd be trouble. His best bet is through Cordell. He will be sure that Cordell will want to contact me; he already has through Hayes. I need to speak to Cordell and I bet Sealy knows that only too well."

"You want me to act as courier? I can shake them off as I go."

"Well, *I* certainly couldn't. Sealy's got me bogged down in areas where it matters."

"You'll have to use someone else's phone or a call box. Give me a number and I'll see Cordell and tell him to ring you at a certain time – you'll have to settle for that. There's a call box just round the corner."

Scott sat back to watch Bulman considering the idea. He said, "Two bloody coppers and they don't know how to make contact or shake a tail. No wonder the crime rate's up."

It was four thirty p.m when Bulman stood outside the call box hoping no one would use it. When a woman came bustling along he dived in and picked up the phone while keeping the cradle pressed down. The woman passed and he hung up. Almost immediately the phone rang and a startled Bulman picked it up. "Yes?"

"That you, George?"

"John. It's a bloody difficult way of doing things but

what else can we do? I believe you want to tell me something."

"I'll come straight to the point. You've read the letter? Right. You've probably guessed it refers to Sealy's son. I'm sure that Sealy is your man but his motives are still unclear. Why is he aiming at the Ambassador? I don't think anybody but himself knows. Connie Taylor was his PA and was suspended about the same time as me. She's seen his reaction when reading the letter and he seems to go into shock, not surprisingly. Connie pinched the letter long enough to make a copy and give it to me. But he knew what she was up to. Connie never met his wife or son but knows he was crazy about both. Apparently he kept the letter in the back of a frame of a photo of himself, his wife and his son which he brought to the office in the morning and took home at night. He doted on his wife."

"That surprises me. My information is that Sealy's wife was a scrubber. I met Cooper, who'd had personal experience and thereby lost his job. Strange, ennit?"

There was a long silence and Bulman thought they might be cut off. Cordell said, "Don't worry about the time, I'm on a card. Yes, I find that very strange. According to Connie, and she was a close observer as she had a crush on him herself, he doted on his wife. Maybe it didn't matter to him."

"You really believe that?"

"No. But then if he's going round wrecking people he can't be that normal."

"Do you think this Connie Taylor can help any more than you've told me?"

"Probably not. She might be able to put a little depth into it but she knows nothing of real importance. I thought you needed to know the background to the letter. It brings us a little nearer to his state of mind and a hazy motive."

"Do you think you should go to Sir Maxwell Swain at this stage?"

Cordell laughed. "I'm suspended, for chrissake. I've brought the game into disrepute, in the short term anyway, and Sealy seems to be satisfied with that. And there is nobody so plausible than the insane when they want to be."

"So you're saying the letter has driven him over the edge? The final straw after the death of his son followed by the suicide of his wife?"

"That would be a logical conclusion but for the fact that the letter has apparently been around a long time. So why now? What sparked what?"

They broke off after agreeing that a simple telephone code would be quickly broken by someone like Sealy, so the cumbersome, but safer method of using Scott as a courier continued, but only if felt to be sufficiently urgent.

Before they hung up, Bulman said, "You've really come off the fence with this one, John. Thanks a lot."

"What else could I do? I'm trying to save my own reputation. I'm now hog-tied. You can't trust anyone around Sealy. That leaves you. Keep out of his bloody way."

Bulman laughed. "I'll never solve it if I do that."

Bulman waited until late evening then caught a cab to East Dulwich again. This time Cooper was at home, invited Bulman in and they entered the comfortable living-room with old prints of fox-hunts adorning the walls.

Nancy brought in a bottle of Scotch and glasses, poured herself one and then left them to it, saying to Bulman as she left, "Don't worry. I got used to all the secrecy, but I would like to have a drink with you before you go. I might get a bit of conversation for a change." She winked and left and Bulman said to Cooper, "So you like hunting?"

"Hunting? I loathe it." He glanced around the walls. "Hunting is when the odds are even and then only justified if there is a real human need. Ever tried hunting a man-eating lion in the dead of night? Using a miner's lamp attached to the head so that the beam can pick out the eyes and go straight down the sights. That, old chum, is really scary, the balance of risk in the lion's favour. It was killing off the cattle and the natives, so it had to go. Nobody enjoyed it."

"So why the prints?"

"To remind me how much I loathe it, and to get silly buggers like you asking daft questions."

"Okay, so you're anti-blood sports." Bulman produced the letter and handed it over. "I know you said you were saying no more until Sealy was dead but this has cropped up, and as it would seem to be personal and not political I hope you can throw some light on it."

Cooper read it without twitching a muscle, folded it and handed it back. "Where did that come from?"

"Isn't it better you don't know?"

Cooper reached for the bottle and half filled his glass. His tie was loosened, the knot halfway down his chest. "You know, you've reminded me that I promised Nancy I'd take those prints down."

Bulman said nothing, waited, gazed round the room and still Cooper was silent.

"Where did you get it?" Cooper asked again.

"Well, I got it third hand. I didn't know of its existence until the early hours of this morning. I believe he kept it in the back of a frame of a family group. He brought it to his office and took it home at night. Day after day, by all accounts."

"You haven't answered me, George."

"Well, as I wasn't there I can't be certain but I think there was an opportunity for someone to take a look and make a quick copy. And before you ask, the same person was concerned because every time he read it he went into deep labour."

"So Sealy had it?"

"That's what I've been saying."

"I had to be sure because I've seen this letter before."

"I thought you were cool about it."

"And he didn't show it to me. It was his wife. It was sent to her. She was hysterical on my shoulder all night."

Bulman could only stare. "Each time I've seen you you've managed to surprise me. Sent to her? Why? It's a strange thing to send to a mother. A horrible thing to do. Who sent it and why didn't she destroy it?"

"I don't think she ever found out who sent it. She might have had her suspicions but she kept them to herself. But you're right about destroying it because in the end I think it destroyed her. It just grew and grew in her mind until she was totally confused, in mental anguish and several times near suicidal until in the end she could take no more."

"Is it now happening to him?"

"Sealy? Suicide? He'd try to get rid of everybody else first."

"Perhaps that's what he's doing. It's his selection that puzzles me."

"It puzzles me too; he's known about the letter from the beginning. It's taken a long time for him to get this reaction. So what's brought it on, George? What's going on inside his twisted mind?"

"Perhaps it's not as twisted as we think. Maybe we're looking through the wrong end of the telescope."

The two men stared at each other in silence as the implications of that possibility dawned.

Chapter Twenty

When Bulman arrived back at the apartment he immediately rang Marvin Hayes even though it was late. Harry the butler said he was still out, probably at the London Clinic and that he would ask the Ambassador to return the call as soon as he was back. Being reduced to the telephone as the sole means of communication was becoming wearing, but the moment he became careless Bulman knew he would have put himself on view. He would wait up.

He sat down and read the letter again and poured himself a drink. He considered that Tony Cooper had been more than useful but had shown, before Bulman left, that he was very wary, if not actually afraid of what Sealy could still do to him. Of course Bulman had no knowledge of what had actually happened at the time Sealy had got rid of Cooper; it could have been a very ugly episode. But Cooper, within the bounds he had set himself, had been extremely helpful and had set a rethink on the whole sad business.

It was half past midnight when Hayes rang back and without explanation Bulman asked, "We provide you with an armed bodyguard, right?"

"Yes. But you know that, George."

"Is he with you all the time when you are out?"

"Most of the time. There are times when it is downright inconvenient. But these guys are trained to be discreet and know when to make themselves invisible."

"Well, don't let yours make himself invisible. Whoever you get, day by day warn them to keep close until you tell them otherwise. And tell them to keep their eyes skinned for a tail. I know they do already but tell them to be extra vigilant."

"Are you expecting this guy to have a go at me? Don't you think he imagines that he's doing enough damage already to my family without actually killing me?"

"He's been using psychological torture from the outset but he might decide that's not enough. It's just extra precaution, Marvin."

"Something must have provoked it for you to try to contact me at this time of night. Do I need to know about it?"

"I couldn't tell you. Motive wise I think we might have been looking in the wrong direction. You see daily what he has done to your wife. What do you think he has in store for you? Ask for double protection."

"I'd have to give a strong reason and produce the whole story and that could bring us right back to square one, the evidence against Don being what it is. Are we on the verge of anything?"

"Yes. Which is one reason why he might get desperate. I wish your people would pull finger and come up with something your end."

"I'm sure they're doing their best. They don't really know what they're looking for. Anything else?"

"Just watch your back."

Tammy Rees had at last got Don Hayes to come to bed with her and he was grateful for her increasing concern. The original group were still supposed to keep clear of each other until the police had made a positive move but as the days wore on the instruction was wearing thin.

The same day, Don received a letter stating that he was a murderer and authority was failing to act because of the position of his father, but that nevertheless he remained the killer of a young policewoman and something was going to be done about it.

The letter had caught him when he was already very low. He had made friends but was not in his own country and from the outset had been frantically worried about the effect it would have on his parents, particularly his mother who had suffered enough back home in New York. He had failed to make contact with his father and now suspected that the evasion was deliberate and, as he saw it, that could only be because there was bad news about his mother. He began to feel suicidal and it was in this vastly depressed mood that Tammy caught up with him.

She was staggered by how depressed he had become and when he showed her the letter she went to work to instil into him all the commonsense arguments against taking notice of anything anonymous. It was deliberately cruel and aimed to unbalance him, which it had. Tammy, aware that her feelings were growing for him even though they came from two entirely different backgrounds, and that in the end it would get her nowhere, could not resist showing her love in the best way she could. In any event she did not think he could safely be left alone for the night.

She cuddled up to him in bed while he had his strong arms about her and was afraid to let her go. She did not mind being used as a prop at this time and had instigated it to get him through these dark days. She was afraid he might do something silly and she intended to cling on.

About halfway through the night, and still in each other's arms, Don said, "It's no use. I'll have to go to London and find out what's happening there. Not knowing is driving me mad."

"I'll come with you."

He gazed down at the top of her head as she nestled on his chest. "No. You'll get yourself in trouble."

"Worse than we're in, you mean?"

He realised his depression had occupied him too much and that but for Tammy he might have ended it. There were still times when he felt like it, but the dreadful feeling floated in and out of his mind now instead of remaining there all the time, the acute heaviness increasing with each dark thought. He kissed the top of her head, only too aware of what she had done for him. "You want to meet Pop?"

"I want to be sure that you will be all right. This thing will end, you know. It's unnatural; it can't go on for ever. But give it a day or two. For me. Something good might happen to us." She wished she believed more in what she had said. In a perverse way she thought that if they went to London and met his father it might be the beginning of the end of their association.

He squeezed her gently. "It's no use, Tam, I must go up tomorrow."

Sealy went straight to the mews from his apartment the next morning. He let himself in to find Wise up but wandering around in his pyjamas. Sealy made no comment except to say he wanted to be left alone with the prisoner.

Wise was at once suspicious and not a little concerned; he could see himself taking the can back for all sorts of atrocities. "Do you think it safe to be left alone with McQueen, sir? He's a strong and violent man. If you're going in I really should go in with you."

"Tommy, I'm armed. I simply want to have a quiet word with him without incriminating you. Enter up in your schedule that I insisted we be left alone for, say, an hour, although it will probably be far less. Now get dressed. Have you had your breakfast?"

"No. This is a late morning, for me."

"Then have a full breakfast out and charge it to expenses. Take your time."

Sealy had called him Tommy and was being amiable. Wise was suspicious on both counts yet there was nothing he could do but protest and that would get him nowhere. He wondered if McQueen would still be there when he returned. He took his time getting ready hoping the delay would force some explanation from Sealy, who surprised him by preparing a breakfast for himself. After that, Wise dressed and left after entering up the instruction on his schedule.

Sealy took his time finishing breakfast. Afterwards he cleaned and cleared up. When he had finished he closed down all the monitors and then went round to check that the only one left operating was the monitor erected above the door of the cell.

He stood outside the cell door and watched McQueen stir between the blankets, awake but clearly with no desire to get up. Sealy saw that as a good sign, for what was there to get up for? However reluctantly, McQueen was showing signs of accepting the inevitability of his lot.

Keeping his eye on the monitor Sealy spoke into the speaker quite softly and said, "Good morning, Wally. I'd like to have a helpful word with you. Just you and me. A proposition."

McQueen straightened in bed almost as if he was lying to attention. He looked towards the camera. "It's a bit early for serious talk, isn't it?"

"Not for me. But I wanted to be sure we are alone. And we will be in there. Now if you're fully awake, go to your usual place at the end of the room and I will enter. I am armed so don't think of trying anything. Even if you succeeded in overpowering me you would be shot to pieces before reaching the street."

McQueen climbed from the bed, taking his time, wondering what was going on. He went to the end of the room, dressed only in pyjama trousers. The bare arms were powerful and free of tattoos. He grabbed a chair on the way and straddled it, arms folded along the back.

Keeping his eye on the monitor Sealy unlocked the door, stepped in briskly and closed the door behind him, turning the key behind his back, his other hand holding a .38 Smith and Wesson. "You look worn out," said Sealy.

"So would you be if you were cooped up here illegally by a Government department. No windows. No exercise. You want to try it."

"How would you like me to let you go?"

McQueen stroked his unshaven face and then scratched

his unruly hair. "That's a stupid question. And if I said I would there would be a catch to it."

"Not a catch. A price to pay. But once that was done you would be free."

McQueen did not believe a word of it. He sat with a smirk on his face and said, "That will be when I get a bullet in the back."

"Your account would be square. There's no money in it, just your freedom. You've got plenty of drug money stashed away. What do you think?"

"You haven't told me what I have to do."

"Something you are very good at. Kill someone."

The smirk froze around McQueen's mouth and he lowered his head to rest his chin on his arms. His eyes were probing Sealy's who was sitting on the foot of the bed.

"I'm a lousy shot. I might miss."

"I didn't stipulate the kind of weapon but you were right to mention the one you use best. The shot you fired at Paula Smith, considering the weather conditions and the number of people around you, was absolutely first class. Of late I've had to resort to foreigners for all sorts of reasons, and there you are, one of our own, exterminating people first shot. And then to have the presence of mind to panic the others away and run with the almost blacked-out American, clobbering him at the right time and putting the gun in his hand to get his prints. And then to pug the gun up under a hedge, just enough to keep fairly dry so that the prints would not be ruined – that was excellent thinking in very tight conditions."

Sealy was full of praise and gave no sign of sarcasm. "It was professional, Wally, and good professionals have to be admired in whatever they do. Of course, most of it was premeditated; the drugging of the drinks, the choice of company. You had picked young Hayes out from the outset. But you could not foresee the cloudburst and you coped magnificently, even turning it to your advantage.

I don't think you will find any problem with what I propose."

McQueen was bewildered. He had not expected anything like this. But he did not trust the man who was making the proposition. "And when I've done the job I stop one in the back."

"That could be arranged. But it would be very stupid of me. My subordinate knows you are here and would report the matter once he knew you were dead. He would have to to protect himself. That wouldn't do me much good and I detest prisons."

McQueen was not convinced. "It seems to me that you are leaving yourself wide open, anyway. And I think you're too clever for that. You have to have an angle."

Sealy eased his position on the bed. "Oh, I realise there would be nothing to stop you pushing off and not doing the job at all. That's quite possible. It would be the first thing to enter your mind. But consider this." Sealy placed an arm over his crossed legs and leaned forward. The gun dangled from his right hand. "If you doublecrossed me I would get the police to order a nationwide hunt. Your photograph would be released and within days the whole country would know about you as a suspect in the murder of Paula Smith. You could not have been imprisoned here because how could you possibly have escaped? And there will be no record of your having been here. Indeed you'll not know how to find the place. You'll be captured, even if you manage to lie low for a spell, and you'll go down for murder. You'll get life."

McQueen thought it over. "Clever bugger, aren't you? I may have better contacts than you realise. I could escape if I put my mind to it."

Sealy smiled. "Of course you could. Are you trying to convince me or yourself? You could last on the run for quite a time, Wally. But during the whole of that time you'll have to be extremely careful, never relaxing. If you manage to get abroad it will be much easier for one of our foreign stations to deal with you. Which sea would you like to be dropped in?"

McQueen had suddenly lifted his head but Sealy continued, "No, I did not get careless when I mentioned foreign stations. I want you to know precisely what you're up against." He paused just long enough to get McQueen thinking then added, "I said I'd offer no money. Nor would I. But there's something more precious I can offer you which would change your whole life. A new identity. A complicated procedure, but forever effective. You would have to sort out your finances before the actual switch unless you want to lose all your money, but that is just a matter of timing. With the problems you have, a new identity must have considerable attraction."

McQueen was at once interested. "Supposing I get caught doing the job?"

"We can help with escape facilities. You tell us what you want. And we can, if pushed, impede the police. Do we have a deal?"

"It needs thinking about. How much time have I got to think it over?"

Sealy studied his watch. "Five minutes."

"It's not enough. My life's on the line."

"Your life has been on the line ever since you shot Paula Smith. I find it interesting that during this discussion you've not made your usual denials about killing her."

"What's the use? You won't believe me whatever I say. I didn't do it and you know I didn't do it. There, a denial. The only reason I'm even considering your proposition is to get out of this place. But five minutes is nowhere near enough time to think over something which will affect the rest of my life."

"Let me persuade you that it is. If you don't do it I will kill you here. Tapes and sound tracks will be destroyed and it will be like you never existed."

"That's what I thought. What about the other guy?"

"What other guy? Your guard? That's for me to sort out.

257

Make up your mind, Wally, before you have no mind to make up."

"You make a convincing argument." McQueen's attitude suddenly changed and he was now presenting an entirely different image. He was still very young but his experience was now beginning to show as he saw only one way out. There was no further point in trying to fool the man at the end of the cell. Probably, there never had been. McQueen was rich in his own right, intelligent, requiring a university degree to add a touch of respectability and authenticity to his general image.

At the age of twenty-three, McQueen was a hard successful man steeped in anything that was crooked and he made a lot of money. He had been streetwise from the age of nine, and clever enough to stay clear of an actual criminal record. This was vastly important to him, to his rising ego and his excessive belief in his own ability. A policewoman lay dead to protect that belief and to avoid his exposure. It did not disturb him in the least. The silly cow should not have been there.

And yet the man sitting on the bed knew all about him and had him cocooned in a way he would never have believed possible.

"Your five minutes is up," said Sealy, receiving a glimmer of what was passing through McQueen's conditioned mind.

"I wouldn't know. You took my watch from me. Do I get to know what I'm up against?"

"The whole element of surprise will be with you. Your target has a police guard and if he plays up you can take him out too."

McQueen's hard eyes reflected alarm. "A copper? Bodyguard? Which means an armed copper. What are you trying to pull?"

"He's hardly likely to have his gun in his hand. You will have. With your standard of marksmanship you'd be away before the bodyguard could react. In any event he's most likely to rush to the victim. It's no real problem to a

258

man of your calibre." Sealy was deliberately pandering to McQueen's vanity. "If you want to spend the rest of your life free we don't intend that you do it on a soft option."

McQueen pushed himself upright but kept his grip on the chairback. He could not fail to notice that the man sitting on the bed raised his gun straight and true at his chest. "You've had this in mind all the time, haven't you? Right from day one. That's the only reason I'm here?"

"I had to be sure that you are the man for the job. You've convinced me that you are."

"So who's the bastard you want hit?"

"The American Ambassador."

Chapter Twenty-One

McQueen, supremely confident in himself, was suddenly engulfed by uncertainty. "The American Ambassador?"

"The actual method you use is up to you. If you want a gun then I will supply one. We can get you to a position of advantage and supply a back-up car with false plates for your escape. As you don't look remotely like an Arab extremist, the bodyguard will barely notice you. You will have every advantage and it will be much easier than you think. Have you anything to say?"

All McQueen wanted to do was to get away from his prison. "Nothing's as easy as you're suggesting. But, okay, I'm limited for choice."

"I've arranged your accommodation: a small central hotel." Sealy smiled briefly. "Nothing as luxurious as this, but comfortable enough. I will be in constant contact."

"You've already fixed the accommodation? You were pretty sure, weren't you?"

Sealy, still seated on the bed, shrugged. "You hadn't a great deal of choice but I knew it was a job which would not offend any scruples you may have. I think we'd better get you to the hotel before discussing the detail. Dress quickly. You can shave later."

For the very first time McQueen noticed an agitation about Sealy, as if now they were agreed he wanted the deal concluded quickly.

Sealy rose and unlocked the door. He put away his gun and turned to face McQueen again. "You are bigger, stronger and much younger than me so there's now nothing to stop you overpowering me. But if you do, you are open to all the threats I made earlier. Don't underestimate me, McQueen. One way or the other I'll get you. Meanwhile you'll be under close surveillance. One slip and you're finished. I'm allowing you to get away with murder by committing another. What could be fairer?" He produced a printed card with the name of the hotel on it. "Put that in your pocket."

When McQueen was ready to leave, Sealy made him tidy his cell, fold the blankets and remove anything that was his so that there was no sign of his presence. It was then that Sealy produced a blindfold.

Sealy guided McQueen to the big double garage doors, told him to get in the front seat of the Jaguar and to get his head below the dashboard. Sealy opened the garage doors and drove out, stopping only to close the doors again. He then drove off, warning the uncomfortable McQueen to keep his head down until told to remove the blindfold. He drove through the London traffic for about twenty minutes before telling McQueen to sit up.

McQueen sat up, stiff and blinded by light; he had not seen natural light for several days and it had turned out to be a bright day. He said nothing, finding everything strange even after so short a time. Not only had the light and the surrounds changed, but the mass of activity around him came as a new experience. But the meaning of life had also changed dramatically: for the moment he was an unpaid assassin.

Sealy pulled in on one of the streets behind Oxford Street, produced a hundred pounds in fivers and handed them to McQueen. "That's just to tide you over until I see you later this evening. You can get a cab just round the corner." He glanced over his shoulder. "Make it quick, the horns are going to blast me any moment. See you later."

Once McQueen was out Sealy pulled away and headed straight back for the mews. He was running out of time now but it was impossible to hurry through the busy streets. He reached the mews, opened the doors and drove in, and immediately went to work. He collected all the visual and sound tapes and dropped them in a plastic bag he had brought with him and put it in the boot of his car. He made sure there was no sign that McQueen had ever been there. It would be impossible to wipe away every fingerprint if ever it came to such an issue, but if it did, and that was extremely unlikely, by then he would no longer be worried.

Tommy Wise returned late and potentially rebellious and immediately checked the monitors to find them blank with fresh tapes inserted. He flew to the cell, saw the blank monitor and rushed back to Sealy who was quietly drinking a coffee.

"What's happened to McQueen?" he blurted out.

"I let him go. I wasn't getting anywhere with him." Sealy gazed up at the confused Wise, a biscuit in one hand, the cup of coffee in the other. "I thought that was what you wanted, not that what you want matters on this issue. He's gone, Tommy. He's free."

"But you said he killed the policewoman."

"I did. And I still think he did. But there's not a chance of ever proving it, not a chance in hell. We would have had to torture it out of him and those days are long gone. Sadly, I think in some respects."

Sealy smiled at the still bemused and highly suspicious Wise. "I took it as far as I dared. And let me remind you that I noticed your disapproval of some of my methods on occasion. He was never here, Tommy. The records have been wiped clean. Tapes, visual and audio and combined, and all written schedules." He dropped the smile and replaced it with an icy stare. "As per normal practice in such cases as this. We can never admit that we ever had him here and he hasn't a clue where he was. It might teach him a lesson, although I doubt it."

Sealy finished his coffee and rose. He patted Wise on the shoulder. "I should think you are relieved. It was a rotten detail." His apparent good humour returned. "I haven't forgotten I promised you a break after being cooped up here. Take a couple of weeks, Tommy. As from now. I'll lock up."

It wasn't until three p.m. that same day that the fax arrived on Marvin Hayes' private machine. It was long and it was informative. He had only just returned from the London Clinic where Zoë seemed still to be in limbo, probably as a way of opting out. He rang his chauffeur to bring the car round and when he picked up his bodyguard outside the house he said, "Keep an eye out for a possible tail, Charlie."

He was dropped off at the block where Bulman was staying, told Charlie to wait in the lobby and the chauffeur to park in the underground parking lot belonging to the luxury apartments. Charlie made sure the lift was empty when Hayes entered and then resumed a watch on the entrance.

Hayes stepped from the lift. The luxury of the top floor came not only from the thickness of the pile of the carpeting but was conveyed by the very silence, as if nobody would dare to break it. Even the doorbell issued subdued chimes. Nobody answered. He rang again, waited with no result then produced a spare set of keys his multi-millionaire friend had left him. He let himself in.

He went from room to room; the place was empty. Not only that, but there was no sign of anybody having stayed there. Was Bulman so tidy? Or was it his policeman's mind leaving no clues? He sat down to face the hall door and was suddenly grateful for the solitude. Even in his own house staff moved about, no matter how quietly; the Embassy was a hive of buzzing personnel and pealing telephones, and the Clinic where he spent so much time lately was only superficially quiet: there was movement all the time.

He was asleep when Bulman came in. Bulman saw him as soon as he entered the drawing-room and was shocked at first, until he realised what must have happened. He crept to the kitchen and filled the kettle ready for a pot of tea. He went back to the drawing-room, sat down and waited for Hayes to wake up, thinking it was probably the first natural sleep the Ambassador had enjoyed since his wife collapsed.

When Hayes finally awoke, Bulman himself was almost asleep but he pulled himself together and said, "Duplicate keys, eh? I'll go and make some tea." By the time Bulman arrived with a laden tray Hayes was fully awake.

Hayes took the proffered cup and put it down. "I slept for over an hour. Just as well I wasn't at a banquet." He pushed himself upright and pulled out the pages of fax. "I'll pick out the parts that matter. These are from my old pals in the Drug Enforcement Agency. They've come up with something."

He drank some tea then fiddled with the papers. "Over the years the DEA and other drug squads have done their fair share of crop-burning in an attempt to stop drugs at birth. Sometimes helping a foreign government out at their invitation, sometimes just doing it when we ran into double standards: you know, the government who pays lip service to the abolition of drug-running yet benefits hugely from its massive spin-off."

Hayes was not reading the fax as he spoke but was merely filling in the background detail he knew so well. "Some operations were successful in that we'd burn down acres of the stuff by dropping small incendiaries. But it was no more than a slowing-down process, we knew we couldn't win completely. The Colombians can take that sort of loss in their stride but it annoys them and holds them up for a while.

"Well, George, there was a difficult period a few years ago. The Panamanians were seemingly double-dealing and objected to our using their bases for flights to Colombia. Guatemala and Nicaragua were making things generally difficult and Costa Rica had plenty of its own problems.

"At that time our intelligence came up with a report that a big shipment was due to leave for the US, but how and when could not be determined. The drug-runners could take their time and would confuse us in any way

264

possible. The usual game. But we knew where most of it was stashed. Meanwhile the Colombian government was doing a massive deal with the drug barons and we could not rely on them. You remember that the biggest baron of all was put in jail with luxury around him and still conducted his business until he felt it time to escape.

"The SIS have a station in Bogotá and confirmed the same news and locale that we had picked up. How could it be destroyed before it was distributed? By fire bombing, of course. But from where?" Hayes shot Bulman a piercing stare. "Are you getting all this?"

"Every word."

Hayes was now partially referring to the fax. "Well, you Brits had given British Honduras its freedom, now Belize; but because Belize was overshadowed by Guatemala who had murmured veiled threats about taking over once the Brits had gone, the new regime begged for a continued British presence, if only a token military force. So it was the Brits who suggested flying out from Belize." Hayes reached for his tea.

"It was a crazy idea right from the start. But nobody at that time came up with anything better. It was a two-thousand-five-hundred-mile round trip, so an old airbase was found by friendly locals which would allow the planes to land after dropping their incendiaries, refuel and take off again. Even then, because of the limited size of the unmarked, old stock aircraft, extra fuel tanks had to be attached for the zero-foot run across the Caribbean."

Hayes shook his head as if reliving the episode.

Bulman probed, "You were there?"

"Only at the Belize end. The safe base. Four planes went out, two returned, one ditched in the sea and the pilot lost, and one never took off again from north Colombia. The pilot of that plane was British. It was the last plane in and the Colombians were waiting. SIS had insisted on some sort of involvement, perhaps to share the credit, as they were supplying the operational base, albeit from a country no longer under their flag. The pilot's name was Ray Sealy."

"Sealy's son? Wouldn't you have remembered when I first asked you about the name?"

"Had he used that name at the time. But they all used cover names. His was – " Hayes glanced at the fax – "Johnny Osborne. The whole goddamn exercise was abortive and we reckoned afterwards that we'd been suckered, both us and the SIS. So far as we could establish afterwards the intelligence report was suspect in the first place. It was what you Brits call a complete cock-up. Sealy was killed and news came through later that he had been thrown alive into a furnace while everyone watching cheered until the screaming stopped. We all know that the Colombian drug cartels make the Mafia look like choir boys. They lived up to their reputation then all right."

Bulman frowned. "Are you saying that Michael Sealy blames you for his son's death and that he is now taking his revenge out on you?"

"Who knows what a sick mind will do? I was certainly in charge of the base operation."

"But this was some years ago. Time for him to come to terms with it. And why activate now?"

"Because I came to London as Ambassador. I was suddenly highlighted to him, a public reminder. I suppose his mind went."

Bulman said, "I understand that as a result of his son dying his wife later committed suicide. She may have got over the death of her son but not the manner of it; that would have been impossible. And of course Sealy lost both, arising from the literal ashes of the first. I suppose it's possible."

The two men sat in silence, while what was left of the tea got cold. And then Bulman slowly shook his head. "You've certainly provided a motive. And a strong one. Sealy's obviously gone round the twist and he's sick in the head. I can accept that. But there's something missing. Something that doesn't gel."

Hayes shrugged unhappily. "It's the best I can do. His son died in gruesome circumstances on a mission I controlled, as a result of which his wife committed suicide and Sealy is still suffering. His aim is to make my family suffer too."

"To the same extent, Marvin? An eye for an eye? If that's the case he's hardly begun. There's something else. I know a guy who might know something but he's mean with his knowledge and is genuinely afraid of what Sealy can do to him. He lost him his job but I think there is much more to it than that. I'll have to go and see Sealy. Maybe a confrontation will sort him out. You see, we can't prove that Sealy is doing anything to you. If we could, we'd be able to go straight to the Home Secretary. I'll see Sealy first and then we'll decide what else to do."

"I don't like that idea, George. You'd better be very careful. Getting there might be possible but it's getting back you've got to watch. It's too risky."

"That's what you're paying me for. I'll take Spider, my good friend and retired cat burglar, with me. I'll ring him now."

He glanced at the time and rang the office. Scott had already left but there was something in the way Joe Weller, the young office manager, told him that made Bulman suspicious. He said, "Come on, Joe, you know me. What's he up to?"

"The police came for him. He's been arrested."

"Arrested? What the hell for?"

"I don't know. It was done in his office but they've taken him away."

"You don't know where?"

"No. The local nick, I suppose."

"Does his wife know?" Bulman was shattered at the news.

"Not from us. We talked about it and decided the police would tell her."

"Okay, Joe. Thanks for telling me. You did the right

thing in not telling Maggie. I'll keep in touch but he'll want you to keep the business going, okay?"

Bulman put the phone down feeling numbed.

Hayes, seeing his shock said, "What the hell's happened?"

"Scott's been arrested. I've got to find out why." He picked up the phone again and punched out a number; he was dreading the call.

A subdued Maggie came on and he wondered at first if she knew.

"Maggie, it's George. How are you . . ."

"Willie's been arrested. Is that why you're ringing?" She never called her husband Spider because it was a reminder of his past. Maggie sounded as if she had accepted it calmly, almost as if she had been expecting it to happen over the years and now that it had it had come as no surprise.

Bulman quickly detected that she was still in shock. "I've just heard, Maggie. This must be a mistake. What's it all about?"

"It's for murder. George, what has he done?" The tears weren't far away now, and Bulman picked up the first faint suggestion of hysteria.

"*Murder*? Who's he supposed to have murdered?"

There was a hesitation, as if Maggie was referring to something, then she said, "Someone called Charles Dubas. He would never kill anyone."

"And he didn't. I know about this man, Maggie. It had nothing to do with Spider. Nothing. And I can prove it. Now hang in there. He'll be okay. It might take a couple of days but he'll be released. Trust me, love. Just trust me."

"Can you come round?" She wanted direct reassurance.

"Not at the moment." Sealy would have someone watching Scott's place now. "I can't give you a telephone number either because I'm not at my own flat. Is there anyone you can stay with?" He knew she would not go to her mother because she had suffered serious family objection to her marriage in the first place.

"I don't know. I just want Willie home."

"He'll be home. Look, I'll phone as often as I can but don't worry. It's nowhere near as bad as it looks and he most definitely did not kill Charles Dubas. I've got to ring off now but I'll be back." He hung up and stared into space. "Oh my God."

Hayes, who had not seen Bulman so distressed before, said, "What's going on? It sounds like this friend of yours is up for murder."

Bulman painfully raised his head. "He didn't do it. I could get him out today if I wanted but I need to be free for at least a couple of days."

"You sound pretty sure, George."

"I am. Spider didn't do it because I killed him. Charles Dubas is an alias for Aleksei Chernov, the ex-KGB hitman."

Bulman looked utterly defeated just then. "I'd better tell you more about that side of things and about Galina and the three women who were killed. But this is going to be Sealy's worst mistake. The bastard. This could do to Maggie what he's already done to Zoë."

Hayes was staring at Bulman as if he did not know him at all, chin sagging and eyes wide with disbelief.

Bulman did the in-filling he had been trying to protect Hayes from, but the time for refinements had passed. He explained it all and finished by saying, "It was self defence. Pure and simple. He was just about to shoot me. My blow was lucky or unlucky, depending on how you look at it. I certainly had no intention of killing him but of saving myself. I couldn't go to the police with it, it seemed too tall a story and I would have been tucked away on remand, and I couldn't allow that to happen. Sealy could pull some powerful strokes. He's just pulled one. He must have given the police something pretty solid for this to happen. He's taken Scott from the scene hoping it will flush me out. He's not sure what I know but he'll assume that I know most of it."

Hayes was still trying to recover. "I had no idea you had

been through all that. Can't you get permission to carry a gun?"

Bulman shrugged. "I'd need four men with red flags round me. I'd shoot myself in the foot, at best. A gun's not the answer to Sealy. I'd better get round there." He stood up, offered a hand to help Hayes up. "If I don't come back you'll at least know where I've been. That might be enough for you to get something official going."

Hayes gazed at Bulman. Of equal height, both were big men but from there all resemblance ceased, except perhaps a stubbornness about the jawline. "I'm worried about you, George. You've been tripping over stiffs all over the place without telling me the full story, until now. And you're in grave danger of becoming one of them. There must be another way."

"If Sealy will oblige us by blowing his brains out it would solve our immediate problems." Bulman gave a bitter smile. "Maybe he can be induced to do it. Meanwhile there's something about the letter that's been niggling and Sealy knows the answer. He'd be pretty stupid to kill me in his own place. Come on, let's get it over with."

They walked towards the door. Hayes said, "I've got my official car downstairs. Can I give you a lift?"

Both men grinned, but beneath the spontaneous humour was weariness, the frustration that had been with them throughout, and the disbelief that one man could cause so much pain and misery. They walked side by side to the lift, sombre and silent as if walking into the unknown world of a crazed but clever man who had out-thought them, anticipated them, and had won every round of the deadly game.

As they rode down together Hayes riffled through the faxes before stuffing them in his pocket. "One thing I should have mentioned: whilst the Colombian débâcle was handled by me at the South American end, the London end was organised by SIS and this report suggests that Sealy Senior would have been in charge at that time. I'm not passing the buck. It all went wrong our end. It was just one of those strange coincidences."

"Really! Doesn't that raise the possibility that Sealy detailed his own son for the mission?"

Chapter Twenty-Two

The advantage of diplomatic plates, although technically illegal, was in hassle-free parking. Bulman and Hayes sat in the back, with Charlie the police bodyguard and the chauffeur in the front. Before he climbed out Bulman whispered to Hayes, "Do you think your chauffeur can lend me a tyre lever? Spider wouldn't need one but I haven't his finesse in opening doors."

Hayes was hesitant. He was about to condone breaking and entering and he was the most senior ambassador in the country. It did not take him long. He told Charlie to stay where he was, climbed out and called for the chauffeur to join him at the rear. "Mr Bulman wants to borrow one of your tools. Will you open the trunk?"

Bulman selected a tyre lever and a heavy spanner. He slipped the lever up his sleeve and the spanner in his pocket and went to the front nearside to say to Charlie, "I'm visiting a Michael Sealy in this block of flats. Will you look at your watch and register what I've said and the time in your notebook? It could be important later." He turned to shake Hayes by the hand and they gripped each other like brothers, knowing that one way or another this day might be decisive. Bulman waited until Hayes was driven away before entering the main hall.

He flashed his old warrant card at Reception and took the lift to the third floor and then walked up a flight. He had expected that Sealy's flat might be secluded and it was, at the end of a short corridor. He rang the bell. Then again. And when there was no reply produced the tyre lever and used it like a jemmy to force the door. It was harder than he thought and he managed to splinter the wood in several places before the door swung open, part of the lock hanging loose. He went in and shut the door.

It was now five thirty. He was not sure when Sealy might get home or even if he would come home at all. He began to search the flat, starting with the small study. He found the floor safe but had no means of opening it, although he did make other discoveries. It was two hours later when Sealy arrived, by which time Bulman was comfortably seated with a drink in his hand.

When Sealy entered the lounge he had a gun in his hand and at once Bulman said, "I hope you have a license for that thing. I'm George Bulman, by the way."

"I know who you are. You've smashed my door and I would be perfectly entitled to shoot an intruder."

"You'd better do it, then. You will have expected me to have informed others, including the police, that this is where I am. So be careful with your threats. You've been exposed, Sealy. We now know who has been causing the trouble and why. And by the way, you'll pay for putting Spider Scott back in nick for something he didn't do. His wife is devastated."

"How sad. I suppose you did it?" Sealy picked out a chair with care as if it had some special purpose, and sat facing Bulman at an angle. "Tell me what you think you know, Bulman, while I consider what I am to do with you." Sealy seemed to be perfectly relaxed except for the eyes; they were somehow fired up, a touch of insanity about them, but there was nothing insane about the way his mind was working.

"Why are you hounding Marvin Hayes and his family? What have they done to you?"

"The American Ambassador? You're off your trolly, Bulman. What on earth are they to me? And aren't you supposed to be telling *me* what's going on? I'm listening."

"Okay. Some faxes arrived from the DEA today. Sit back and I'll fill you in." While Bulman related their content and produced the connection between Sealy and

Hayes he watched Sealy closely. He detected the early alarm and the darting eyes sweeping the apartment. Sealy had not known that Hayes had made the tie-in.

Sealy made no denial and gathered himself sufficiently to say, "But that was years ago. Long forgotten. These things happen, not all missions are successful. We don't usually get involved in drugs but there are times when there are political links we can't ignore."

"I find it interesting that you haven't dived for cover behind the Official Secrets Act. You've made no denial of your intelligence connections."

Sealy smiled, feeling more in command now. "Really, Bulman, do you expect me to insult your intelligence? You've done your homework but you've somehow branched off the wrong way, applied the wrong assumptions."

"That must be the detective in me. We're always making cock-ups. The courts are full of cases of police cock-ups and downright corruption. I wonder what a jury might make of the typewriter."

"Typewriter? What aberration are you suffering now?"

"The one that's in your desk cupboard. The one that was used for the nasty little notes you sent to people like the Hayes family." Bulman smiled but was at a high point of wariness. "I've typed out all the characters on your machine so that the typeface can be compared with the notes."

Up till then the gun had been held loosely on Sealy's lap. The hand round it noticeably tightened, and Sealy lost composure. For the moment he seemed incapable of answering.

Bulman pushed home the advantage. "Routine detection. The boring old stuff. Nothing clever like you do. Oh, and the copy I made has been passed on to an outside source. Just in case you lost your senses and tried to find it on me. The gun might go off accidentally. You're bloody mad, Sealy. You need putting away. But you're very cunning too. Why did you send that terrible letter to your wife describing how your son died? And why did you send him out to die?"

Bulman saw no obvious change in Sealy but he felt it; a strong sense of evil spread through the room and just then he would have been prepared to assert that he could smell it. Sealy wasn't even looking at him. Bulman felt that he should either back off or press on to send Sealy completely over the edge. He realised that the turning point had been the faxes; Sealy had still believed that he held complete advantage and was master of the game, but suddenly, and perhaps his arrogance was such that he could not believe it could happen, it was falling about his ears.

He gazed over to Bulman in a frightening, unstable way, his head tilted at a strange angle. He had arrived to see the broken door, guessed who had done it, but still felt sure of the whole situation until the remark about the letter and his son.

"You fool. I loved my son. I've had nightmares about him."

"About what you did to him? Or the terrifying manner in which he died?" Bulman was ready to jump and he was gripping the heavy spanner in his pocket.

"God, I loved him. And nobody could have loved my wife more than I did. She was everything to me."

"And to others too?" Bulman was ready to leap.

Sealy rose on shaking legs. He stood unsteadily, gun hand waving in all directions, and eyes glaring with an all-seeing madness. "I loved her." It was a scream but directed at himself. "The others meant nothing to her. Nothing."

"Did she love your son as you did?"

Sealy stared blankly at space then the roving glare returned. "What did you say?" It was a whispered accusation and the focus fastened once more on Bulman. "What did you say?"

Bulman had never been so scared yet he could not stop himself. He had pressed a self-destruct button and the sudden insight of the terrible truth had really sprung from

275

Sealy's own reactions. He was afraid to rise, should Sealy shoot him then. Yet he felt he was uttering his last words when he was compelled to say, "Did she love him like you did? Or did she have the passion for him that you had for her?"

Hayes seemed to be paralysed, saliva slipping from a corner of his mouth.

Bulman, realising he had struck the truth, continued, "Is that why you had him killed? You could close your eyes to the others but not the relationship with your own son. And she never forgave you. She hated you so intensely at a time you needed her to return your love. And when she killed herself after you sent the letter to torture her out of crazy revenge, you had to find someone to blame and to convince yourself that your son died as a result of a futile mission which had been conducted by Marvin Hayes. After your wife killed herself, that was down to Hayes too, because it all stemmed from your son's death. My God, it's been eating you all these years and then Hayes came on full view and the rot deepened and deepened and there he was to blame for the whole murderous tragedy of your life." Bulman rose from the ashes of his own disgust.

They stood facing each other but it was doubtful if at the time Sealy really knew what was going on. Bulman knew he had better leave, for surely as Sealy came out of shock he would turn to someone else to blame, and he still had the gun in his hand.

Bulman walked towards the door and as he passed Sealy the choked, wavering words followed him: "Stop or I'll shoot you."

"In the back? That would be your style, Sealy. You've got worms in your brain: clear them out with that gun. It's the only thing that can save you now."

Bulman strode on, feeling the mad eyes and the direction of the gun follow him and desperately wanted to run. He reached the door in a cold sweat. A shot was fired, the door lintel splintered near his head, a sliver of wood piercing his ear. And then he ran. And as he reached the lift Sealy screamed after him, "It's not over yet." Bulman had no intention of waiting for the lift; he took to the stairs in a manner he would have considered beyond him.

Don Hayes stood at the entrance to the London Clinic with Tammy Rees by his side. He had finally discovered his mother was there by ringing home. His father was still unavailable and Don, in desperation, had threatened the butler that if he did not tell him what was going on he would go to the Embassy and raise all hell there. The butler told him his mother was at the London Clinic, that she was not in danger and that his father was probably there; his father had been trying to spare his feelings at a time when he himself had so much on his mind.

He had gone straight to London, Tammy insisting on being with him, saw his mother lying there and clearly not recognising him, and had found out what he could, not getting beyond the fact that Zoë had suffered severe shock. His father was not there but was a frequent visitor and he could wait if he wanted to.

Don took Tammy's hand and stepped out into Devonshire Place and wondered what to do. His inclination was to wait for his father because he would learn nothing unless he did. The traffic was building up with the evening rush hour and they stood there watching it. It was more comfortable inside the clinic but he wanted to see his father before his father saw Zoë.

It must have been about forty minutes later when Don called out, "Here's his car." He had spotted it at once, the flag furled in its holder. He recognised the chauffeur, and the bodyguard as one of the regular detail and, of course, his father on the rear seat. He hurried towards the car as it pulled in and the chauffeur and the bodyguard climbed out. The door was opened for his father who showed controlled pleasure at seeing Don, his gaze slipping to the girl whose hand he held. And father and son moved to embrace, just as Tammy said, "Isn't that Wally McQueen?"

Don followed her gaze and bawled out, "Get down, Dad." He hurled himself at his father as he saw the gun rising in McQueen's hand behind a parked car across the road. Tammy screamed as she, too, saw the gun, and Charlie the bodyguard helped Don push his father to the pavement while drawing his own gun.

Two shots rang out and Charlie spun round as he was hit and jackknifed to the pavement, his gun sliding towards the street. Cars screamed to a halt as brakes gripped, there was a crash of metal as one ran into another, and then the running of footsteps as McQueen dashed through the chaos of piled-up cars to finish the job.

Tammy, who was rooted, screamed out again, "He's coming."

Don reached for the gun which had slid near him, grabbed it, rose from his father's prostrate body and levered himself against the Embassy car just in time to see McQueen reach their side of the street. McQueen rounded the car, pushed Tammy away and levelled his gun at Hayes. There was a crazed expression on his face and it remained with him as he took two rounds in the chest from the police gun Don was holding. McQueen sank to his knees, tried to raise the gun again and then fell forward on his face.

They met at Marvin Hayes' residence. There was Bulman, Tony Cooper, Sir Maxwell Swain, John Cordell, Marvin Hayes and Don. Between them they were able to reasonably complete the picture. Sealy had fired a second shot after Bulman had gone, this time into his head when he finally realised he had nowhere else to go. He had destroyed his own family, had people killed, ruined the lives of others and, in the end, had almost achieved his objective.

Tony Cooper confirmed that Sealy had never been able to accept blame and had definitely been responsible for his son going to Belize and taking part in the abortive mission. He'd had a brilliant career in the SIS which had enabled him to rise so high but in the end had been destroyed by a crazed love for his wife who had enjoyed her own brand of love, and it was their variation of love which had finally killed the family.

The Bomb Squad had been called out to disarm the illegally parked car McQueen had waited behind in the certain knowledge that sooner or later Hayes would appear. The car had been wired up to destroy him had he succeeded in killing Hayes, and would have exploded half an hour after the ignition had set the timer as he drove off. Tammy's recognition of him had most certainly saved the Ambassador and had probably confused McQueen sufficiently to cross the street to finish the job.

Spider Scott was still in jail and until Bulman reported in to confess to the self-defence manslaughter of Chernov, would remain there. But it was only a matter of hours before a reinstated John Cordell had already set the wheels in motion. Zoë was still in the London Clinic but Don's voice had got through to her and she at last began to believe in his innocence.

There was still much to unwind but the danger was over for Marvin Hayes and his family and he was never to forget George Bulman's part in it all. The killing of Paula Smith was now down to McQueen, who was still alive and who confessed that he had been set up by Sealy to kill the American Ambassador. He was more reluctant to confess to the killing of Paula Smith and the opportunist use Sealy had made of the murder. But Tommy Wise came down on the side of common sense and self protection and was able to relate the various interviews Sealy had held with McQueen and which referred in part to his killing of the policewoman. McQueen, too, had come to the end of the road.

When Scott was released, and Bulman allowed out on bail while the unhappy business of Chernov was sorted out, the two of them, with Cordell and Hayes, had a quiet dinner party at the latter's house. There was no celebratory air about the dinner, but humour burst on the scene when

Bulman asked if he might stay on in the penthouse until the owner returned, and was given an affirmative. The mood grew lighter from that point and the near past began to disappear. It was over.